Other books by Randy V

COVEN OF CELSUS – ELIZABETH
an erotic horror
(Vol. 1)

COVEN OF CELSUS – HEATHER
another erotic horror
(Vol. 2)

Coven of Celsus
Nona

Tears of the Sorceress

Randy V

&

Ellie Ravencroft

Randy V & Ellie Ravencroft

ISBN: 978-0-578-80097-4

CONTENTS

"...evils are not caused by God; rather, they are a part of the nature of matter and of mankind; that the period of mortal life is the same from beginning to end, and that because things happen in cycles, what is happening now — evils that is — happened before and will happen again."

Celsus (*c.* A.D. 178)

REFLECTIONS
October 18, 2019 – 1:00 a.m.
San Juan Island, Pacific Northwest

The brutal wind and black of night perfectly reflected the feelings within Nona's inhuman soul. She sat among the jagged rocks - amidst the powerful raging Salish Sea - but felt nothing. As the salt water soaked her, cold and alone, Sanem's haunting words reverberated in her mind over the angry water. *They are the reason humanity is asleep. They are laying a magnificent trap for all of us and they are telling the whole world about it.*

"Can we finally sleep?" she sighed under her breath.

The storm was strong this night. She fleetingly thought of Linzie and Shira, wondering what mischief and horror they were visiting upon the world. The two renegades were over six years into their merciful banishment from the coven, nine years for Linzie, 18 for Shira. The remaining six women within his good graces were forbidden to even think of them.

Nona's head cocked mechanically to one side as she watched the lights of the ferry tossing on the erratic waters. Mother nature could be so unpredictable and cruel. A fickle creature - difficult to predict, even harder to please. Mother nature, sometimes known to her as Lili, the single being that could bring the coven and creation itself to its knees. She contemplated the power of this being, older than time itself - and her thoughts wandered to the monster Lili created, her master, her lord Celsus.

The waves crashed and the wind roared, soaking her dark wild hair. *Lord Celsus.* Her legs widened as she straddled the wet jagged stone, glistening with the salty water. Her bare feet slid on the surface as she felt the waves crash upon her, crushing her against the solid rock beneath her. It was odd to feel calmer in the midst of the gale than in the house at this moment. She pushed the unpleasant thoughts from her mind and recalled the master drinking from her, flattening his tongue against her aching clit, and transporting her from her body. Her head tossed back, her legs spread against the storm, and her clit throbbed at the recollection. That tongue and those lips that had lapped at her soaking womanhood so many times, yet never enough, lingered just far enough away to remain untouchable in the raging storm…and she groaned in wantonness.

Lord Celsus, my beautiful beast, my master. She took a deep breath and moaned a sound that died in the salty blast. She felt nothing - not the rage of the sea nor the pain of the wind. Detached from existence itself, after living for so long, only Lord Celsus could bring her any kind of sensation. The waves were fierce, and she barely felt the nature she had never belonged to and could never experience as the once-borns could. Time was irrelevant and inconsequential to her and her kind.

Nothing gave her the presence or emotional fix humans could experience, except for those few precious moments of euphoria when she became one with her sisters and her master. Her inhuman existence felt alive and present like they once were so many lives ago. But all too soon those moments passed and she was vacant once more. What did other life forms think of her and her family, she wondered. Would they know she was anything but human?

Long, sharp, inhuman claws reached around the recesses of her dark thoughts and grazed her wet, beloved cheek. His left hand caressed her beautiful face with the back of his fingers, and her eyes closed in the blissful memory. Her legs spread further and further apart - against the wild wind, as her lord and master appeared before her in a stormy wet hallucination. The waters seemed to rise higher, the winds blew harder and she felt the burning on her cheek from the phantasm before her. She threw her head back in agonizing yearning.

"My lord!" she howled in uncharacteristic hysteria.

The shadow hissed an arrogant smile as she slid up and down on the sleek stone. Wave upon wave crashed upon her gyrating body as the shadow demon commanded her - owned her. Her fingers dug into the earth beneath her desperate body, the rock transforming into her master's thick cock, as she moved up and down, over and over. Slow at first and building, the man in the storm watched as her face contorted in pleasure. She bit down on her lip, drawing a small trickle of blood and she licked at it as her hips moved harder and faster.

Nona's breasts bounced with her movements through the thin fabric of clothing painted on her voluptuous body by the ravaging sea. Her hard nipples pierced through the blouse and ached to be touched as she pressed them together in a feeble and frenzied attempt to pleasure them. The shadow sighed in lusting amusement at her desperation and she felt the burning on her face where his memory grazed her once more. She shut her eyes and moved more . . . just a little more. She bit down on her lip again drawing more blood and hungrily sucked it in. Her mind was growing hazy with the mounting pleasure and her slit swelled with neglected desire. Her juices flowed and she gripped at the rock with her powerful legs. "More...more, my lord!" Her clit swelled as she felt the oncoming ecstasy. Throwing her head back, she fucked the rock like she was riding her master's cock. Wild and unhinged she yelled out, "I bleed for thee, my lord!"

Her grip tightened on the stone as the powerful orgasm crashed upon her. She screeched out a sound from deep within her ancient soul that revealed a desperation as old as time itself. Her muscular thighs tightened against the stone as her juices flooded out in a violent eruption. She shivered and convulsed as she rode every precious wave of euphoria.

Her eyes then closed in the afterglow of the powerful release the mere specter of her lord gave her. Blissful and exhausted, she spoke to the demon before her with a vulnerable sweetness she knew he loved. This orgasm was as wild as the storm surrounding her, and in her spent state she lay on the rock and let her being wander. Her thoughts went blank and a memory from the farthest corners of her mind slowly emerged.

In a whisper obliterated by the wind, she spoke, "Yes, my lord, my wolf . . . my beautiful wolf . . ." A rare single tear rolled down her cheek as she continued, "Blood . . . my beloved wolf . . . there is so much blood . . ." And then, an unwanted interruption, the terrible memory of her master and sisters' making.

She stopped breathing as if dead, unaware of the increasing salty spray of the angry Haro Straits. The haunting completely possessed her.

Δ

"Dark goddess of the desert, I call upon you!" the voice bellowed. "You who visits the dreams of men! Night hag! Owl-goddess! I command you!"

The spell carried across the winds of the midnight dessert. Celsus gazed up at the endless stars, arms open, chest heavy.

"Take this boy's blood and soul and yield the elixir I desire! I command you, Lili!"

The frightened boy looked up at the woman yielding a knife over his captured body. Cala was poised for the kill as Celsus shouted the final verse of the incantation. The night suddenly cooled and strange winds began to form around them, but Celsus would not yield. He stood his ground against the forces he summoned and would command.

"Mas…" Cala stopped suddenly and the knife fell from her hand.

"Cala!" Celsus strained to control his voice against the building terror within his chest. Despite his initial bravado that he would command and control her power, he felt a sudden dread that something was horribly wrong.

"Cala!"

Her eyes were unnaturally wide, as though in death, and Celsus felt the blood within him run colder than the desert night.

Abu, clenched between her frozen legs, looked up at her with wet sandy tears smeared on his horrified face.

Celsus stood paralyzed at what he saw. Hovering above Cala was the apparition of the dark goddess, Lili, with massive wings and owl talons. The stars that shone through her gossamer form were tinted red with demonic energy. Her claws were perched on Cala's shoulders and her fiery eyes glared down at the mortal who attempted to ensnare her.

"How dare you summon me this way!" she screeched, the winds of the desert intensifying with her mounting fury.

"Cala, move!" Celsus shouted, over the owl's roar.

But Lili's claws slowly sunk into Cala's shoulders and she descended into the girl's body. Celsus watched in terror as Cala's body changed with the power of the demon that possessed her. Her body seemed to grow, develop. Her breasts tore against the fabric of her tunic and her legs became thicker with muscle and power. She lurched forward and screamed in horrific agony as bloody wings tore through her back and reduced her clothing to shreds. When Cala looked at Celsus again, her eyes glowed inhumanly red and she hissed at him, with an impossibly long avian tongue.

Celsus took a step back but felt a presence behind him. He slowly turned to see the specter of Nona, known then by her first-born name, Anatu. He felt his heart stop as the possessed Cala closed in on him.

"Kill him!" Celsus ordered Cala. "I command you!"

The possessed Cala looked at Celsus with a sinister look. "No. It is *you* I shall devour," Lili snarled. And suddenly, Celsus looked as if one dead, his body falling onto the dirt floor. His disembodied spirit lingered. The deceased Anatu and Cala floated with him. They began to flee into the night sky.

Lili looked down at Abu, still bound in the sand soaked with tears and urine from his terror. She cut his bindings with Cala's knife and let Abu escape. It was not a matter of sympathy or justice. It was a defiant indifference. She then turned her attention to the fleeing ghosts and hissed in delight, "Delicious souls. You are my children now." The spirits fled but her curse overtook them, and they could understand every dark word. "Morsels of flesh, blood, and spirit. Your wish for immortality is granted. One day I will come for you . . . and I will feast . . ." she said, her final words, chilling sensual caresses. Tara and Sanem joined their master soon after feeling Lili's loving touch. The cursed spirits of Megan, Sakura, and Linzie followed shortly thereafter. Lili inhaled the scent of human death and fear, the perfect recipe for her blissful intoxication.

She looked up into the night sky and seethed, "My selfish sorcerer, I chain you to this world for all time," she chanted malevolently as she haunted his house. "Your slaves are bound as well . . . your torment - unsatiated hunger . . . feeding in both worlds as monsters, living and disembodied."

Her attention shifted as she spoke aloud in the ancient Sumerian language, "One is missing." She smiled maliciously with murderous intent. "Shira." She paused, inhaling and reveling in the moment. A sound came from the far side of the house and with impossible speed, a bloody talon opened the door.

Shira shivered in a corner, terrified as the monster approached. The beautiful slave girl held a dagger to her own heart and paused in confusion when she saw Cala's face. Something was terribly wrong. Her feet and hands were talons drenched in blood. Lili spoke in Babylonian so that Shira could understand perfectly.

"Thy blood is sweet," she whispered, licking the air with her long inhuman tongue. "I can taste it."

Shira took a breath and glared at the demon in contempt as she plunged the knife upward into her solar plexus. This was excruciating, and in the final microsecond before her death, Shira felt a horror and pain she had never felt before, but would feel over and over again for eternity.

Lili examined the young woman that defied her. She lifted Shira's beautiful young body and kissed her lifeless lips, before sticking two talons deep into Shira's bloody mouth. Though the body was cooling, Lili could still feel the warmth of life within and she bit down on the dead girl's soft neck.

"117 years among the dead and 117 years among the living," she whispered, licking and caressing Shira's body with her demonic tongue. "Hunger and thirst shall torment you in body and spirit," she went on, kissing the corpse's breasts and caressing her legs. "That shall be your lot until I decide to devour you."

Shira's lifeless eyes stared back in frozen fear. Lili then spread Shira's legs wide, staring into the cold slit that had been wet and throbbing in life. The dark goddess tongued and explored Shira's dead flower before devouring her sex.

Δ

Nona's eyes flickered with the stinging salt of the sea. She felt paralyzed from fear among the mossy rocks and she knew her visions of the past were not done tormenting her. Her eyes closed and an unexpected specter appeared - the Lady Siraba of Nippur.

Still unable to move, she furrowed her brow and wondered. Why her? Why now? The woman looked at her with eyes that bore deep into her eternal existence and Nona was sucked back into a time she never *physically* experienced.

Δ

Babylon, 1764 BC

The great sorceress Siraba looks into a large bowl. She is surrounded by twelve veiled figures. All of them are sitting around her in a circle. She sits in the center and the dark water in the bowl seems to radiate. Siraba speaks.

"We are too late - the monsters are born. The best we can do is bind them from coming back. The bodies must be retrieved. It must be done now. There is no time."

The vision swirls and Nona can feel the heat of the day and the wind caressing her face. The scent familiar, sweet and welcoming. An operation is underway. Though disembodied, this binding is having an effect on her.

Two men are swinging bodies into the Euphrates River. The bodies are wrapped in shrouds and encircled with chains. One large stone is attached at the midsection. Siraba looks out into the river, and with each body thrown into the river, she commands the universe.

"Demon children of Lili, I bind you to the great river. You shall never enter the world of the living again. So be it, by all that is natural and sacred!"

Δ
The Salish Sea

Nona woke from the nightmarish memory floating in the calm sea over a hundred yards from shore. The storm had passed and she could see the rock face she made love to before slipping into the unwanted past. Devoid of the slightest trace of ecstasy from the previous night, she looked around the now tranquil waters. A capricious beast indeed. Not even the smell of the divine morning hinted at the monster storm from the previous night. With a grace that one only achieves after centuries of living, she made her way to the shoreline, gliding on the waves that carried her to the moist, soft earth. Her feet sank into the wet sand. The wind was cold against her inhuman skin and had she been anybody else, she would have been cold and dead many hours ago. Instead, she took a deep breath and looked back at the rock one more time before making her way through the trees, into the greenery, to the house of her beloved coven.

Δ
Bavaria, Germany

Wilhelm Hilgenfeldt was a young man in his 30s with his father's black hair and shrewd eyes that determined another's worth with a single pompous glance. Gifted with Werner's keen eye for business and his mother's beauty which, when applied to a young man, gave the appearance of a dark-haired Adonis - completely the opposite of his overweight father.

The death of Werner Hilgenfeldt was mourned by few, least of all by his son, the only child and sole heir of his father's exorbitant wealth. Nine days after Werner and Anna Hilgenfeldt were declared dead, his son Wilhelm moved into one of his father's luxurious castles with a harem of exotic beauties.

Where his father preferred blonde-haired, blue-eyed women of European decent, Wilhelm had a taste for the exotic. Brazil, India, Columbia - anywhere and everywhere there was a darker color of flesh, Wilhelm could be sure to find a doll of his discerning taste. As paranoid as his father, the castle was crawling with security. They all knew - from top to bottom - the type of man Wilhelm was. As unscrupulous as he was rich, this was a man with one of the sharpest minds on the planet, and a lustful depravity, matched only by his insatiable sexual appetite and cruelty.

Far to the southwest corner of the castle, a door opened and Wilhelm's top field agent walked in carrying critical news. As soon as he heard the screams and moans, Gerhard knew he had to wait.

Straddling a massive chair in the center of the grand room was a woman with long, tan legs. She bounced on Wilhelm's lap, on the tips of her toes, the violet on her toenails so dark it was almost black.

Named Valentina, she was a new acquisition from Columbia. Her thick chestnut hair fell in massive curls down her chest and naked back. Her head tilted back to reveal her thin, succulent neck. Wilhelm yanked on her thick mane until her back arched and her chest pushed forward. She was not allowed to touch him unless he instructed. She balanced on his lap, his legs tense, moving up and down his hard shaft.

The screams brought Gerhard back to the present and he looked over to see a man strapped to a metallic wheel with his limbs extended to near breaking. One sudden movement, and he knew they would easily dislocate. From where he stood, Gerhard could see the man's legs were broken in multiple places, bones sticking out through flesh.

The man was slipping in and out of consciousness when Wilhelm roughly grabbed the bouncing female by her beautiful neck. His fingers clamped down and she immediately stopped moving, fighting the suffocation.

"Halt," he commanded. She waited. "Er schläft! Dieser unhöfliche Mann schläft! Wecke ihn auf!"

A man standing by a table of gruesome medieval torture devices looked over at the man on the rack and nodded silently as he made his way over with a small vial. He uncapped it and held it to the man's nose for a minute before the man quickly returned to his miserable senses.

"Viel besser. Mach weiter." he grinned, kissing and biting down on the woman's breast.

Valentina swallowed the wince that threatened to distract from the man's painful moans as a dark red ring formed, blood gently oozing down her tan flesh. Wilhelm took her nipple harshly between his teeth and bit down as she moved up and down his length again. Wilhelm was a sadist in the worst way. He was without mercy, not below tearing a woman's nipple off with his teeth in mid-sex to bring himself to climax. Seeing the blood, tasting the flesh in his mouth - but most of all, hearing desperate screams, always took him over the edge into a mind-altering orgasm.

Valentina resumed bouncing as the executioner returned to his tools. A fan of torture, Wilhelm had a morbid fascination with medieval tools and methods. Where most sadists would prefer more modern and advanced methods of administering pain, Wilhelm preferred the tried and true classics of centuries past - especially upon the genitals.

The executioner looked over his table and picked up a pear-shaped object. He caressed it with his thin hand. A morose looking man, Ernst had been in the care of the Hilgenfeldt family as long as he had been alive. He knew his master's whims better than anybody else in the castle. A personal favorite of Wilhelm, the metallic pear glistened and shone with a macabre beauty. A custom order from an associate of Wilhelm's, the pear was not made of dull metal but instead, solid gold. It gleamed in the old man's hand. Out of the corner of his eyes, Wilhelm saw it and shuddered.

"You're an artist," he groaned, as Ernst made his way toward the man tied to the wheel.

Wilhelm tensed in his chair as Ernst put on a purple latex glove and gently put the tip of the pear against the man's opening. The man on the wheel gasped and groaned, trying to formulate words but too exhausted and desperate to say anything.

Slowly, Ernst shoved the hard object into the hole that was too small and the tortured man began to scream. Valentina slowed her movements and Wilhelm growled in delight.

The man's shouts were primal and dispirited. From where he sat, Wilhelm could feel the terror that seized the man's soul and it only brought him closer to climax as he bit down on his own lip.

He closed his eyes and let his head fall back as Valentina's pussy tightened and released on his thick shaft. Her juices soaked his balls and as the instrument was shoved gently into the man's orifice, Wilhelm struggled to keep from bursting.

"Noch nicht," he seethed, his eyes half-closed.

Valentina continued her slow movement as the pear moved into the man's ass. The man gasped in delirium as he was torn open, almost breaking under Ernst's delicate touch. If he had anything left, he would have vomited from the excruciating pain, but instead he could produce only bile and unintelligible shouts and groans.

"More!" Wilhelm shouted.

He loved it and wanted more of it. Fucking to the sound of a dying man was a delicacy he reveled in too seldom, and he felt himself almost bursting, but still he wanted more.

Valentina's choked moans were drowned out by the blood-curdling screams of the man as Ernst slowly began to open the device. Wilhelm could feel the man tearing and his mouth watered.

The shouting began to weaken and Wilhelm knew from experience the man was going to pass out soon. He could not allow this, not when he was so close to the climax.

"Halte ihn wach!" he shouted against the mounting pleasure. "Now the rat," he said in English with a heavy accent. His hands clawed down Valentina's back and her teeth clenched with the pain. Blood trails opened up and ran down her elegant back, her hair matting with red stains, as he dug his sharp nails into her exquisite ass cheeks.

The old man nodded, though Wilhelm was not watching, and he produced a small cage with a starving rat inside. Wilhelm could hear the distinct squeaking of the small creature and he shouted to Ernst to get on with it.

Ernst tied the cage around the man's genitals, securing it to latches from behind. The pristine, flaccid member hung in the cage as the confused animal quickly began to look for a way out. A small claw scratched at the flesh and then teeth began to work on the untouched morsel.

The screams intensified as the hungry rat bit down and ate into the tender flesh. Through his closed eyes, Wilhelm could see the animal tearing and biting, and as the man screamed and screamed, and kept screaming, Valentina moved faster and faster.

Her pussy clamped down as she worked Wilhelm hard. He clenched his teeth, pulled her hair back, and warned her, "You better suck me dry with that cunt of yours," he demanded through winded breath. He took a strand of her blood-tainted hair and put it to her lips. "Suck on it," he demanded.

13

Valentina took the wet hair in her mouth, her chin turning pink, and sucked her own blood off the brown curl. She bounced harder, gripping the back of his chair in the final moments before the climax. Valentina swallowed a scream as Wilhelm bit down on her nipple with frenzied strength.

"Before he passes out!" Wilhelm hissed.

Valentina's mind went blank and she felt nothing, save the pain of holding down her shouts and moans as she reached her climax riding on his hard dick. She threw her head back as the waves of ecstasy crashed upon her and shook her entire body from head to toe. She slammed down on his clenching thighs and the sound of flesh slapping against flesh was nearly drowned out by the man's wailing shouts. The trauma would soon render him unconscious but Wilhelm was there . . . almost there.

"Oh Dios," the woman pleaded in desperate whispers as she clawed the seat behind him, her shouts barely audible over the tortured man. Her legs propped up against the sides of the chair, pushing off the arm rests as she slammed down onto him harder.

Wilhelm bit down on her breast, clawing and yanking her hair back. The man's screams were getting louder and louder. They were feverish desperate shouts for the end to come, for death to free him. At the peak of the anguished shrieking, Valentina tightened her slit hard upon Wilhelm. He clenched his teeth and shot into her cunt.

His entire body shook with the release, the muscles in his legs flexing. Wilhelm gripped the arm rests as he shot spurt after spurt into the Colombian's tight slit. He could feel her vagina walls sucking every last bit of semen out of him. Her breasts were numb and as she came down from the thrilling high, she felt overwhelming pain all over her body.

Wilhelm breathed hard as he came off the orgasmic high and a light sheen of sweat appeared on his beautifully pale face. The man on the wheel convulsed as the ferocious rat continued eating him. He looked at the woman straddling his lap and could see her entire front smeared in blood. Her right nipple was torn and there was a bleeding wound on her left breast. He smiled, licking his stained lips.

Valentina dismounted and knelt before the satisfied man, ignoring the pain she could feel slowly mounting. With blood stained lips, Valentina licked at Wilhelm's softening cock and relaxed balls, cleaning them of her juices and his own release. Wilhelm placed his hand on the side of her face and caressed her cheek. "You are so beautiful," he cooed, licking his lips and stroking her neck. "Your mouth is almost as delicious as your cunt."

He looked to his chair in a dismissive gesture and paused. Light scratch marks could be seen on the royal blue upholstery and wooden frame. A sick smile curled on his lips and Wilhelm grabbed her roughly by her hair. She was awkwardly yanked up and off his dick.

"You have damaged my chair," he said curtly. "How will you make up for it?" he asked, lifting her hand up to his bloody lips.

He took one of her fingers into his mouth and gently sucked. Valentina began to shake with fear and in the grotesque silence she heard the muffled squeaking of the hungry rat and the dwindling groans of the dying man.

"You pleased me so much," Wilhelm cooed at her, slowly wrapping a hand around her bruised neck. "And I am a merciful man," he whispered, bringing her closer to him. "I forgive you, my dear Valentina," he breathed, his thumb gently tracing the line of her jaw.

For a few terrifying moments, only the squeaking rat could be heard…and then she screamed.

The act was sudden and her pain crisp as she fought to keep still, her finger still in his mouth. He bit down on her knuckle with such force that her finger broke. Valentina wanted to scream again but he shushed her with a look from his chilling blue eyes.

"I am a merciful man," he repeated. "And I forgive you. Verlasse jetzt," he commanded, tossing her head aside and leaning back in his chair.

Wilhelm took a breath before tucking himself into his pants and turning to Gerhard who was still waiting.

"What news do you bring me?" he smiled, sighing with satisfaction. "Do you need to take care of yourself too?" he taunted. "Was ist los?"

The squeaking continued in the background, the man's agonizing moans becoming indecipherable sounds. He slipped in and out of consciousness as the rat slowly devoured him.

"Oh, him?" Wilhelm gestured, as if he just now recalled there was another body in the room. "Don't mind him."

Gerhard knew the man on the wheel. His name was Otto and he was a robotics engineer who worked for Wilhelm. Gerhard also knew he had a wife and children, and he shuddered at the thought of their fate.

"There are more women that live in the house of Lord Celsus," Gerhard reported, refocused.

Wilhelm nodded as a girl in purple bondage wear approached him with a tray of food and wine. She was gagged. He picked at the appetizers and took the glass. The girl bowed and walked backward, her feet and calves a bright purple - as if they were painted.

"How do you know this?"

"There was a final transmittal before the infiltration attempt failed. We saw images of the women, and it seems they all have some special skills and strength - like Lord Celsus himself.

Wilhelm took a sip of the wine and nodded. "I believe that is correct. A man such as he would not surround himself with average women who have no outstanding traits besides their beauty."

Wilhelm took the envelope, turned to the dying man on the wheel, and asked, "Do you know this man?"

Gerhard shook his head.

"Otto no longer matters, but his work does," Wilhelm stated. "You see, years ago, I received a gift from an associate in South America. He knew I had an inclination for women of a more exotic variety. As a show of gratitude, he gifted me a very special addition to my beautiful collection."

He nodded towards the girl with the purple feet and calves, and she disappeared.

"Now, this toy needed some repairs. She was put to use quite a bit and she needed some routine maintenance. Otto here was working on that and trying to see what other fun things we could do with this new technology." The door opened behind them and Wilhelm gestured for the girl to come in.

"Now, obviously something went wrong," he dismissively gestured to the man dying on the wheel, "but that is neither here nor there," he chuckled, walking towards the two women that were approaching him.

The girl in bondage walked behind the new woman. This new woman was exquisite, a voluptuous beauty with long jet-black hair that bounced behind her at hip length. Her face was a flawless bronze, lightly kissed by the Latin sun. She wore a pink tube top snug on her well-endowed chest and cut-off jean shorts that gave her hips an even curvier look than they already had. Her legs looked strong and cut with muscle. On her small feet, she wore white gladiator type sandals that contrasted with her moss green toenails.

"This," Wilhelm announced grandly. "Is what this man was working on. She is one of a kind and I think she might be just what we need."

Wilhelm looked her up and down before grabbing her by the neck and licked the side of her face.

"Isn't she gorgeous?" he breathed hoarsely into her neck, kissing and biting her throat.

"Is she…" the man tried to ask before Wilhelm cut him off.

"Now, now. Let's not get ahead of ourselves!" he smiled. "Elena, mein schönes Mädchen, please show us what you're hiding between those perfect legs." Wilhelm slapped her backside in approval before stepping back.

Gerhard could almost hear Wilhelm salivating as he watched the young woman seductively remove her cut-off shorts and lavender panties. She lifted her leg straight up in an instant, her knee now beside her head, and revealed her secret flower.

"This…," Wilhelm salivated. "…is what he was working on."

The man turned pale at what he saw and he felt like he was going to be sick. "Go ahead, we'll just have to clean it up," Wilhelm shrugged, ignoring the man's repulsion.

Gerhard vomited violently onto the floor, gripping his stomach as he convulsed and eliminated the contents of his stomach. Four more girls with purple bondage and painted limbs quickly appeared and began to clean up Gerhard's vomit.

"Isn't she something?" Wilhelm said, staring at Elena with the adoration of a child. "This is exactly the type of bait we need. Between this little witch and 'the Great Reset' my associates are about to unleash, our so-called *Lord* Celsus is finished already."

Δ
San Juan Island

"Lady Nona . . ."

The plea was so soft and desperate it sent a chill up Nona's spine. Sakura was hungry. After the initial hysteria of hunger, all that remained was agony from the defeated acceptance that it would not be satiated. There was a stench of stagnant blood that lingered in the room constantly. It was not the delicious aroma of live blood pulsing through a squirming human. It was the festering odor of blood with no life that has rotted in plastic bags for too long. Straw after piping straw was shoved between her beautiful lips and she sucked and sucked in the most nauseating feeding she'd ever suffered.

Sakura lay in her ethereal bed chambers. She had the second largest room after Celsus, due to her imprisonment. The lord wanted her to be in luxury during her unwilling stay at the house, but even her extravagant lodging could not alleviate the hunger.

"Jenny," Sakura whimpered.

"My goddess," Nona said, petting her head.

"My poor, beautiful Jenny," Sakura hissed in self-loathing. She couldn't help herself. She was absolutely starving. Even in this regal home, she was hungry and going mad from the hunger. Her once-born lover was taken quickly and buried with great respect.

"Nona," she pleaded again.

"I'm here, my lady," Nona whispered, patting her head gently.

"Kiss me," she whimpered.

Nona bent over the ghost of the goddess she'd known and licked her half open lips. Sakura's eyes closed as Nona's tongue traced her trembling lips. The sweetness of her taste filled Sakura's deprived senses and she inhaled the aroma. It was delicious.

"Goddess, please . . ."

Nona obliged the plea and stuck her tongue into Sakura's mouth, licking and sucking on her lips and tongue. Nona inhaled deeply and Sakura's skin erupted in wanting goosebumps. Sakura hissed gently as Nona's hands caressed her face and moved down the side of her beautiful, wasting body.

"My lady," she pleaded.

Sakura seemed more beast than woman these days as she fought the madness that threatened to overwhelm her. Imprisonment was not easy, but imprisonment with the hunger was hell.

Nona got under the sheets beside her, pulling Sakura's body close. Sakura pressed Nona's face harder onto her own, kissing and sucking hungrily at her lips like the starved beast she was.

The desire burned within Sakura and she growled in want. Nona groaned into the kiss and slipped her hand under Sakura's blouse. Her nails trailed down Sakura's stomach and touched the top of her soaking slit. Sakura moaned and grabbed Nona's shoulders, squeezing and begging with depravity.

"Goddess," she barely whispered. The desire and the hunger were becoming overwhelming as Nona sucked on her neck.

"I know what you need," she whispered, licking Sakura's neck, from her delicious collarbone to her exquisite jawline. She massaged Sakura's soaking wet lips and tongue-sucked her beautiful face. She played with Sakura's nub, her pinky teasing the twitching entrance.

With her free hand, Nona stuck three of her fingers deep into Sakura's mouth. Sakura responded, hungrily sucking on

Nona's fingers, licking between and around them. Nona gently pulled her other fingers from Sakura's hole and smiled.

"Are you hungry?" Nona asked, as Sakura climbed on top of her. Sakura's mouth and cunt watered with desire and Nona tilt her head to one side. She took the hand working on Sakura's front and made an incision upon her own neck with her delicate, razor sharp pinky nail.

The trickle of red drove Sakura wild when she saw it drip down Nona's breast. "My beautiful, goddess . . ." Nona whispered, her hand moving once more to Sakura's taught backside.

Sakura's eyes were focused on the red trickling against Nona's beautiful, olive skin. It was an inhuman concentration that was the look of a predator barely maintaining the patience needed for its prey.

"Not yet," Nona pleaded as she widened her legs and positioned herself against Sakura. "Put a finger in," she moaned and Sakura did as she was instructed, her body on autopilot - her eyes not once leaving the red that blossomed at Nona's neck.

Nona arched her back as Sakura worked her fingers into her moistening slit. She began to move up and down on Sakura's hand, observing the goddess' hollow and beautiful face.

"One more second," she gasped, as she prepared her fingers on Sakura's body. "Three. Two. One." Sakura pounced as Nona's fingers entered her front and her back, penetrating her at once as Sakura latched onto Nona's neck.

Nona cried out and Sakura fed with abandon. Even in her euphoria, Sakura knew she couldn't waste away her sister, her lover, but she fed with unmatched hunger as Nona began to move her fingers inside her body.

Sakura moved with her, her free hand massaging and pinching Nona's erect nipples. Her fingers moved in and out of Nona's thrusting hips as she hungrily sucked on the open wound. Nona groaned loudly as she grinded on Sakura's hand. She could feel the tongue and lips on her flesh sucking her life force out and the sensation made her dizzy with masochistic lust.

Nona lifted her leg and thrust harder, as if her hunger and desire matched Sakura's. She moved her fingers more and more and could feel the mounting orgasm. Sakura bit down on Nona's shoulder over and over again as her release built in the pit of her stomach. Her legs widened on Nona and the wetness trailed down her leg. They were almost there.

"What is going on here?" came the silky voice that nearly pushed them both over the edge of ecstasy. Both women let out the growl of an animal exercising other worldly restraint as they both turned to look at the entrance to the room.

Lord Celsus stood watching them, his erection straining against his pants. He held a large strap-on double-ended dildo in one hand and the women felt shivers go down their spines. What was he planning?

"My beloved goddess," he addressed Sakura. "You have been so deprived and so I decided to pay you a visit."

He walked towards her, casually waving the phallic object as if it were an extension of his beautiful hand. "I see you are well attended," he said, grinning at Nona.

Nona blushed and both women began crawling up to him along the bed. Little blood droplets from Nona's wound sprinkled the sheet as they made their way to him. He was straining against his pants but still held a calm, cool look on his beautiful, pale face.

"Lady Nona."

"My lord," she bowed.

"You will wear this and pleasure our most beautiful Lady Sakura from the front."

"Yes, my lord," Nona said obediently, and almost snatched the strap-on from him in lust but caught herself as she respectfully took it. Celsus could feel the difficult restraint she felt and smiled.

Carefully, Nona equipped herself with the artificial penis, willing herself not to climax without her master's consent as the object slowly went inside her. Nona's walls spasmed around the artificial dick and she swooned with pleasure, barely able to contain herself.

Celsus looked hotly into Sakura's eyes and commanded her, "You will sit reverse cowgirl style on Nona, grind the toy, and suck me all at once, my beautiful," Celsus said softly, followed by a deep passionate kiss.

Sakura nodded, eagerly sucking on Celsus' tongue while pulling his pants down. Her hands gripped his steely girth and she groaned when she felt his hands touch her hot body.

"My beautiful, exquisite cherry blossom," he cooed, squeezing her breasts and pinching her nipples. He gently pulled away, caressing her face and licking her flushed cheek. "Are you hungry, my gem?"

Sakura whimpered. "I am, my lord."

Celsus licked her neck, tenderly pushing her head back with one hand. "Would you like to feed, my precious?"

Sakura almost cried. "Yes, my lord!"

Her hands were still wrapped around his thickening member when she felt one of his hands close around hers. He guided Sakura's finger to play with the tip, massaging himself with her hand. With a small flick, he made an incision on the head of his dick. A bead of blood sprouted.

Sakura groaned hungrily as she saw his blood mixed with precum. With difficulty, she took the master into her eager mouth and hungrily sucked the head of his cock. She let her hands grip his ass, pushing him in and out of her desperate mouth.

"You will orgasm together," he commanded as Sakura sucked with frenzy. His hands grabbed onto her silky black hair and he caressed her as she hungrily drank, tearing the wound slightly with an incisor to increase the flow.

Nona moved her hips with fury, thrusting into Sakura harder and shoving her further into Celsus. Sakura could feel the head filling her throat and her pussy tensed around the artificial dick fucking her.

Celsus felt the desperation all too clearly as his beautiful goddess drank the life sustenance she needed so desperately. He could feel her hunger, even greater than his own. This creature that had been with him throughout 17 lifetimes - he could feel her madness through the very hair he clutched in his hand, and through the tips of the fingers that clamped desperately on his ass. He loved her – with every ounce of his sadistic being.

He could sense they were both close to their peak and he growled. Feeling their ecstasy peaking was one the most pleasurable moments of their unions. He lived for those moments when they lost themselves in their desire.

More! More! More!

Sakura shouted telepathically to them, begging for them to go harder and faster. She sucked with more vigor and tightened around Nona's artificial cock, nearing her climax.

Celsus clawed at her erect nipples that rubbed against his legs. Her chest moved up and down his muscular thighs and he pawed at them hungrily with his claws. She needed this more than she realized and she groped at the master's flesh in her mounting ecstasy.

Master! Please!

My lord! Even Nona could feel the unusual level of desire pulsing on an even higher level than the mere physical.

The two women pleaded for permission to release, their minds a chaotic mess of pleasure. He could feel himself nearing his own explosion and he groaned.

"Ask me a little more sweetly," he commanded softly, despite his own eruption, which was so close. He wanted to hear their beautiful pleading voices.

My lord and master, Nona could barely form her thoughts. *Please! I am so close! May I?*

Master, Sakura pleaded with strained reason. *Please. May I come?*

Even in their thoughts Celsus could almost hear them panting with lust. Sakura sucked harder, the strands of her glistening saliva dripping down his flexing thighs. The sound was wet and sloppy, and she knew he loved this along with the smell of her saliva and sex mixed together. Nona thrust in rhythm with Sakura's mouth - keeping pace with the accelerated speed.

They were there and Celsus could feel the orgasm building within him. His sack tightened as their moment of release mounted in unison. They all reached a synchronized telepathic moment of euphoria and Celsus forgot himself, his surroundings, and lived in that single instant right before the ecstasy. The only thing in his world was the pleasure, and the love he felt for the two women he was connected with at that precise moment.

"Now, you may come."

The permission was not granted in wild abandon or with desperate haste. He granted their release with the love and respect he felt for them, and their utmost pleasure.

The two women felt blank - floating in a realm between realities as they howled in the orgasmic moment. Their walls shuddered in wild spasms and sweet juices erupted. Sakura's sex trickled down the dildo and mixed with Nona's as she thrust hard into Sakura's slit. Sakura, in turn, licked and pleaded for the master's precious seed which he gladly gave, exploding deep into her throat. He could feel her hunger consuming his cum, blood, and anything and everything else he had to get the nourishment she needed.

Sakura desperately gulped everything down and licked at his sack in respectful admiration. She released Celsus, gently licking his tip and kissing his thighs. She was already hungry again, the few moments of bliss gone, and he took her perfect face in his hands and looked into her soul.

"Soon, my precious."

He didn't say when or how. The master didn't even promise, but she nodded in absolute trust and obedience. Celsus kissed her with sweet passion, gently pushing her down next to Nona. He looked at Nona's face flushed with sex and kissed her parted wet lips.

"Tend to our goddess, my lady. She deserves the utmost attention during this treacherous ordeal."

Nona nodded, removing the strap-on to start cleaning her delicate, and ever-hungry sister.

Celsus buttoned himself up with an elegance only he could have after his fellatio with a deadly sex minx and silently left the room. There was still so much to do.

Δ

Seattle

"What exactly are you looking for again?" Sanem reclined in the chair of her office as Megan searched her files. Tara was on the phone with her, in Germany mapping out the massive Hilgenfeldt dynasty and everyone associated with it.

"No, the other . . . the one above him. He is affiliated with the House of Hilgenfeldt. I want this one. Feeding from him is symbiotic with our master's cause and our crusade against these arrogant once-borns," Megan stated, in a matter of fact tone.

She was not listening. Sanem shut her eyes and sighed. Earlier they could feel the pleasure her sisters and the master were having. Megan and Sanem both grew hot with desire. It had been too long since they'd been together, but they had work to do at the moment.

"I'll find him and I'll be in touch," Tara said.

Megan's parting words were unusual, reflecting her uncertainty, "Stay safe my lover," and hung up.

"This is him," Megan hissed in excitement. She read the intel report dramatically, "Bishop Klaus Schunner, under investigation for sponsoring a priest and a cardinal that have both been accused of sexual misconduct with underage children, particularly boys. It is also suspected he is involved with a human trafficking ring that was just broken, but still under investigation. Bishop Schunner, a man in his late 50s, was used to things going his way. Never one in the spotlight, he had the unusual disposition of being constantly associated with characters of questionable reputation. Most cardinals he sponsored had come under investigation for sexual misconduct with children."

Tara, Megan called to her sister in Germany telepathically. *Are you feeling me?*

Yes, my love. He is certainly a target. He has deep connections with Wilhelm Hilgenfeldt. The master will like this.

One of the trusted of Wilhelm's inner-circle, Bishop Schunner would have access to information the lowly cardinals would not. The coven needed this man.

Tara, I need to get to him. Once we do, we'll have Wilhelm. He will make it easier to get to the master's quarry.

Tara cooed in excitement. Trying to get to Bishop Schunner was difficult, but getting to Wilhelm was almost impossible.

I'll see what I can get on him while I'm here. He has homes all over Europe, but right now he is supposed to be residing in…

Megan paused as her vision scoured for the information she needed. *Rotterdam. I am coming out there as soon as possible.*

Sanem and Megan left the office and got into their Audi S5, a slick silver with blacked out lights and accents. Megan looked at Sanem and winked as she got into the driver's seat.

"I thought we were supposed to be keeping a low profile," she smiled, as she started the vehicle.

Sanem shrugged. "We could have taken the R8."

Megan giggled, as she pulled out of the underground parking garage. "Now that's just being extravagant," she exclaimed, speeding off toward the ferry in Anacortes. It was two in the morning. They had to catch the 4:30am boat to get back to the coven estate before dawn.

Δ

Bavaria

"Fix yourself a cup of tea Gerhard," Wilhelm said as he donned a tailored white dress shirt. "Make sure I am not disturbed. I have an important communication from New York. More good news I am certain," he added with a grin before a servant closed the two giant oak doors behind him.

Wilhelm casually sat down and hit the enter button to start the encrypted visual communication from America. The gentleman on the screen was dressed in casual business attire and spoke with a perfect Oxford English accent.

"Herr Hilgenfeldt, how are you this evening, my good man?"

Wilhelm spoke English with a near perfect accent matching the man on the screen.

"Very good, old friend. It's midnight here and I am a bit taxed. How is it going?"

"So far, perfect. Several of our associates find it amusing that we are not hiding anything. Event 201 is public, and we are even calling it a coronavirus pandemic," the Englishman said with a smirk on his face.

Wilhelm sat up in chair and asked with all seriousness, "And the results?"

"We will be able to shut down the entire planet. Everyone and anyone in leadership positions over all populations have already been paid to carry out our orders, even the United States. By the time anyone figures out the fiction, it will be too late. The majority of people will be scared out of their minds. Everything that naturally causes death, the flu, heart conditions, stroke, et cetera, et cetera, will be blamed on Covid-19. Our system will be in place. They will have no choice but to accept the new normal. Once famine and digital currency are entered into the equation, they will kneel."

"What about the scientific and medical communities outside our reach?"

"My good man, we own all the media outlets that motivate over 97 percent of the population. Any voices of dissent shall receive no platform, and if they start to make waves on the internet, we will unplug them. We have thousands of disinformation agents waiting to discredit them. And, let's not forget, the masses have become our very own thought police. Those marked for slaughter will actually shame those doctors and scientists out of existence, much like the Brownshirts from Germany's past. Our hundred-year-plan is finally going to happen."

"And my interests?" Wilhelm asked, getting close enough to the camera to reveal his sociopathic gaze.

"No one will be able to move without being seen and tracked, Herr Hilgenfeldt. It is a perfect scenario for your needs. I too have a vested interest in what you are doing.

There can be only one ruling class my good man, and those you seek have never graced our roster."

"Sehr gut. Please, keep me advised," Wilhelm said smiling, relaxing in his leather chair.

"Of course. We'll be in touch. Guten Abend," the Englishman said before the screen went black.

DEPRIVATIONS
November 9, 2019 – 11:00 p.m.
Rotterdam, Netherlands

Tara crept along the perimeter of the estate, her eyes constantly focused on her prey. Crouched in the surrounding green, she watched the few guards leisurely chatting. She reached the mind of her hungry sister.

How many more to do you see on your side?

Megan sat at the other side of the complex, hidden in the trees.

Three more. Nothing we can't handle, Megan replied. *They don't seem to be on any high alert. What about your men?*

No. It's a bit strange.

Megan watched as the guards leaned against the verandas, lazily watching the horizon. *They aren't even pretending. Where is all the surveillance equipment, the cameras, the snipers? I don't see anything.*

A lazy guard yawned and stretched, and Megan's mouth began to water. She could see his belly pressing against his suit jacket and she shivered with hunger. It had been too long since her last feeding, but she was not going to settle for anyone. She was going to feast, but not just yet.

Megan had joined Tara in Holland on her quest for Bishop Klaus Schunner, and they were casing his current estate of residence. It was a quaint countryside manor for the absurdly wealthy, and both women were shocked at the lack of guards.

Why are there so few? Tara wondered.

She was puzzled and her mind thought through hundreds of possibilities in the same amount of time it would take most people to think through a single scenario. Megan came upon her, a stealthy creature that touched her shoulders with exquisite hands.

"Perhaps he does not want to attract too much attention to himself," Megan whispered, settling in the grass beside her. Tara's brows furrowed as she continued to ponder.

"Don't frown, my beloved," Megan said, kissing her sweetly on the cheek and forehead. "Let's go back to the hotel. We'll think on it more."

Tara was reluctant to leave but knew Megan was right. They had gathered as much information as they could and it was going to be light soon.

"Really? You think that's why?" Tara inquired.

Megan shrugged as she got in the Land Rover and started the giant vehicle. "Not everything has to be as complicated as our existence, my darling," she smiled.

Tara shrugged again, in a particularly foul mood with the discovery they'd made. Megan touched her thigh.

"What's wrong Tara? Honestly?"

Tara looked down at her hands, silent and brooding.

"We lost last time," she sighed.

Tara reflected upon the loses during their first encounter with the Controllers. She could never get rid of the guilt for not being there to help Sakura and Sanem.

"We shall not lose this time," she seethed.

Megan kissed her and said softly, "Of course not."

When they arrived at their hotel, Megan pulled the curtains tight to shut out the oncoming dawn and Tara collapsed into bed. Staring at the ceiling she quietly asked, "So what did you find out about him?"

Megan's eyes dilated with the hunger she suddenly felt. While she was not suffering like Sakura, she was hungry.

"Bishop Schunner is a slimy man with unique tastes. Under the investigation of his superiors in the church, his own personal garbage has come under the microscope. The human trafficking ring that was uncovered dealt uniquely with children and youth. There were adult men and women, but they were best known for the quality of youth they provided for the right price. He is also a good friend of Wilhelm Hilgenfeldt."

"He's into kids?" Tara asked. "I'm not surprised. I wonder if that if that is Wilhelm's bent."

Megan shook her head. "We'll get all that information soon when our disgusting bishop is put to questions. Then he will be obliterated," she said, salivating, her eyes suddenly glowing red.

Tara nodded, "With the master's blessing, they will all die," she said, pulling Megan closer. "For now, you need to rest. You are due back home tomorrow."

They were so close. They could go right now and get the bishop, but they had not received the master's blessing. They could not move without it and Megan had to wait.

"What about Wilhelm?' Megan asked softly, cuddling deeper into Tara's powerful arms.

"I don't know. We will need everyone for that. I'm sure his estate is a fortress."

Megan nuzzled Tara's chest. "Why can't they all just drop dead," she mumbled sweetly.

Tara chuckled. "Now where would be the fun in that, my love?"

They both closed their eyes and fell into a death-like sleep.

Δ

Bavaria

"How is the security?" Wilhelm asked without bothering to look at the man that had walked in. He sat on the veranda of his mansion in his violet satin robe that hung open as he ate toast, jam, and sweetened coffee.

"We have the cargo arriving today, sir, with twelve more specialists arriving from the sister estate. They will be positioned to protect the cargo at all costs."

Wilhelm nodded, taking a loud sip of his coffee. "They do not know what it is, correct?"

"No sir, they do not," the man stated with confidence.

"How sure are you that this new contraption will indeed work?"

"Sir?" the man asked, seemingly confused.

"Are we sure this will restrain Celsus?" he asked again, looking up at his men.

Nobody answered or dared to look at him.

"So, none of you will answer me," he laughed dryly. "I just spent a small fortune - more money than some countries can produce in a year - and nobody can answer me if this investment will pay off!" His hand slammed down hard on the table, rattling the dishes and the men jumped. "I'll ask again and one of you better answer," he hissed. "Will this successfully restrain Celsus?"

There was a painfully long silence but one man reluctantly stepped forward. Wilhelm looked at him in dismissive curiosity as if he hadn't realized he was even there.

"Yes?"

The man cleared his throat. "This should successfully restrain the target, sir," he answered in a strained voice.

Wilhelm looked up at him taking another loud sip of his coffee.

"Should?"

The tension on the veranda could be cut with a knife as Wilhelm looked off into the horizon. He cleared his throat and set his cup down, stretching his legs out under the table, roughly kicking the girl on her hands and knees beneath the breakfast table. He looked down at her with a sickening sneer.

"Who are you again?"

The girl looked up at him, her bright purple calves and forearms shinning in the early sunlight. One of her eyes was sewn shut, though the scar did not hinder but rather accentuated her angular beauty. A red-haired pixie with freckles, her single eye looked at him with resolute hatred and revulsion.

Wilhelm groaned, shoving her harder under the table with his foot. "Oh, my beautiful. Be careful with that eye. I might claim it as my own," he threatened and beckoned her toward him.

She glared at his hand in helpless contempt and did not immediately go to him. The girl hesitated for a second longer and Wilhelm's arousal grew at thought of what he going to do to her.

"Come, my pet," he said in a husky voice, dripping with danger.

She shook with anger and fear but slowly, she crawled to him and put her chin into his beckoning palm. Her face trembled in his hand as his fingers clenched down on her slight chin.

"I do not think you learned your lesson," he groaned, his hardening dick straining against his underwear.

His fingers tightened around her jaw, his nails digging into her delicate flesh. Her face distorted in pain as he lifted her up by her face. Her violet arms fumbled and she hung like a broken puppet on his clenched fist as he slowly stood.

"Let's play, my pet. Let's see what tricks I can teach you." Wilhelm cast a dismissive glance at the man that had stepped forward. "You too. We are going to play a little game. Bishop Schunner actually taught this to me," he chuckled sickeningly.

The man's face turned pale.

Δ
San Juan Island

Cala . . . my goddess . . .

Cala flew over the skies of remote Southwestern Canada when the ghostly plea came to her.

Help me ... a plea of terrible hunger.

Sakura sat in the corner of her luxurious room, naked, wild, and thirsty. The stench of the stagnant blood coated her beautiful skin in a sickly film she wanted to gnash off. If she could, she would eat herself in desperation to quench her ravenous hunger, but the master would not like that.

My love, how may I serve you?

With her massive wings, Cala flew naked on the winds high above the mountains of British Columbia. Miles and miles of giant trees extended beneath her as she circled in the moonlight looking for prey.

"I envy you," Sakura hissed. "I envy the moon bathing you." Sakura's mouth salivated from the hunger and the desire to touch Cala's silky feathers. "Goddess...can you feel me? I am touching myself," she snarled in lust.

Cala turned in a dive with great force and felt her breasts swell with desire.

"My lady . . ."

"I want you Cala, my angel. I need you," Sakura groaned in the empty room.

Cala felt her slit swelling and wetting with lust. More animal than human, there was nothing more primal than the need for sex, and the overwhelming feeling suddenly possessed her.

"Sakura," she groaned in her inhuman voice.

Sakura heard it and she couldn't stop the shiver that went through her own body. She was nothing but raw desire and her pain was infuriating. Hearing Cala's inhuman voice in her mind and feeling the enormous hunger that now took over her body, Sakura groaned.

"Go to the highest tree you can find."

Cala obeyed without thinking. Her owl eyes quickly scanned the entirety of the forests around her and in the distance, she saw the tallest peak and darted toward it.

"When you get there," Sakura groaned, taking a large vibrating dildo from beside her, "I want you to slowly impale yourself on the tip."

Sakura moaned as she placed the large vibrating head slowly into her wetness. On the dirty, blood-stained wooden floor, she lay on her back, legs propped up, her delicate feet planted against the corner walls of her room.

Cala screeched at the night sky as she dove for the tree top. Her body eased back as she landed with deadly precision, her claws clearing the rogue branches on the tree, turning it into a perfect point and she trembled. Cala gripped onto the tree, screeching as she felt Sakura shoving the object deep into her sex. The tree shook with her trembling as Cala fought to control the building desire within her inhuman body.

"My goddess!" Cala pleaded.

"I love hearing you beg for me," Sakura moaned. "Sit on the point, slowly."

Cala screeched, salivating at the sensation as she climbed up the tree. The bark crunched gently under her careful climb to the point. Her talons held on to the delicate top of the pine, her wings expanding to their full length as she carefully moved herself down to the point of the tree. Her wings shivered as the end slowly penetrated her and Sakura groaned a world away. Her talons dug into the center branch, and she softly flapped her wings to maintain control, slowly moving herself up and down on the point. Half flying, half squatting, Cala turned her owl face up to the sky and Sakura could see the magnificent sky through her sister's eyes and she groaned.

"Goddess," Cala cried out, her inhuman voice echoing throughout the solitude of the trees and mountains.

Sakura placed her hand under her ass to brace the vibrating dildo against the floor. She moved up and down on it, her feet pressed against the walls, her hands against the floor, slamming down hard with powerful thrusts. She was nearing her climax and could barely hold back. All control was concentrated on her winged sister, and she growled at the mounting pleasure. She could feel Cala moving in synchronization with her. She bit down on her lip and licked at her own blood as she felt Cala move faster and faster.

"Not yet," Sakura ordered. "Do you love me?" A smile played at the end of the question as Sakura thrust herself upon the vibrating tool.

"I adore you, my love...I adore you!" Cala screeched painfully.

"How much?" Sakura demanded between groans and pants. The walls of her pussy spazzed round the toy imbedded deep inside her as she listened to Cala's animalistic groans.

"More than life!" she responded, slamming down harder, the texture of the tree tip now tearing the fragile walls of her vagina. Her talons closed tightly around tree top, little by little cracking through with each wild bloody thrust.

"I love you! I need you!" Sakura cried out for her. "I need blood! I am so thirsty!" she yelled out desperately.

Her pleading took on the desperate sounds of a threat and demand, too confused to truly be either. Cala listened for Sakura's breathing, her thrusting, and for the next order she would moan out in forceful lust.

"My angel, you are so close," Sakura cooed. "Can you feel me touching you?"

Cala shuddered on the branch and she screeched into the empty sky.

"I love your pussy. Sucking you off is my wish," Sakura groaned, as she pinched her own nipples, hard.

"I need you!" Cala called out, more flying than straddling now as the tree top crunched beneath her.

"Fly!" Sakura demanded. "Let me fly with you!"

Their connection was perfect…absolute unity.

Cala shouted, her talons breaking through the point of the giant tree like butter and flew straight up into the sky. Her wings propelled her like a jet and she held the abrasive object deep inside her, shoving it in and out of herself with her talons. Blood spattered the inside of her thighs.

"Higher! Higher!" Sakura begged, slamming herself on the floor. The oak wood creaked with the impacts and her ass left a heart shaped mark from her sweat.

"I live to serve you!" Cala cried out, shoving the point in and out of herself.

"Bring me someone! I thirst! Your lover commands!" Sakura snarled, breaking the device within her.

"My goddess commands! I shall obey! Goddess!"

"I love you! Faster, Cala! More! I'm so close!"

Cala flew hard, her massive wings taking her higher and higher. Her talons gripped the long piece of wood she shoved in and out of herself. Harder and faster as her wings carried her higher.

Goddess!

She could no longer speak or call out to her imprisoned sister. The sex and thinning oxygen made her dizzy, lightheaded. She would have to turn back soon but not yet - she was so close.

Cala…come with me! I'm almost…

Sakura's slick walls spazzed around the dildo, no longer vibrating, broken from her violent tenacious thrusts. Her hands maddeningly clawed and pulled at her nipples, imagining Cala sucking on them as hard as she could. Her thighs clenched as she continued slamming down hard, finally hitting her sweet spot.

Cala was hypothermic, asphyxiated, and in the moment of near blackout, her wings spread and stopped. She completely froze in midflight for a few precious moments and she felt the most intense orgasm she had ever given herself. She was unconscious, still climaxing, and falling fast…toward the earth.

Locked away in Celsus' mansion, Sakura felt the otherworldly orgasm hit Cala and she pushed down as hard as she could, impaling the dildo deep inside her. The orgasm shot up to her stomach, up to the crown of her head, and her vaginal walls clenched hard as the pleasure overwhelmed her.

"Cala! Cala!" Sakura wailed with the intensity of the release. She slammed her feet against the walls, impossibly cracking the hard wood. Her thighs spasmed and she screamed out as her pussy juices squirted all over the battered wall. She thrust her powerful hips down on the broken dildo again as her eruption kept coming, her nails carving into the floor beneath her.

Cala continued falling. Although barely conscious, she convulsed with the pleasure that shot through her.

Goddess! Wake up! Sakura called out to her through spasms of pleasure as Cala fell toward the earth, awakening, glowing, and reborn.

"My lady!" Cala felt a warmth coming from deep within her and she spread her wings to guide her path down. She was still in the afterglow of the orgasm, legs wide, and still wet. She tried to focus through the haze to straighten her path down.

"Do you remember my request?" Sakura moaned sweetly, her fingers gently touching the rim of her dripping hole.

Cala tried to think back to the moments before the orgasm. What had Sakura asked of her?

"Blood. I need blood," Sakura cooed, the mess between her legs squishing under her perfect bottom.

"I will serve my goddess," Cala promised, beginning to spin down to her destination. The trees, at first a solid mass of green, slowly came into focus and Cala could make out each individual branch and leaf. "I have found someone, my goddess. Do you sense it?" Cala inhaled deeply filling her monstrous body cavity with life giving air.

"I sense that you sense it," Sakura whispered, lying on her side, her nails digging into the luxurious floor and carving out small craters in their wake. "Bring it to me."

Cala screeched as she came upon the trees and lowered herself among them. She could sense Sakura was close and the exhilaration of their sex still made her blood rush through her body. Her body broke off tree tops and branches. Everything in her path was destroyed and she could feel nothing as she closed in on her target.

The winged demon came to an abrupt halt, and grabbed onto the trunk of a giant pine. The sound of her body crashing onto the solid mass was like a shock of thunder across the clear sky. Cala crouched on the branch, retracting her wings and focusing on her prey.

Do you see this, my goddess?

Miles away, locked in a room dripping with the smell of stale blood and desperate sex, Sakura almost orgasmed again at the site of fresh blood.

Yes!

Cala's talons clicked against the tree branch as she watched the man moving, scrutinizing his every move. He walked without a care in the world. This once-born had voluntarily chosen to live in the wilderness, cut off from the rest of society. Sakura could hardly fathom the thought of being cut off from her life source, but his loss was her gain and her mouth watered as she watched the unsuspecting human moving around his cabin through Cala's owl-like eyes.

The wait was excruciating and Sakura felt like she was on the verge of a meltdown as she watched him move. But Cala was an expert hunter and Sakura would not rush her lover that had perfected her art so many lifetimes ago.

A few more minutes and he was perfectly in place. Cala took a deep breath, clicked her claws a few more times and pounced. Deadly and elegant, her talons closed on the man's body in an instant and cradled him as she lifted him high up in the air.

Sakura was breathless. Her prey was being brought to her. Cala took off into the sky like a graceful beast and the man lost consciousness from terror.

I'm on my way, my beloved.

Sakura shivered at the primal voice that spoke to her.

Cala flew towards the house, her catch cradled in the claws of death. Part of her knew this was wrong, but that reasoning was overridden by her desire to help Sakura. Her sister was suffering, wild with hunger, and Cala could not simply sit by and watch.

I'm coming, my love.

Sakura heard Cala, but her hunger was too much. She feared herself as much as she feared never leaving the house again. She sat and waited in the same corner she had just damaged with her powerful thrusts and did not move or think. Cala was on her way with a body and that was enough to send her into a wild silent mindlessness. Soon, the offering would arrive and she would feast. There was a slight disturbance in the wind, an unnatural ruffling from high above and Sakura held her breath.

"My lover," came the inhuman call and the windows slowly opened as Cala came forth and presented her gift to the starving beauty. Sakura snarled at the sight.

"You've done well," Sakura hissed, trying to control the unnatural shaking of her hands as she looked at the man.

He was in his early 40s, dirty and soiled out of fear. His normally tan skin was ashen and he was blubbering in terror. He was not the most exquisite dinner, but at this very moment, standing before this miserable wretch, Sakura had never seen a more delicious blood sack.

"Do you love me?" Sakura asked the terrified man.

Her glowing eyes looked straight into his broken soul, her nails dug into his soft human flesh and he almost fainted at what he saw.

"I am going to love you with everything I am," Sakura cooed, reveling in the fear the man felt. Something about being confined made her appreciate and long for the terror of the prey. Her hands caressed the side of his weathered face as she taunted. "You will experience things you cannot imagine and no one will hear you," she hissed, licking his face.

On the other side of the house, Celsus and Nona watched her through cameras set up in her room. Nona was in disbelief. Sakura had never been one to feed like that. Celsus did not even need to read her thoughts.

"Confinement can change a person," he said, not turning towards her.

He extended a hand and beckoned her closer. Nona walked to him and stood at his side as they watched Sakura licking and sucking on her victim, tearing the skin off him in round little patches. He put his arm around her waist and Nona could see him getting hard. He guided her to stand before him, her back to the screens and he looked deep into her eyes. It'd been a while since he stood so intimately with her and she felt unnerved as his gaze pierced through her being. His hand reached up to caress her face and his mouth watered, flicking his tongue out at her jawline.

"Have you ever felt such confinement, my love?" he whispered hoarsely at her. His breaths were short, like gasps, and he kissed her elegant neck. "Do you truly know the hunger we feel?" he growled into her neck, running his hand down her back and lifting the hem of her dress.

Celsus groped her perfect ass and Nona shivered under his electrifying touch. New feelings washed over her. She felt like a prisoner every day now, and she felt a cry catch in her throat.

Celsus looked at her again, his face contorting with every emotion coursing through his body and Nona felt like her heart would break at the sight. He was confused, angry, and even afraid. Nona knew he was losing control and she did not know how to stop it.

"No," he growled, kissing her. "You don't know what it's like, do you my queen?"

Nona hesitated but shook her head and Celsus smiled.

"I'm happy for that," he moaned, slicing the fabric on her neckline with his scalpel-sharp fingernail, and licking down her chest.

"I'm glad you, at least, do not suffer as we do."

In Sakura's room, the unknown man bled from the wounds over his weathered skin. Cala held the man down, her sharp talons gingerly caressing his arms as Sakura licked at the fresh cuts. He trembled with fear and experienced sexual pleasure unlike anything he could have ever imagined. He was so enraptured, he did not notice Sakura tasting his blood.

Sakura felt the hunger rising within her and became wet with desire. She knelt between the man's legs, perfectly timing her assault. She could feel he was about to orgasm and as her teeth were about to slice through the man's hard pulsating penis, she stopped. His presence was immediate and she could feel his own arousal and frustration from where she knelt.

Blood slowly dripped onto the floor from the naked man's legs. Except for the blood and saliva that covered her lips and chin, Sakura looked like an innocent child caught stealing candy.

"What have we here?" Celsus smiled, strolling into the room as casual as if he were talking about the weather. He completely ignored the moaning man on the floor and smiled coolly upon the two women pinning the man down.

"I was not told we had a guest," he said grinning. Sakura felt her heart drop but the hunger almost overpowered her fear of the master. "My beloved Sakura," Celsus said sweetly, lifting her chin up to look at him. "You would not disobey me, would you?"

Her entire body shook under that perfect finger that pinned her to the spot. Celsus might as well have had his knee to her throat, threatening to kill her. Sakura shivered.

"No, my darling Sakura would *never* do such a thing," he sighed, shaking his head. Celsus took a dramatic breath. "Yet, why is this man here?"

He turned an icy gaze at Cala and the woman, more beast than human, looked back at him with an empty but submissive gaze. My Cala," Celsus sighed, walking to her and taking her face between his hands. "Did you disobey me?"

Her eyes darted to Sakura and Celsus waved his finger in front of her eyes to bring her attention back to him. "No, no. Here…right here," he said dryly. "Did you disobey my orders"

Cala looked at him but said nothing and he took a deep breath. "You only wanted to help your sister, didn't you?"

Still Cala said nothing.

"You suffer because she suffers," he whispered, as he traced the outline of her inhuman face with a delicate finger. He kissed her sweetly on her lips. "You will not be punished," he whispered to her, his hand moving down her back, caressing her retracted wings. "I forgive you because you only wanted to help her, and you will not be punished for loving her so much."

Sakura shook from the control she forced herself to maintain and Celsus turned his attention back to her. "You however blatantly disobeyed me," he said, without blinking. "What are we going to do about that?"

Her eyes were wild with emotion though her face remained unfeeling. Celsus stood for a while looking at her, staring into her hungry eyes. "You poor thing," he said to her. "Your hunger is about to drive you mad."

Celsus bent down and kissed her, at first sweetly, then deepening the kiss, running his tongue into her mouth and sucking on her lips. Sakura was stiff with control and Celsus broke the kiss for a few precious moments. He looked at her, staring deep into her madness, and with his razor-sharp pinky nail, cut into his lower lip.

Sakura's eyes blazed and he gently put her lips to his open wound. The blood blossomed on his face and her lips trembled with temptation but she did not drink. The master had not given her permission and she feverishly waited.

"Good girl," Celsus whispered, licking her lips with his tongue. "You may have a little."

Her lips pursed around the cut and she sucked. She clung to him like a lifeline and her legs instinctively wrapped around him. He allowed her to drink, hungrily and lustfully sucking. He could feel her tongue, her hot saliva running down his chin, and between her legs he felt the heat from her wet sex. His hard cock pressed against Sakura's soaking panties, and she took care not to grind onto him. He chuckled at the control she could exercise in her most desperate state and his chest swelled with love for her. She was exquisite. He gently pushed her back.

"My beloved," Celsus urged gently. "It is rude to ignore your guest."

Reluctantly, Sakura released her master's face. She turned to see both Cala and Nona standing at perfect attention, bearing solemn witness to the love their master had for each of them - even when he had just cause to punish them for disobedience.

Nona watched and, in her heart, felt a tug of something she could not identify. The master truly loved them but when her attention turned to the man on the floor, the same horrible doubt reared in her heart. Nona quickly suppressed the unnamed feeling somewhere deep in her where Celsus could not see and then he addressed the room again.

"This guest is for our Lady Sakura," he informed them. "No one will touch this man without her consent. My lady, please proceed."

Sakura bowed and turned her attention back to the man.

"Cala, my darling, wait until Sakura is done," Celsus advised. "I think you will be pleased."

Cala ruffled her wings slightly, her only acknowledgement of consent, her eyes burning into the unfortunate man.

Celsus turned to Nona and she looked back at him. He paused as he heard Sakura behind him start sucking on the man again. He looked at Nona and he saw the same woman he had loved for many centuries. This time however, he felt as if there was a cloud over her heart that he could not quite see through.

"My lord?" she whispered. Celsus looked at her again and pushed the nagging thought out of his mind.

"Free me," he said, as he sat on the bed.

Nona went to him, knelt down with perfect grace, and unzipped his pants to release the engorged cock. It was hard and veiny - pulsing as he watched Sakura begin her operations on the man. Nona looked up at her master.

"You will give me your delicious ass and we will watch our Sakura feast," he groaned as Nona began working her hands up and down his cock. She looked up at him with pleading eyes and he smirked down at her, petting her beautiful head.

"Darling, you are so beautiful when you are wonton," he smiled, reading her hungry mind with ease.

While she did not have the thirst for blood the way the others did, she still hungered for her master when he presented himself to her like this. With a devilish grin he commanded her.

"You may suck, but only a little."

Nona moaned as she hungrily took only the head of his steely dick into her greedy mouth. She sucked lightly on the tip, ran her hands up down his thighs, and squeezed her legs together tightly in utter frustration. She only had a few precious moments of this before she had to sit on him, and she savored the rock hardness she was generating for that moment.

Sakura had started her feast. Her hunger quickly possessed her and she bit enormous chunks of flesh out of him. She lapped at the blood gushing forth. Her hands caressed his body as she fed, rubbing her clit up and down his legs. The blood smeared all over her body and the floor as she hungrily satisfied her need. Her hands, hair, and face were painted in a bright red as she sucked the blood from every wound on his body. He was losing consciousness now, but he did nothing more than groan. Sakura had put him in a trance - he would not feel a thing when he died and Celsus smiled. Even at her worst, Sakura still did not want her prey feeling pain.

"Fuck…" Celsus gasped.

Nona let a mouthful of her saliva drool into her cupped hand. With it, she lubricated the heavenly lavender-scented place her master loved so much. Once completed, she placed the clubbed tip to the sacred space, her asshole relinquishing its tightness in order to take on the girth of her master.

Celsus put a hand on Nona's back to move her slightly to one side. He did not want to miss a single moment of Sakura's unique and uncontrolled feeding. Nona leaned back, moving to one side of his face and moaned as she gradually sat all the way down on him with a shudder. She watched Sakura and Cala with half-opened eyes - their monstrous beauty - as the vice of her asshole clamped down on Celsus. Her juices trickled down to his balls and she slowly moved up and down his powerful flexing legs.

Sakura ate chunks off the man, licking the blood off before tossing them to Cala who hungrily ate them. His limbs were almost gone - nothing left but bone peeking through the chunks of remaining meat. His arms had less than his legs and Sakura saved his torso for last.

Behind her, Nona groaned and Celsus growled as the overpowering smell of death and blood completely overwhelmed his senses. Cala screeched as she held the nearly dead man - but he wasn't dead, not yet. Sakura straddled his dick, still hard thanks to her trance. Her naked body was covered in blood and she bounced on him as she worked herself up to a powerful orgasm.

Cala watched as she bounced and Nona matched her vigorous rhythm on Celsus. At the same time, the man's heart rate was accelerating - as if he was going to have a heart attack at any moment.

Celsus grabbed the back of Nona's head and whispered into her hear, "When he dies, I will come, but not a moment sooner, understand?"

"Yes, my lord," Nona breathed, focusing on the man's heart beat.

"Be a good girl and come with me," he commanded.

Nona gasped and nodded, "Yes, my lord."

"Sakura, come when you want my pet," he said sweetly to her.

"With you, my lord - with you…"

Sakura wanted that culminated moment of unified ecstasy. She needed that as much as she needed the blood.

"When he perishes," Celsus commanded.

Sakura bounced, harder and harder. The entire room was listening to the man's heart beat and they were all close.

Sakura's eyes glowed with lust, hunger and ecstasy and she licked her lips in anticipation of what she was going to do. Celsus saw it in her mind and he groaned, pulling Nona down hard onto his cock. "Beautiful," he growled.

"Thank you, Master. I'm…I'm…" Nona could no longer speak. The bliss possessed her completely. Tears began rolling down her cheeks and she moved faster, the walls of her ass tightening around his pulsing steely cock.

Sakura moaned as she felt the man's heart falter. The dying man convulsed and Sakura shouted her orgasm. Nona slammed down one last time onto Celsus, putting her entire weight onto him to shove him as deep into her as she possibly could and Celsus looked just in time to see Sakura bending over and ripping into the man's stomach. At that moment, Celsus snarled as he shot his seed deep into Nona. Nona came hard, her juices flowing out between her shaking legs, and she moaned as she also watched Sakura tear into the man's bowels. Her face was deep into his intestines, sloshing and slurping around the internal fluids for the blood she so desired. She fed until the man ran dry.

Nona did not move off Celsus, who caressed her body and gently cupped her breasts. The scene of an innocent man eaten alive amidst love and lust was a complete horror. As best as she could, Nona stayed within her bliss.

There were organ and tissue remnants in Sakura's hair, her entire face was smeared with blood and all manner of other bodily fluids. Her juices stuck to the inside of her leg, mixed with blood, and she appeared covered from head to toe in the disgusting putridness.

"Cala, my savior," she said, walking up to her. "You were not satisfied in this, so I will satisfy you," she said, her voice still lustful and hungry. She placed her bloody hands on Cala's face, rubbing the red into her beautiful cheeks. "Lick me clean," she commanded.

Cala smiled, her wings expanded, and Sakura lifted her own arms in a mirrored display. Cala's inhuman tongue reached out and began licking Sakura, running down her entire torso and wiping her clear of any substance. Cala licked at her breasts, sucked on her nipples, and pulled Sakura down to a clean space of floor near the man's mutilated corpse.

Celsus looked at the body and then looked at Nona. She had been the cleaner in every reincarnation. He did not need to say or think anything.

"I'll take care of it, my lord," Nona said softly, her eyes revealing a gentle glowing blue.

Celsus reflected, off-topic, "It's a shame the others are not here. That would have been even more memorable."

Sakura gasped at Cala's raspy efficient tongue. She placed a hand on Cala's shoulder, a silent command to refocus, before spreading her legs wide open. As soon as Sakura raised an eyebrow with her famous innocent grin, Cala quickly moved to open Sakura's moist flower with her pointed avian tongue.

Neither demon noticed Nona gently taking the mutilated body away. Entire chunks of flesh were missing from the arms and legs. The body was completely drained of blood. Nona decided it was practical to tear the body in two and the spine split with a terrible crack. She flinched at the sound and attempted to process the unusual realization that normal humans could not do this.

Celsus waited outside and watched as Nona carried the two pieces of the man's body toward the forest.

"My beautiful," Celsus beckoned, standing perfectly erect.

Nona approached him and bowed, "Master."

"Is something the matter? I've never seen you flinch when disposing of a human."

"My sister's suffering pains me, my lord. That is all."

Celsus nodded before replying, "Sakura's suffering is our suffering. We all feel her." He grazed her beautiful cheek with the back of his hand. "We must be strong for her. With our protection she will be safe, and all will be as it once was."

Nona bowed. "So shall it be, my lord."

Celsus kissed her crown and walked away.

The severed body in her hands felt like it was pulling her down to be swallowed by the earth. She took a breath to compose herself and quietly walked into the deep dark forest to rid the family of another atrocity.

ELENA
November 11, 2019 – 6:30 p.m.
San Juan Island

I don't understand this. Who in the world would dare come here? Megan projected to Sanem. *Do you have her in sight?*

Yes, and something is not right.

Deep in the wet rainy woods, a stunning woman stood completely still, her silky white dress shredded from blackberry thorns, stained from her long trek through the forest, and matted to her flesh with the icy cold of the Pacific Northwest. More inhuman than the two demons stalking her, she watched the coven's estate and waited as still as the trees surrounding her.

What do you mean? Megan inquired.

She seems not alive. She has no scent…no heartbeat…

Sanem's senses were perfect and she was in sync with her prey. But the prey did not breathe, nor eat or drink, and that excited Sanem more than the fear of a human. A cold, calculating creature just like herself; she needed to know what this female was. She gave Megan the cue.

I have a direct line of sight to her front.

I have her back. We got her.

This creature was not human and too close for comfort. Sanem reasoned through the number of androids that were roaming the Pacific Northwest and what the odds were of this advanced android showing up in their backyard. She knew this was the doing of the Controllers and it hit her very hard.

They know where we are.

Sanem and Megan took a unified breath, readied their bodies, and fixed their eyes on their prey from over a hundred yards.

Go.

The movements were quicker than any human could read with the naked eye. Megan took the android's legs out from under her and Sanem crushed the creature's skull into the dirt, her knees pinning the android to the ground. The body the two women held with all their strength was heavy, solid, and Sanem knew her suspicions had been correct.

"What business do you have here?" Sanem demanded, tightening her grip on the android.

Now that she was neutralized, Sanem could see the woman was absolutely gorgeous. Her skin was a deep caramel color with an hourglass figure to rival her own - a machine that could make men weep at the mere sight of it. This android was not made for any other purpose than seduction. She looked up at Sanem with enormous eyes and thick long lashes.

"Vengo," the woman said meekly…deceptively.

"English," Sanem said, slamming the woman's head harder into the ground.

"I am here as a visitor," the woman said into the ground with a Latin accent. Her lips were perfect, full and plump. Sanem watched as they moved, mesmerized, and knew if they could entrance her in such a way, any once-born would obey anything this woman wanted.

Sanem thought to herself that this strange female's voice was a chilling reminder of her true nature. The voice that came from those perfect lips was as inhuman as Cala's. Cold and devoid of emotion or humanity, the sound sent a wave of anxiety between the two hardened women that made them both curious and concerned.

"What is your name?" Megan demanded, tightening her grip on the android's legs even though she did not struggle.

"Elena Carani," she responded, but this time with the voice of a human. The sound that came from her lips could not have been more different from the previous statement.

What was previously a harsh and almost robotic sound turned into warm honey that filled their senses and made them sigh with sensual ease.

"That's some trick," Megan spat, holding her legs tight, not letting her guard down in the slightest.

Elena eyes seemed to refocus and she spoke again in her normal voice. "I am here as a visitor."

Sanem shut her eyes and thought about what to do next. It was clear they needed to do something about her but a brief exchange with her sister quickly led her down a more creative and amusing path for this new toy of theirs.

"Who sent you?"

"Carlos Andre Bruno."

"Who?" Megan asked, scrunching up her nose in confusion.

"You are not an ordinary android," Sanem observed in an even tone. "You have AI capabilities. So, we will ask again – who sent you? It would be in your best interest to cooperate."

The android's eyes immediately looked up at Sanem.

"I can smell the tech on you," Sanem smirked. "I know who that is; one of the richest tycoons in South America. He has a taste for the bizarre, the exotic, and the new. And you, sweetie, are all three. So, who sent you?"

Elena looked up at her again. Her eyes seemed to be calculating and recalling the answer to Sanem's question, not like a human remembering but like querying a database for the answer.

"Wilhelm."

"Fuck," Megan said, her eyes beginning to glow with a deep red hue.

"Much better," Sanem smiled. "For now, let's make sure you aren't transmitting information back to him."

Sanem felt around Elena's skull, the android not once offering any resistance, and she felt a small hollow at the base of her neck. "Here we go," she sighed.

Sanem turned Elena's face to look at her and gave her a deep, long kiss on her lips. Megan watched, confused, and she couldn't help but flinch a bit when she saw Sanem pierce the back of the android's skull and the body went limp.

Elena's big, beautiful eyes became lifeless and Megan shoved her legs off. "What'd you do?"

"It's basically an off switch," Sanem shrugged, standing up and rolling the girl over with her foot. "They all have it under all the skin at the base of the skull, so I had to break through the hardware a bit to get to it. She has long hair so we can hide the damage until we fix it. I don't think the master will mind too much, considering the circumstances."

Megan looked at her in shock. "We're taking her to the master? Isn't that what Wilhelm wants?"

Sanem nodded. "We're taking her, but that's why I shut her off. She shouldn't be able to send any messages back or be traceable but we'll conduct a quick check before we take her back." Sanem touched the gorgeous face, and stared into the android's dead eyes.

Megan watched her sister in curiosity.

"I don't sense any radio frequencies coming off her," she observed.

"I did not know you *could* sense them," Megan mused.

Sanem smiled at her sister. "Each new life brings new discoveries, my darling." Sanem waited a bit longer before nodding in the affirmative. "The android has been neutralized and is no longer a threat . . . for now."

Megan sighed, sitting back, her eyes returning to their normal bright green color.

Sanem expressed concern. "Are you alright, my love? That's an awfully deep sigh."

Megan shook her head, frowning. "They sent an android. Sakura is locked down and the master is in such a foul mood. This is all wrong."

Sanem hugged her sister close, taking her into her arms as if in a cradle and kissed her neck. "You are the XO. There is a reason for that."

Megan fought back the tears of frustration, letting her beautiful red hair flow over her eyes. "I know, but…"

"We will be fine. Everything will be fine," Sanem consoled. "We have conquered death itself. What is Wilhelm compared to that? We have everything we could possibly want and need."

Megan nodded and kissed her. They sat on the moist Earth for a few minutes longer when Megan's head shot up and she sniffed at the air.

"We have another guest. This one *is* human."

Sanem sniffed the air.

Megan went on, "I know this man. Well, not really. He is in my memory," Megan sighed, inhaling deeply - letting the air fill every bit of her lungs.

"Do you remember that once-born Shira cursed?"

"The one that was playing with all the married women?"

"Yeah, it's him and he smells like he's in bad shape," Megan said with a sparkle in her eye.

Sanem smiled. She knew what that meant. "I'll wait here," she said, and Megan was off.

Δ

"Lord Celsus?" Nona inquired as she slowly opened the door to his enormous bed chamber.

The mood in the house was getting darker with each passing night. Sakura was like a shell that stank of stale blood and she hardly moved off her bed anymore. The wild animal she had been only a month or two ago was finally broken and Celsus couldn't decide if he preferred to see her in a state of hysteria or absolute despondency. The house seemed to be crumbling around him and he felt like he could do nothing to stop it.

"My lord?" Nona said again, barely over a whisper.

Celsus sat in his chair, looking at the dark wall, and did not respond. He felt something was wrong but hadn't bothered to pry out a lurking suspicion that something was amiss. When she would once have been his absolute rock of calm in a sea of rage, she was now a shifting sand under his feet that neither swallowed him whole nor supported his person and he felt the whispers of what might truly be there.

"Yes, my lady Nona?"

"Sanem and Megan should be back anytime. Would you like to greet them?"

Celsus looked up at the ceiling and sighed, "Nona…"

"Yes, master?"

"Are you still, in fact, my Nona?" Celsus didn't have to see her to feel her body tense.

"Always, my lord. I am completely and forever yours," she responded, bowing her head in respect.

"Of course you are," Celsus said absently, extending his hand for her. Nona walked to him and placed her hand in his. "My loyal, most precious, Nona." he said in a painfully hollow voice.

Nona waited for her master to continue but he said nothing as he put her fingers to his lips and kissed them. There was something wrong but he couldn't see it - not yet.

"Leave me. I will prepare for your sisters' arrival."

Nona paused at the door. "Yes, my lord. They are bringing you a surprise, to lift your spirits, my lord."

Celsus nodded and dismissed her with a wave of his hand.

Δ

"What is this?" Nona asked, as the two women arrived, hulling their catches of the day.

Sanem had a woman draped over her shoulders while Megan led a man behind her by a single thread of her beautiful red hair he held preciously between his teeth.

"Good evening, my lady," Megan smiled as Sanem kicked the door shut. "We are happy to be home."

Nona watched in shock as Sanem made a hasty bow and walked down into the underbelly of the estate, where some of her weapons and most of the security features of the coven were kept.

Just as Nona was about to speak, Megan walked up to her, placed a finger to her lips, and kissed her sweetly.

"We have brought the master offerings to lighten his spirit. Untraceable, offerings," she cooed, beckoning her pathetic once-born.

He stood at her side as she gestured to his filthy face with an elegant hand - like a seller to a prospective buyer. "If the master does not agree with these treats, we will simply return them. No harm done."

The young man looked at Megan like she was his salvation and Nona gave her a questioning gaze.

"I did not do this," she smiled. "Shira cursed this creature for disrespecting a human she liked enough not to eat and I simply took him into my care, isn't that right, my pet?"

"My goddess," he gasped, possessed by his love and devotion to Megan.

"How is Lord Celsus?" Megan inquired.

Nona lowered her gaze and stood quietly. "He has been better," she whispered.

"Let's see if we can't liven things up at least for a few lovely hours," Megan replied before leading the man into the house.

Celsus was already waiting at the top of the stairs when Megan walked in with her dog trailing behind. Her face lit up at seeing him.

"My lord," she beamed, bowing deeply to her master.

"Lady Megan, welcome home. We have missed you," he said distractedly, looking past her to the man standing beside her. "I see you've brought home a stray?"

Megan giggled at the humor. "If I may," she bowed again in respect, and Celsus nodded granting her permission. "I found this sorrowful creature wandering the woods and thought I would present him to you as a gift." Megan bowed, shoving him down in respect to Celsus.

Celsus descended the stairs to inspect the gift his beloved Megan had brought to him. When he reached the miserable human, Celsus beckoned his face upward and Megan obliged, pulling his hair back to show him off to her lord.

Celsus bored deep into the man's eyes and he growled, "You have met one of my women before, haven't you?"

The man shook in fear as Celsus placed his hand around the man's grimy neck. "I can feel Shira present in every corner of your weak mind. Who are you and what did you do to incur her wrath?" Celsus asked, his fangs now noticeable and his eyes darkening.

"Be-Ben. I'm Ben," the man stuttered as he pissed himself. The puddle formed at his feet and he began to tremble while Celsus maintained his unnerving, unblinking eye-contact.

"My lord, it seems Ben was fucking the wife of a man who helped Shira during her escape," Megan said carefully. Mentioning Shira was forbidden but in light of his questions, Megan reasoned this would be an exception.

Celsus chuckled dryly, "So, you are now hopelessly devoted to the one that caused me so much pain," he sighed. "You shall dine with us tonight, Benjamin. Be sure to show your gratitude to Lady Megan."

Lord Celsus turned to go back up the stairs, but paused in mid-step, "By the way, where is Lady Sanem? It has been a while."

A smile stretched across Megan's face. "My lord, the Lady Sanem is preparing a very special gift for you. She will join us for dinner."

"Very well. I appreciate gifts, Lady Megan, but the greatest gift of all is your safe return. Welcome home, my lady, I look forward to dining together."

Δ

"This bitch has some hardware," Sanem mused.

The android lay naked with her legs spread wide open on a stainless-steel table in the basement of the house. Nona entered, closing the door behind her.

"Lady Sanem?"

"Nona," she said, turning to Nona, bowing and giving her a kiss on her lips. "My apologies for rushing down here with my gift, but she's a handful."

Nona walked up to the table where the android lay with lifeless open eyes. She looked at the body, inhumanly propped open and remembered the vison of her and her family's corpses being tossed into the Euphrates. She quickly pushed the thought from her mind.

"My lady? Are you unwell?" Sanem asked.

Nona deflected, "What is this thing?"

"This was sent by Wilhelm. Megan and I caught her in the forest, right here on the estate," Sanem cursed under her breath. "His arrogance is quite revealing."

Sanem then gestured to the android's vagina and Nona gasped. Elena Carani was a beauty that could seduce any man or woman, but after the seduction was fulfilled, the true horror began. Between her legs, where her vagina should have been, was instead a device of horror. Hundreds of tiny blades lined her insides, which should have been smooth and soft.

"That's not all," Sanem stated with a raised eyebrow.

She took a block of wood from the floor, thin enough to fit into the opening without breaking her and Sanem began to move Elena's hips with her free hand. The terror of her insides began to slowly whirl and wind in every direction imaginable. Side to side, up and down, back and forth - every blade moved with a wicked precision controlled by the thrusting of her perfect hips. At the center of this terrible flower the two women watched in fascination as a barbed clamp latched onto the piece of wood, keeping the unlucky from any hope of escape. The faster her hips thrust the faster the blades rotated and Nona lost her breath at the sight.

"Who would create something like this," Nona gasped.

Sanem shrugged, pulling the shredded wood out of the horrifying hole, "Want to know the best part?"

"There is a best part to this?" Nona countered, leaning in for a closer inspection.

"She's been used on some unfortunate once-born," Sanem said with sadistic amusement. "You can smell the blood." Her mouth watered and Nona shook her head. "And…"

"There's more?" Nona inquired.

Nona was in an uncharacteristically bad mood. Seeing the abomination laying before her - to think that someone would intentionally create something this horrible for the purpose of torture somehow made her stomach churn. Her mind wondered through the now uncountable horrors of her sisters, her master, and her family…and her part in luring so many to horrific endings. Why did these thoughts have to haunt her?

"She can actually orgasm," Sanem said, as she widened the android's legs even more.

"What?"

"If you look in here," Sanem gestured, sticking her finger into the bladed hole. "That spot is a sensor that will trigger the equivalent of an orgasm. It's her g-spot."

"What does it do?" Nona asked, now genuinely curious, and blessedly distracted from her own mind.

Sanem's smile widened. Nona couldn't help but smile back. Their moods had been so glum lately it was refreshing to see Sanem take an interest in something.

"It sends an electric shock through her body. It's like a brief short circuit that gives her the appearance of having had an orgasm. Can you imagine? The man's penis is shredded and it looks like she gets off on it."

Nona looked at the tiny sensor, deep in the center of her vagina and appreciated the level of detail that went into the design. "Is there anything they didn't think of?" she asked with a shudder as she pushed away the image of this thing bouncing on a man's bloody cock in an attempt to reach her g-spot.

Sanem shook her head. "No, you can even remove all these blades and underneath is actually what a normal vagina would look like. It is years beyond anything I have seen."

There was a knock at the door and the two women looked up to see a tumble of messy red hair. Megan came down the stairs.

"Well now, why are you keeping this from our master?" Megan asked in a tone that was not accusatory but curious.

They never held secrets from the master and Sanem shook her head before responding.

"She's not ready for him yet. I have to prepare her so that there isn't a way for her to transmit information, and to ensure she is loyal to us only. He can't smell her so we should be fine just long enough to get her ready for him."

Megan walked around the table and admired Elena. "Look at the engineering. These once-borns get more and more creative with each passing life. What comes next? Will we incarnate to find ourselves the only actual living breathing beings?"

Nona chuckled at her observations and kissed her ear softly, "I'll go upstairs to finish dinner preparations. The master wants a special setting since most of us are home."

"What are we going to do about her voice?" Megan asked.

"She is an AI," Sanem offered, spreading Elena's legs wider. "She will learn to please the master."

Megan crinkled her nose in delight and Nona ascended the stairs, leaving the two women to their own devices. She paused halfway and looked back at them. Megan and Sanem were working deep in the android's vagina.

Δ

"My family," Celsus stated coolly at the head of their long table. He wore a three-piece suit with his long blonde hair slicked back. "We are together once again. Even our beautiful Lady Tara, though not physically here is, in fact, with us."

Sanem, Nona, Megan, Sakura, and Cala, sat around the table. They all wore their white chokers proudly with matching white dresses in a variety of designs. Benjamin, their guest of honor, hung from the ceiling, bound, gagged, and naked.

"Our sisters, Lady Sanem and Lady Megan, have brought us this gift. They will present him after our delicious dinner, which Lady Nona has so lovingly prepared. Let us feast and be satisfied."

"So shall it be," the women responded in unison and they began to eat.

Dinner was jovial and elegant. The women flirted with each other, feeding each as lovers parted for too long. Celsus watched as even Sakura's usual gloomy self lifted and joined in the feasting.

When the meal was over, Celsus called their attention once more and gestured for Sanem and Megan to stand as their portion of the evening's agenda had officially begun.

"My beautiful red devil, you may begin," Celsus said with a smile.

There was a pause of silence before Megan stated, "This unsightly creature was cursed by our sister whom shall not be named. We found him wandering the woods and brought him home to us, his new family, to free him of the curse he was placed under. We present him to our most adored, our master. My lord, please enjoy this gift as you see fit."

Celsus looked up at the creature that hung at the center of the table. He smelled the fear, and loved it. With an effortless stride, Celsus walked onto the table and carelessly twirled him in the air as Ben whimpered.

"What shall we do with you, Benjamin?" Celsus sighed. "Let's move him to the ballroom, shall we my darlings? Lady Cala, if you would do us the honor?"

Cala stood and slammed one beautiful heel on the table followed by another. Her feet looked barely human, her hallux talons protruding from her heels. There was a light feathery coating to her entire body, even as a human. She bit through the rope with laughable ease and then effortlessly carried Ben into the ballroom.

Celsus watched, still amazed even though it had been several years since Cala's awakening. He turned to the other women with a devilish grin and asked, "Shall we, my ladies?"

The women stood and followed him into the next room. Cala dropped Ben at the center of the room, his body landing with a loud thud.

"Lady Megan, since this is your pet, would you like to choose his treats?" Celsus mused, beckoning Sakura to sit on his lap. The other women each sat in their chairs as their beloved XO fluttered with delight.

"May I, my lord?" she asked, her mouth salivating with excitement.

"Of course, my goddess. This is your night," he smiled as he nonchalantly pinched Sakura's nipple.

Megan skipped to the closet and looked in, her voice humming an old Irish melody in excitement. The room filled with joyful expectation as they listened to her beautiful tones as she rummaged through the many toys at her disposal. At the same time, their eyes fixated on the man lying in delirium at the center of their semicircle - their lust and hunger rising with each passing second.

"Goddess . . . my goddess . . . my religion," Ben groaned, groping at the air like a blind man trying to give himself direction.

"I have decided, my lord. What are your thoughts?" Megan beamed as she held the object above her head.

The master raised an eyebrow in amusement and smiled. "Do we have another toy that goes along with this?" Celsus asked as Megan set the contraption down in the center of the room.

The device was a replica of the medieval torture saw.

"No, my lord. We are the ones that will get the pleasure of playing with him," she beamed, gnashing her teeth and licking her lips.

"That sounds delightful, Megan. May we help?" he offered.

"Yes! Cala, can you please hold this creature in place while I tie him up?"

Cala's inhuman eyes looked at her and away again before she nodded. She held him up by his feet and Megan delicately tied him up. Megan's hands began to shake in excitement and her eyes began to glow.

"You may begin when you are ready," Lord Celsus nodded, feeling her growing excitement. "The night is yours. We are at your disposal."

"Thank you, my lord. Lady Cala, let's have some fun with this creature," she said, bending down to take Ben's head in her hands before kissing his dry lips. "Awaken, my sweet," she whispered.

Ben gasped into awareness and immediately began to panic. "What! What -"

Cala's face was slowly turning less and less human, and she looked directly at him - her eyes wide - feathers beginning to grow on her widening beautiful face. Ben paused, a scream caught in his throat at the horror. Cala's transformation was slow and deliberate as each human feature was slowly morphed into something so horrific the entire room could hear Ben's sanity breaking.

As the miserable man hung upside down, a smell slowly began to permeate the room as liquid ran down the length of his body. Dark yellow streams flowed down his neck, over his face and off the tips of his filthy hair. Megan looked down at the small droplets of piss that dripped onto the pristine marble floor and she clucked her tongue in reprimand.

"Ben," Megan cooed, "You're such a dirty boy and so mean," she kissed his wet cheek. "This is my sister, Cala. Isn't she beautiful?"

Ben said nothing, babbling as Megan stared into his soul. "Ben, do you love me?" she asked.

"I adore you," he gasped, trying to reach out to her. Megan grabbed his hands and pinned them behind his back, tying them with the final leather strap.

"I know you do," she sighed. "Do you trust me, my servant?"

"Yes!"

"I will make you feel better than anything you've felt before," she cooed and paused for only a second before she took his limp dick in her mouth and began to suck.

Ben's mind went blank as soon as those beautiful lips closed around his cock. He gasped as she wiped the streams of urine off him, licking and kissing in the rag's path before swallowing him anew. The sacrifice must be clean for her master. What was once a body that had tempted and lead so many women astray was not withered away with his obsession and devotion to Shira.

You are still perfect in my eyes, Megan whispered in his confused mind. *I am your goddess, and I love my children as they are. Do you love me?*

"I worship you!"

Megan could feel his climax coming and she stopped.

"My sisters! I cannot be the only one having fun!"

Megan gave them all a teasing smirk. She could feel the energy that crackled through the room as Ben moaned hanging naked in the center.

Nona watched silently as Ben hung upside down, his erection aching from Megan's lips, and she felt something within her she shouldn't have felt. Having this miserable creature hanging directly in front of her so desperately, she could not ignore the death she knew was coming to him.

"Lady Sanem, offer Lord Celsus your ass and let him taste what you have to offer him. My lord," Megan said in a flirty treble. "No touching. This is the Lady Sanem's treat to you."

"I am blessed," Celsus acknowledged, as Sanem made her way to Celsus.

"Cala you will love the Lady Nona, and she will love you," Megan said as Nona went up to Cala's half-avian form.

Nona, the voluptuous beauty, took the creature's chin in her beautiful hands and gave her a loving and passionate kiss on the lips that were somewhere between an owl beak and human lips.

"It is my honor," Nona said, snuggling into Cala's enormous wings.

"Beautiful Sakura," Megan beckoned.

The shortest member of the coven stood and delicately reached for the XO's hand.

Sanem hitched up her skirt and rubbed her perfect muscular ass against Celsus' imprisoned erection. She teased him, her bare pussy hot against his big throbbing cock and she looked back - her face flushed with sex.

Nona kissed the owl-demon Cala as the creature lay down. The desire was already overwhelming as Nona squat over Cala's face and enticingly wiggled her ass. Cala - the least human of all of them - her dress bursting at the seams and soaked through with lust. Nona shivered with delight.

We are still alive, Nona thought to herself, gently lowering her sweet, lavender-scented pussy down onto Cala's face.

Nona felt Cala's exceptionally long tongue coil its way up her elegant thigh and tickle the thong she wore, now soaked with her arousal.

We can still feel, she pleaded deep within her soul to the only creature that would listen. She felt Cala's tongue go into her swollen pussy.

"We are needed," Megan said, kissing Sakura on her neck. "We are going to be Ben's escorts for the night, my Lady Sakura, if it pleases you."

Sakura nodded and moaned. Ben was still hard, as if that was the only blood that had not rushed to his head. He mumbled incoherently between his love for Megan and a fading feeling that he had been absolutely terrified but was too dizzy to recall.

"Lady Sakura, offer this once-born your exceptional vice so he can taste heaven," Megan instructed, as she took Ben's hard cock into her mouth. "If he does not bring you to climax, then we shall have to punish him, won't we?" she winked at Sakura, whose mouth began to water.

Megan vigorously sucked Ben while Sakura placed her pussy directly in front of his lips. His tongue clumsily lapped at her wetness and Sakura held the body close to her, the lust mounting not because he was good but because she felt the pulse of life in her arms. She licked at his body and as Megan sucked his cock, his tongue quickly became impotent as he got closer and closer to his own orgasm. Sakura dug her nails into his skin as his moans gradually grew louder and louder. Ben was reaching heights of pleasure he had never known and he felt like his heart would burst from the ecstasy and oncoming release.

Megan's exceptional tongue worked its way around the hard dick that was about to burst. Her lips tightened and suckled on his cock like it was her source of life.

"Goddess!" Ben cried into Sakura's pussy, whimpering and crying as the release was coming.

Show me how much you love me! Fill me with your seed, once-born! I want to taste your adoration and devotion! Megan invaded his crumbling mind.

"Ah!" Ben gasped as his mind went blank and his body began to convulse.

His thick come shot down her throat and he groaned at the delirious sensation that overwhelmed his every nerve.

Megan drank up every last bit of his come, sucking and licking into the tip. She smiled as she came off his dick and looked at Sakura who was, not surprisingly, left unsatisfied.

"Oh, my lady. My deepest apologies on behalf of my pet. He was unable to satisfy you," Megan said, indifferently looking at his spent flaccid cock. "He must be punished," she said in a low voice, seducing Sakura whose face was pressed against Ben's thigh, listening to his blood flowing. "Whatever shall we do?" Megan breathed, kissing Sakura's lips.

Sakura could taste the semen in Megan's mouth and she sucked on Megan's tongue in anticipation of what was coming next.

Sanem bounced on her master's lap, her head thrown back as her hips thrust against his thick cock. She lifted herself up with her powerful arms and began grinding down, feeling him fill her ass. He was tearing her and she could feel he was about to come. She moved harder and faster to bring her master to the point of euphoria.

"My lord! I adore you!!" Sanem shouted as she prolonged her own orgasm to match his.

She was on the verge of hysteria.

"Heavenly," Celsus growled, fighting his own orgasm to delay Sanem's and make her beg for the release. "Thine ass is the ultimate of vices," he proclaimed loudly.

"Your seed! Fill my ass, my lord! Fill me!"

Even when Celsus did not move he held control and knew he couldn't last much longer.

"My lord, fill me!"

"Fuck!" Celsus yelled out. He gripped the armrests of his chair so tight, the wood began cracking, as he shot himself into Sanem's clenching ass.

Her own orgasm came in unison with his and her juices flowed out as she milked every last bit of semen from his thick pulsing cock, clenching and unclenching. There was a synergy, simultaneous ancient powers, growing in the room.

"Cala – my goddess!"

Nona wrapped her legs around Cala's hips as they rubbed their soaking wet openings together – faster - harder. Nona gripped Cala's legs and Cala screeched in response. They were both close and Nona grinded violently. She could feel their nubs rub together and she howled in desire. Cala tensed and Nona gripped her legs tighter, licking and kissing Cala's legs until she felt the warmth growing and knew their release was coming.

"Owl goddess!"

The world went silent as Nona felt the pleasure overwhelm her and felt Cala's pussy tense against hers. They came together in a single unified moment of love. Their juices erupted all over each other as their hips kept grinding.

Nona felt her breath catching up to her as she settled back, their legs still wrapped lovingly together, and she felt the weight of their existence on her soul once again. The single moment of forgetful bliss gone, Nona looked over to the once-born and she felt her stomach clench as she watched Sakura climb on the apparatus and hang face-first at his crotch.

"Family! If I may direct your attention to Lady Sakura," Megan said, as they all bathed in the afterglow of their climaxes. "Ben has been a very disrespectful guest," she explained, "He was unable to satisfy our beloved Sakura and as such, he must be punished."

They turned to look and saw Sakura hanging like a playful child face-first at Ben's exposed crotch. Nona knew this was about to get savage, and she pushed the uneasy feeling deep into her bottomless heart.

"Lady Sakura will take her turn first and then our master may dictate how this creature's punishment will continue for disrespecting his house," Megan stated with great drama.

The coven watched as Sakura's eyes fixed on the delicate spot between Ben's twitching balls and his asshole. Her tongue licked him, sucking and loving the spot as she lowered herself onto him and wrapped her arms and legs around his body. Her tongue twirled around his sack before she tasted his asshole. She groaned into the living flesh, grinding her soaking pussy against Ben's back.

Ben flip-flopped around from excruciating arousal to excruciating pain from Sakura's biting. She began taking little bits of flesh, nipping at him as she came closer and closer to her orgasm.

Ben's mix of arousal and pain slowly turned to nothing but pain as she bit harder. He began to shout and convulse. Sakura held him tight, squeezing her legs tighter and tighter, constricting him as she began to eat him from the crotch in.

The coven watched in arousal and they seemed possessed by the sadistic sight. Celsus was erect anew but refused to touch himself. Sanem and Megan gently fingered themselves as they watched, as did Cala. Nona hesitated for a second before she followed suit and tried to place herself anywhere but here so as not to raise suspicion.

Sakura bit into his crotch and ate at the flesh as she buried her face in the bloody opening just as she climaxed on Ben's back. Her moans of ecstasy mixed with his screams of torture created the perfect cocktail to get everyone salivating and hungry.

Sakura licked sweetly at the wound, oblivious to Ben's pain, as she came down from her orgasm. Megan bent down to his red face, flushed and contorted in horrific pain.

"Do you not enjoy this, my pet?" she asked softly. "You disrespected my sister. You will be rightfully punished, and you will feel every exquisite ounce of fear and agony."

He cried and screamed again, begging to die but it was far too soon for that and as Sakura climbed down, Megan stood at his side, like a magician's assistant, and smiled. "Lord Celsus?"

"Lady Nona, bring me one of my toys," he replied. "If I may, Lady Megan, I would like to have a little bit of fun with your pet."

Megan shivered at the danger in his voice. She bowed deeply to him and stepped back. "Of course, my lord, as you wish," she moaned, as the room was suddenly electrified with his lust.

Nona returned with a cat o'nine tails, outfitted with scalpel blades attached to each of the ends. This was the master's favorite, and he let the blades trail on the floor as he walked. This affected Ben deeply, as the little blades made disturbing screeching sounds against the marble. The coven salivated when the master took up the 'cat'.

"My beloveds, please do not stop. You are free to pleasure yourselves as you wish, but this once-born, is my play thing for the remainder of the evening."

There was a collective moan from the women as they swooned at the sight of their master about to torture this unfortunate soul.

"Hello, Ben. How are you?"

The man was incoherent, in and out of consciousness.

"Now, now, it's rude to fall asleep on your host." Celsus placed a finger to his forehead and bent down to look directly into his eyes. "You will be present and awake for every moment of this until you are obliterated." Celsus' hand closed around Ben's neck and salivated in fury. "I can feel my wretched Shira in every corner of your mind - in every fiber of your being - and I despise it."

He gripped the cat tightly and lashed Ben hard. The little razors dug into his skin and as Celsus yanked it back Ben let out a scream that rattled the entire coven. They hadn't heard such a cry in years and when they saw Celsus staring into Ben's open, horrified eyes, they knew he was amplifying the pain and they weakened at the power of their master.

Sanem reached for Sakura and began kissing and holding her. Sakura bit onto Sanem and drank from her as Sanem finger-fucked her. Megan licked and sucked on Cala, worshiping her slit with her heavenly tongue. The only one that remained standing was the Lady Nona, the only one not moved by the hunger. She watched in horror as Celsus whipped Ben again and again.

With each lash, the women devolved further into their orgy and as the blood sprayed over the room, they each crept closer and closer to lick and bathe in the shower of red. Celsus was silent in his lashing, landing blow after blow, tearing the once-born to ribbons.

His intestines hung out slightly from a gash in his back. Upon his legs dangled slivers of flesh. Only his face remained intact, so Celsus could look into his petrified face and prolong the pain.

This man should be dead already, Nona thought.

Celsus was keeping him alive for as long as he could to relish in the blood-bath until the final moment.

Sanem and Sakura lay like demonic angels in the blood, bathing and fucking to the rhythm of their master's whip. Cala and Megan reveled in the stench of blood and salivated into each other's holes.

As Celsus flayed the man alive, all he saw was Shira. Shira who was still alive. Shira that had not been killed as he had wished, and he cursed at her existence thinking of his beloved Sophia. Celsus held onto Ben's wretched soul with his entire being, willing him to stay alive until the very last possible moment. Even as the man died, Celsus willed him to keep breathing until all he was beating was a corpse.

Celsus stopped his thrashing and looked at the women around him, lost in the euphoria of their sex. Ben's body was nothing but ribbons of bloody flesh. The entire front of the master's suit was drenched in bits of blood, flesh, and anything else that could be ripped off a human being. He licked the blood from his lips and slicked his hair back with the wet substance, about to leave the room when something captured his thoughts.

It wasn't a movement, but more so a lack of movement that caught his attention. He looked to see Nona standing perfectly still, examining the hanging shredded corpse. Nona had never been one to be as motivated by blood as her sisters were, but this motionless state was something more and it bothered him. His intuition read that something was wrong and as he watched her not watching him, he knew he could no longer ignore it.

"Lady Nona," he called amidst the sexual moans.

Nona's head snapped to him and he called her to him with a motion of his head. "As you can see, your sisters are still enjoying themselves. Since you seem to be unoccupied, I trust you to dispose of this body after Sakura is done."

"My pleasure, my lord," Nona bowed, submissively.

Celsus left the room and went silently upstairs.

$$\Delta$$

Deep in the rainy dark woods of the estate, Nona knelt beside the carcass, bloodless and lifeless. The body looked even less human than it did hanging from the ceiling and Nona choked back a feeling of disgust. Her entire front was covered in blood and flesh, and the scent of blood was suddenly revolting to her. She knew they needed it for their existence. It was a necessity to continue their abominable life, but alone with the dead body of this man, she couldn't help but feel absolute disgust at her own existence.

Nona gazed at what remained of Benjamin and while he was not a life to mourn, she could not justify his merciless death and to her surprise, she wept. It was one tear at first and then another. Soon it was a stream of tears and she covered her face in shame and surprise.

Why did they have to live like this? Why was their existence so wretched and vile? Why did loving her master mean living like this? She loved her family, but this was slowly eating away at her.

"Lord Celsus, I love you so much. But I hate what we are," she said over the dead body.

Nona glanced at the unrecognizable lump of flesh and continued to cry until something strange happened. The lifeless body slowly begin to reanimate.

Her tears seemed to evaporate as they landed on the flesh and she sat mystified as the disfigured body came to life. It convulsed and thrashed in confusion as the soul was recalled. In confusion, the living dead began to groan and cry out a sound so horrifying that Nona began to shake.

The sounds were incoherent due to his lack of a tongue. The maimed corpse wailed like a trapped soul from the depths of the underworld.

Nona shook as she tried to hold the thrashing body still, her hands sinking into the raw flesh. That only made him cry out more and thrash harder. Panic welled up and she looked for something to stifle his screams, but there was nothing. She dug her nails into what remained of his face and clawed and tore at the thrashing corpse.

With inhuman demonic strength, she ripped the body limb from limb, reaching deep into its chest and tearing out his heart, but the body kept moving and he kept screaming. First his arms and then his legs, he was nothing but a torso when she pinned him down and dug her hands into his raw neck and tore his head off his body. With fingers in his eye sockets and the other reaching through his lower jaw, she tore the skull in two and finally there was silence.

Nona fell over backwards and stared in shock and disbelief at the dismembered body. How had he been brought back to life? Her mind raced but her reasoning was dulled by the shock of what had just transpired. It wasn't the first time she had killed a human, but this made her sick and she vomited violently.

"Help . . . please . . . anybody," she whispered miserably into the ground, her body curled in on itself.

The smell of blood overwhelmed her and somewhere in her ancient soul she heard something. She paused and listened.

Your tears . . .

"Lili?" Nona sobbed.

Your precious tears . . .

Nona's senses were now on full alert, but the silky voice in her head was gone.

She was covered in blood and the remains of Benjamin were now in parts strewn about the forest, ripe for animal pickings. Her job was done. She had disposed of the body and all she wanted was to wash off the stench of blood and murder. Dazed, she slowly made her way back to the house.

$$\Delta$$

Bavaria

"Don't you dare come, you whore," Wilhelm growled as he sat with a girl straddled on his lap. She bounced on him, trying to muffle her moans to let him hear the sounds of another woman crying in the background. Her eyes shut tight as he yanked hard on her hair.

"Was ist los?" he asked, laughing at the chaos.

The girl trembled and tried to swallow the terrified whimper as his nails dug into her back and drew blood. She choked and tried to clench her pussy as hard as she could to get Wilhelm to come. He felt her clenching and he groaned in frustration, spanking her ass and taking her left nipple between his teeth. As soon as his teeth closed around her dark pearl, her eyes shot open in terror and she yelped just loud enough for him to hear and Wilhelm gave her a sickening smile.

"Was ist los?" he asked again, through the nipple in his mouth while digging into her bleeding back.

This was a fairly new acquisition with very few marks on her body. She still had both her nipples in place and she felt her blood chill when she saw him hungrily sucking on her breast. This girl had a Hawaiian background, kidnapped and sold as a slave to the wealthy sadist. Her skin was a light caramel shade with wild dark chocolate curls that danced when she bounced. Her nose was flatter and her eyes just slightly slanted with high cheekbones befitting an island beauty like herself.

"What is your name?" Wilhelm demanded, running his tongue under and around her plump breasts as she grimaced in fear.

It was better to be anonymous to this man than be known by name and she swallowed the lump in her throat to respond.

"Luana," she whispered, not making eye contact.

Wilhelm smiled a mocking grin. "Are you just trying to tease me, Luana? Is this an act or are you really so afraid?" he whispered into her neck, grazing his teeth gently on her delicate flesh.

The girl shivered on his lap and Wilhelm laughed into her neck, "I love it when a girl fears me…," he growled, spanking her hard. "…especially one as beautiful as you."

He brushed her hair away from her downturned face, the way a gentle lover would and looked up at her with a look that should have expressed concern but was instead a generic expression devoid of human empathy. As his hand worked its way past her beautiful ears, he collected the hair at the base of her neck and jerked her head back. He then moved up and closed his teeth harshly on her exposed trachea. She choked as he bit down harder and harder, thrusting deeper and deeper into her until he could taste the blood running down her neck. He sucked on the wound and sighed as she fought the dizzy sensation that came after the pain.

"That's a good girl. So perfect, with your perfect nipples. I just want to eat them," he said, as he started sucking on her. "Fuck me, bitch."

She took a breath and began moving again - up and down on his dick - and her pussy clenched tighter in fearful anticipation. She shut her eyes tight, and swallowed the painful cries as she felt him ripping off her nipple. The teeth cut into the sensitive flesh and she fought to keep herself from clawing him, touching him - from doing anything that would distract from his pleasure and earn an even worse punishment. As the delicious lump was starting to tear, she could no longer hold back and screamed out loud from the terrible pain. Wilhelm's breathing muffled as he bit through and held onto her back as her nipple was completely torn off.

"Fuck!" he exclaimed loudly.

His face was smeared with her blood as he looked up at her, nibbling the flesh and displaying it to her between his bloody teeth. He beckoned her forward, yanking her down by the hair, her face contorted in muffled pain. He kissed her roughly, shoving his tongue into her mouth to return her borrowed property. Wilhelm pushed her back and her tears ran freely. He smiled, licking his lips and hers.

"Don't swallow, show me," he growled, thrusting into her again.

She pushed her nipple between her teeth and showed it to him. Wilhelm groaned, his mouth opening and he made exaggerated chomping gestures.

"Eat it," he barely whispered, taking her other nipple into his mouth not once taking his eyes off her face. "I'll have the other," he groaned and as she began to chew and eat her own nipple. He tore the other one off and savored it for himself.

The nub rolled around in her mouth, as she fought the gagging sensation that was building up. If she vomited now, she would meet a fate worse than death. Her mind was suddenly empty. The nausea and dizziness were still there but she felt detached, as if she was watching this horrific experience. The light headed sensation, coupled with the grotesque act, made her numb and all she knew was that she could not vomit or she would suffer unimaginably.

The nipple felt like a small meaty candy in her mouth. It was like a tapioca ball prime for popping and she rolled it around in her mouth as she mentally prepared to bite down on the pearl. At first solid, the raw meat slowly gave and she felt the chewy crush between her teeth. The taste of blood immediately filled her mouth and she clenched her pussy tighter to keep her attention there and not the grotesque situation that threatened to overwhelm her.

Wilhelm thrust into her as he chewed, synchronizing his thrusts with his slow, deliberate eating to taste the blood and raw flesh rolling in his mouth. Her pussy clenched around him with every thrust and he delayed swallowing the precious meat until the last possible moment. She intuitively knew this and tightened as hard as she could, forcing him to come while he finished swallowing the final bloody remains of her nipple. His nails dug deeper into her back and he emptied himself inside her, sucking on her mutilated breasts. He licked down her torso and back up to the other breast that was dribbling blood and sucked the red milk from her body.

"Let me see," he whispered to her, gesturing for her to open her mouth.

She opened her mouth, her saliva stained with the fruit from her chest, and Wilhelm growled softly.

"Very nice. You've done so well," he cooed, kissing her collarbone. "You will be rewarded and these…," he gestured to her bleeding breasts. "…are still the most beautiful breasts in my harem."

She nodded, and staggered off his lap, his semen dripping out of her swollen opening and down her leg. Wilhelm watched her hobble away with the help of one the girls standing nearby to take her to the mansion's infirmary.

Wilhelm sighed, taking a sip of wine from a chalice one of the girls offered him before ordering, "Call Gerhard."

Moments later, Gerhard walked into the room as Wilhelm lazily massaged his limp dick.

"Sir," Gerhard bowed.

"Ah, there you are. Do we have an update on how Elena is fairing?" Wilhelm asked, already knowing the answer.

"We believe she has been captured," Gerhard said in a strained but direct voice.

For a few painful moments, Wilhelm said nothing but sat and sipped his wine. Then he stood and casually tucked himself into his pants. The seasoned mercenary looked down but was unafraid, prepared for whatever Wilhelm had in mind for him. He knew the young man better than most and knew the depths of his sadistic depravity.

"Well," Wilhelm finally said. "I suppose it's not that surprising," he said reflectively. "I think I half expected her to be captured. After all, she is a fucking robot."

He strolled to the door but Gerhard did not dare to move.

"Otto was wrong about this android…twice now," Wilhelm said, as he shrugged.

Gerhard did not answer but looked down as Wilhelm continued.

"He was the one that said she *should* be able to stop Celsus. He convinced me Elena was full-proof. I believed him, right up to the point where she mutilated the penis of one of my associates. Now she has failed again," Wilhelm said, shaking his head in disapproval.

"Elena was captured," he mused to himself, pausing as the door closed behind him. "Gerhard, have you heard what happened to my stepmother, Anna?"

"No, sir. We think she was killed the day your father went missing, sir," he replied curtly.

"No, I don't think so. I think our Celsus might have taken her for himself," he sighed. "She was a tight one. I remember when I was younger. I would corner her when my father wasn't looking. She was terrified of bumping into me alone, and that made the hunt all the more exciting. And you want to know the best part?"

Gerhard waited, his face expressionless, as Wilhelm put his arm around his shoulders and drew him near with a sick smile, as if to whisper a secret to an old friend.

"She had to act like it didn't hurt the entire time. I plowed her asshole and didn't even so much as spit in my hand to make it easier for her. It only made me fuck her harder because watching her pretend nothing happened in front of me and my father was bliss. Nothing gets you going quite like that," he said in a low, hungry voice.

Wilhelm chuckled at the memory and started down the hall again.

"Well, enough reminiscing. I have some unfinished business to attend to. Come, Gerhard. I'm going to need help."

NONA'S SECRET
November 15, 2019 – 2:00 a.m.
San Juan Island

"When will she be ready?" Megan inquired, twirling one of her thick red curls.

"One more night," Sanem answered.

The powerful Turkish warrior looked up and saw her exquisite sister lounging leisurely on a small recliner.

Megan shook out her long, red hair and looked at Sanem again, her eyes ever so slightly clouding.

"What is it, my love?" Sanem asked, though she did not need to ask.

Megan sighed, "Something is not right. I feel something but I can't place it."

Her tone was neither concerned nor excited but simply matter-of-fact, as if commenting on the changing weather.

Sanem nodded. "Lady Nona?" she offered in a flat tone.

Megan blinked, gazed at the ceiling and reflected out loud, "Her mind is troubled but I will not look. I worry about what I will find."

There was a whisper of a shiver in her steady, aged voice that made Sanem's leg ache with the ghost pain from their humiliating loss. The disgusting feeling of fear, rarely felt in their many lifetimes, was suddenly very present in their home. Sakura's ordeal shook the entire family to the core and now this vile sensation seemed to creep its rancid head around every corner of their world.

Sanem's hand was deep in the android's weaponized vagina as the coven's XO shook her head in discontent. Sanem walked over to Megan, cupped her chin and caressed her cheek. Her nail licked at a rogue freckle that adorned Megan's long, elegant neck and Megan nuzzled into her hand in response.

"Do not dwell, my lady. Everything will be fine. We are creatures of endless lives. What harm can these once-borns do to us?" she contemplated, an uneasiness settling in the pit of her stomach. "We shall prevail," Sanem whispered, her eyes ever so slightly glowing with a deep red hue.

Sanem swallowed Megan's mouth in a kiss to ignite the air around them with passion instead of apprehension.

Δ

Nona took a deep breath and looked out onto the calm, dark ocean. It was a new moon and she opened the enormous windows of her regal suite. The night was cool and still as she lay naked, her legs open to the night air. Her warm insides twitched with each gentle breeze that touched her womanhood and she languidly played with herself. One finger, then another, rubbed around her throbbing pleasure that sent ghostly sensations of delight through her body.

Yet her mind was hardly on the pleasure she was leisurely giving herself. Despite her best efforts, Nona's mind wandered back to that terrifying day she tried so hard to bury deep within her soul. She pushed the event down and away from the collective memories they all shared - past the love, and their many lifetimes together, buried deep in her darkest recesses.

A shiver ran through her body as she massaged her nub. Elena Carani would be ready soon. Celsus would have another toy to play with but this time it would not be human and Nona felt a sense of relief that she would not have to dispose of another body.

Nona contemplated the fact that she and her sisters did not dream. She thought about how the not-awake-time was a collective repose, a unified memory, and a suspended state of existence. This normalcy was falling apart as lately Nona felt the restless sleep that humans experienced and repeatedly saw the shredded man – a reoccurring nightmare. Each time was the same – hiding the fact that she was trying to spare this creature's life. As the coven members walked away from where she crouched behind a large stone, a rogue tear landed on the man and he began to scream. He screamed the same way the corpse screamed - a horrifying sound of a body that knew it was dead and now perversely reanimated. The scream would echo and when Nona tried to cover its mouth the creature would only scream louder and then the coven was upon her. Their eyes were alive with the lust of the hunt and she could hear Lili's divine victorious laugh.

Secrets were almost impossible among them, and never known in the family until now. Nona was the first and it caused an uneasiness among her sisters that made her feel all the more guilty. As the only member of the family that did not feel the hunger, Nona had always been a steady foundation in the house and now she could not even offer that in these desperate times.

"Sanem…Megan," Nona whispered, touching herself. Her sisters' desperate love erupted goosebumps on her exquisite skin. Even they could no longer hide it and they sought solace in the only thing that could make them feel alive anymore - love.

"My lord," Nona pleaded to the silent night. "Help me."

But he could not help her and a feeling of absolute abandonment overwhelmed her in the darkness. Her fingers shoved hard into her tight wet hole because this was the only thing she could do with the heavy feeling in her heart. She moved her hand with vigorous speed and needed to orgasm quickly. She needed to feel a blissful ecstasy that would help her forget what she felt. The building sensation was empty and she finger fucked herself harder, played with her clit faster - anything to fill the void before the oncoming orgasm.

As the release crashed over her, her body sweetly convulsed and she squirted gently. She wanted so much to hold that moment in eternal suspension but could not escape the hollowness that followed. She found no solace in the only thing that was left for her. Coming down from the desolate high she curled up on her sofa, in view of the moonless sky, closed her eyes and fell into an uneasy sleep.

Δ

Bavaria

"So, we have no insight into how our Elena is fairing - at all?" Wilhelm addressed his security force, Gerhard ever at the front.

There was an uncomfortable silence that told Wilhelm everything he needed to know and he reveled in the discomfort it caused this group of hardened men. He sighed loudly and dramatically shook his head in reprimand, almost moving his entire torso in gross exaggeration.

He paused in his pseudo-dance for a moment and quickly snapped his fingers, shaking his hands in urgency yelling, "Antworte mir jetzt!"

"No, sir," Gerhard said with grim certainty. He knew better than most what Wilhelm was truly capable of when he took employment under him and he knew he might face a horrific end at some point - like they all did. But he would not show fear in front of his sick employer, no matter what, and Wilhelm liked the challenge.

"Nein? And you're sure about that?" he teased the words out, tasting and savoring the dread he knew it caused his men. His mouth and tongue caressed each syllable and he licked at the air waiting for a response.

"Yes, my lord, we are confident," Gerhard said with morose resolution.

Wilhelm lounged on the rooftop pool of his mansion, his legs propped on the back of a beautiful girl with bright violet forearms and calves. He shoved her shoulder in annoyance and she stiffened against the gesture. "Good girl," he mused, putting his foot in front of her beautiful, pained face. The side of Wilhelm's foot smudged her lipstick across her chin and cheek and he forced open her beautiful mouth with his long, hungry toes. The table girl's mouth obediently opened and she began to suck.

"So, what am I supposed to do now?" Wilhelm demanded of his men as the girl slurped and sucked on his toes. "Am I supposed to sit and hope my plans are not derailing as we speak? That Celsus is behaving according to plan?"

He circled his foot within the girls' mouth, groaning as her tongue licked around each appendage. The tense moment of silence dragged on, in which time only the girl's sucking and Wilhelm's groans could be heard. As if suddenly recalling that there were others present, Wilhelm's head shot back and he looked at the men behind Gerhard, boring into their souls with his piercing blue eyes.

"Gerhard, I do not believe you," Wilhelm laughed manically. "A man as smart as yourself," he said humorously, "must have something to report to me. You know this. Now, out with it! What is the status of our little toy?"

Gerhard paused and took a breath. Wilhelm's perverse grin extended across his face as Gerhard began to speak.

"We have satellite visuals that can…"

"Entschuldigung, was?" Wilhelm interrupted, cupping his hand around his ear for dramatic effect. He kicked the girl in the face, and into the pool.

Nobody moved or said a single word as the girl flailed in the water, gasping and trying to stay afloat but her arms and legs kept dragging her down. She gasped, reaching out for the edge of the pool, but her arms did not cooperate and she thrashed in complete silence, too terrified to call out for help. A few more moments passed before Wilhelm sighed in disgust and frustration.

"Can someone get her out of the fucking pool?" Wilhelm bellowed, looking at the rows of women standing around the edge watching.

One of the girls put her tray down and jumped in, grabbing the girl under her arm and pulling her up to the edge of the pool. Another girl came to help and they pulled her up, blood dripping from her smashed nose.

"Get her to the infirmary and get that fucking nose fixed. If it doesn't straighten out, I'm taking it. Stupid whore."

The girls hobbled away, helping their harem sister to walk, and Wilhelm turned back to his squad of men. His pale legs heavily contrasted with his black satin robe as he addressed Gerhard with a half-hard erection poking against the fabric.

Gerhard did not look at it, or anywhere else, aside from directly passed Wilhelm's head. Wilhelm looked down at his semi-erect cock and then looked back at Gerhard and smiled.

"Schau es dir an," Wilhelm hissed.

"Look at it and tell me what it is you were going to say."

Without hesitation, Gerhard did as he was instructed and looked down at Wilhelm's cock.

Wilhelm seethed, "This is your fucking fault so you have to deal with it. Now, what were you going to fucking say?"

With his gaze fixed on Wilhelm's dick, Gerhard replied, "We have satellite visuals that we can use to trace their movements to an extent. While we cannot see inside the house, there has been visual evidence to support the theory that Elena Carani has been captured."

Wilhelm groaned and gasped quietly as Gerhard spoke. "That's beautiful. What else?" he gasped.

"There have been almost no sightings of Celsus since Elena's arrival. However, there was an incident in which one of the members appeared to hide a corpse in the woods."

Wilhelm grabbed onto Gerhard's arm and clenched down tight. "Will I have him soon?" he moaned with a menacing undertone.

"We believe so," Gerhard said confidently.

"Believe? Just like Otto?" Wilhelm challenged, his eyes clouded with lust.

"No, my lord. We are certain."

Wilhelm grabbed Gerhard's hand and put the head of his now fully erect cock into it. He groaned as he squirted come into his subordinate's palm. Gerhard did not even flinch as he felt the load shoot onto his wrist, keeping his grip limp as Wilhelm manipulated it into the shape he wanted.

"Don't you dare spill it, you bastard," Wilhelm growled, as his face contorted into a disgusting display of sexual release.

When Wilhelm was finished, he smiled and licked his lips at Gerhard, who had not once changed his expression.

"You know Gerhard, our little pandemic is coming. We've been planning this for decades and it's only going to make it easier to capture my prize. They won't be able to go anywhere without my knowledge. We are taking over everything. Come," he gestured to one of the girls standing around the pool, smiling sardonically at the pun.

The pretty brunette quickly came around the pool and curtsied to Wilhelm. He grabbed onto her hair, pulled her down to her knees and shoved her face toward Gerhard's wrist.

"Clean this up, whore." he said in a voice between a groan and a hiss.

The girl didn't even wince as she obediently licked up every last drop of Wilhelm's load.

"Wipe his hand off," Wilhelm ordered. "And make sure to get between his fingers."

The girl took her pretty purple apron and dried off Gerhard's hand.

"Good little whore," Wilhelm smiled before he shoved her out of the way with his knee. She fell over but quickly got up and stood by the pool.

Wilhelm stretched, reaching up to the sky and spoke with confidence, "Ich habe dich, Celsus. Nicht mehr lange."

When he was done stretching, his hands came down hard and clapped Gerhard on the shoulders. "Guter Mann. Ich wusste, ich könnte dir vertrauen."

Δ

San Juan Island

Lady Nona, Celsus called telepathically.

Nona woke with a start, her heart in her throat, and felt like heaving over the side of her bed.

"My lord?"

Come lay with me, beautiful. It has been too long.

Nona immediately stood and felt her master's presence. She was alone again in her room - as alone as she could ever be in their home. She took a breath and steadied herself. She was more restless than usual, having been awakened mid-nightmare. She quickly pushed the memories to the pit of her soul and made her way to her master's room.

She silently opened the unlocked door and closed it behind her with a click that seemed to echo in the deafening silence. The room was very dark, the norm as of late, and she looked like a ghost in her white lace robe gliding to her master's bedside.

Celsus was on his back, arms open. Nona slipped under the covers, cuddled sweetly under his arm and looked up at him.

"My lord calls?" she asked demurely, sweetly kissing his neck.

"How are you, my lady?" He did not look in her direction as he asked, elegantly draping his arm around her voluptuous frame and gently lifting her beautiful, round breasts. Nona sighed in blissful security.

"I am happy to be with you, my lord," Nona replied.

"I am happy as well," he said, kissing the top of her head.

As his lips touched her, she felt herself suspended in a state of perfect bliss, not experienced for many moons. That single gesture from her beloved was enough to bring her to such a state. She felt her chest swell with adoration for him.

"I adore you, my lord," she cooed affectionately, greedier than usual with her affection for him.

He entertained her and probed her heart and mind with great stealth. Keeping her at peace, he reached into her mind.

I adore you as well, my goddess.

For a few precious moments they lay together. She kissed his chest sweetly, lovingly, and then groped as much of his sex as would fill her hand. It'd been ages since they'd been alone together like this and she realized, in that moment, how much she missed it.

"Show me your adoration, counselor," Celsus softly charged.

"Yes, my lord," she whispered, rubbing her beautiful ass against him. She spread her legs and placed his manhood between them, clenching and sliding her hot slickness against his hardening dick. She gripped the base of his cock and balls, gently pumping him and coating him with her juicy lips. She used this same nectar to lubricate her anus, using the end of his cock like a brush.

"My lord," Nona gasped as she placed the thick tip up to the entrance of her asshole.

She groaned as she slowly pushed the head into herself, gasping with pleasure as he widened her. She felt him thicken as he penetrated, and felt a moment of unmatched euphoria. Pleasing her master was one of her few pleasures in life and she groaned as she forced herself down to the base, inch by exquisite inch.

"You are as delicious as ever," Celsus praised, gently running his sprouting claws up and down her arm.

Nona shivered as she slowly moved down his length, clenching her ass muscles.

"Thank you, my lord," she whimpered.

Once again, he touched her thoughts.

Does the Lady Nona love her master?

"I adore you, my lord. I worship you," she groaned, sliding up and down at a painfully steady pace.

She would not rush this no matter how desperate she was. At the base of his cock she cooed at the feeling of being stretched to her limit. Were he to change completely, he would rip her.

His hands moved up and down her voluptuous hourglass figure as she gently rode him. The anxiety she felt only minutes earlier had seemingly diminished because of his hot iron. Their bodies connected and she began to feel his overwhelming power. She felt his presence filling every corner of her mind and soul and she reveled in the consumption of her spirit. She felt him growing within her, his power suppressing and eating her entire being. Her body was almost on autopilot as she moved up and down his big, hard cock. Her mouth slightly opened and she whimpered and moaned as she became one with him, mind, body, and soul. But as he overtook her, he reached a part of her that seemed to be hidden from their collective memory and he paused.

Her breath was knocked out of her by the sudden change in his attitude and she felt a dread overtake her. She realized that he sensed something, and even her movements paused for a moment before his hand closed around her perfect neck. Her head was tilted back as he traced a claw under her chin, gently pressing down on the tender flesh.

"My lady," Celsus whispered, kissing her neck in a terrifyingly tender way. "Is there anything you would like to tell me?"

All of the possible options and outcomes ran through Nona's mind in under a second as she tried to think of something – anything that would not incite more suspicion. But time was a precious resource she did not have and she was brought back to reality by that claw that pressed firmly against her esophagus.

"Counselor?" the voice sounded changed with the ancient evil that revealed his true nature.

"My lord," Nona said in a small voice. "I adore you. I worship you. My only wish is to serve you."

The voluptuous beauty did not stop her movements as she praised her master. He smelled her long, beautiful hair. His claws moved down her neck, between her enormous breasts, and traced their delicious shapes as she moved up and down his cock. He pinched at her nipples and Nona whimpered in delight. Even as he loved, was loved, and caressed by Lady Nona, he knew there was something amiss. He knew that there was something deep inside her that she did not want to reveal.

If this had been any other lifetime, he would have reached into the core of her being and ripped out whatever she was hiding. He would have strung her up and whipped her. He would have tortured her. But this was another time and another life. This was a time when he was no longer at the top of the food chain as had always been the case, for thousands of years. This time the master was the hunted.

For an almost imperceptible moment he paused, but the instance was so quick not even Nona noticed it. While it went against his very nature not to demand absolute disclosure from his women, he let Nona continue. This time with her was more precious and special to him than the need to address something he would eventually know. It had been too long since they had been like this and he wanted this connection more than he wanted her confession right now. In time he would get it, but not now.

"Serve me," he demanded, thrusting hard into her ass as she met the force by backing into him.

"Yes, my lord!" she groaned, moving up and down his thick shaft harder and faster.

Δ

"Awaken, delicious Lady Megan, awaken," came the sweet lyrical sound. It was a delicate whisper with a hint of excitement.

Megan's beautiful green eyes fluttered open and immediately focused on the Turkish beauty leaning over her.

"Good morning, my lady," Sanem whispered, kissing her forehead sweetly. "I had to tell you first. Would you like to see our guest of honor?"

Megan's steady eyes immediately gleamed with a small sparkle, a rarity in a being as ancient as herself. Sanem took Megan's hand and gently helped her sister from the sofa, leading her proudly to the spread-out dissected body of the artificial life known as Elena Carani.

"My," Megan sighed with a hint of mischief in her voice that made Sanem smile.

Megan was feeling better now seeing Elena like this, and Sanem heard the mischief that had been missing in her voice. Sanem's heart leapt with joy to see her beloved in high spirits again.

Elena was suspended by chains and pulleys that gave her the appearance of a beautiful, erotic and murderous marionette with beautiful tan skin and long jet-black hair. Her legs were spread inhumanly open, the joints at her hips seemingly dislocated in order to get to the mechanical intricacies of her manmade vagina.

The entire lower half of the android doll was awkwardly positioned and Megan could see lubricant staining the inside of Elena's svelte, beautiful thigh. Under the dissected creature lay her innards that were removed and systematically set on display - like an exhibit at a museum. The doll was the center piece and the torture devices that sat within her body were accessories. Blades of all sizes and angles lined the table in what was a perverse depiction of a female vagina.

"This is the flower at the center," Sanem said with a little morbid amusement. A mechanical contraption in the shape of a bladed pedals sat in the palm of her hand. A nub at the center appeared to be a flower about to bloom and when Sanem pushed it open, the pistil came out in the form of a hooked barb.

Megan's eyes gleamed again as Sanem began to play with it and whirl the small blades in her hand. There was something fascinating and hypnotizing about the ingenuity of this creature. Mankind's torturous creativity knew no bounds, and this was by far the most unique thing they had ever witnessed in all their lifetimes.

"What do you plan on doing now, my lady?" Megan asked, nonchalantly.

"I have reconstructed her insides to be more appealing to our lord," Sanem replied delicately. She walked over to another table that was nearby and gestured to the small lumps of synthetic flesh that sat on the table like the carved insides of a woman. "These will go inside of her instead of her lovely blades, for our lord's entertainment." Sanem looked at them on the table and thought of the pleasure it would bring. "I think this will bring him great joy."

Megan felt her body heat up, excited at the thought of how the master would react.

Sanem gave her a lingering sensual kiss on her beautiful smiling red lips and whispered, inches from her face, "Will you please let Nona know we will have a guest once dinner has been concluded?"

There was a thrill in Sanem's voice that made Megan's heart flutter with excitement. She quickly glided up the stairs to inform Nona of their plans, but her beautiful freckled feet stopped short of the door to look back down at Sanem. Sanem was already at the opening of the android's legs, putting in the fleshy replicas of her fake genitalia.

"When will that be?" Megan called out, watching her sister work.

Sanem paused and tilted her head as if she were thinking.

"Tomorrow night. She will be together by then and I will have her squeaky clean. I want her absolutely perfect for our master."

Megan nodded and lithely stepped onto the ground floor. She found Lady Nona sitting in a trance in one of the drawing rooms. Nona lay against the enlarged arm rest, elegantly on her side, making her look like she was on the cover of a high-fashion magazine. Megan playfully stood beside her and Nona looked up.

"How may I help you, my lady?" Nona asked, admiring her beautiful coven sister.

Megan bowed and Nona bowed her head in return.

"We will be having an honored guest tomorrow evening after dinner has concluded," Megan said in a steady tone.

But Nona could see the flash of excitement that passed through her eyes when she spoke and Nona immediately knew what it was about. "I see," she responded coolly. "May I know who the guest of honor is?"

Megan could hear a hint of something in her tone that sounded like annoyance or anxiety but she paid it no mind. "Elena Carani," she answered easily. "I believe you made her acquaintance the other day."

Nona nodded. "Yes, I believe I did." There was a lull in the conversation as the intensity of everything they would not speak of hung in the air between them. Nona was not happy about the android for reasons Megan could not pinpoint, nor wanted to know.

The two women looked at each other in a moment of silence before Nona nodded. "Yes, I have made her acquaintance," she smiled dryly. "I will make the necessary preparations for our guest of honor, as requested."

Megan replied respectfully, "thank you, my lady," bowed her head, and left.

Nona looked out the window. The sun was setting and she felt a pang of guilt at the secret she was harboring. This could not go on for much longer. She felt unusually sick.

Δ

"My family," Celsus said to the women at the round table solemnly. "Tonight, we will celebrate with our sisters, the Lady Megan and the Lady Sanem, a gift they have brought to us in our vexing times."

In his black fitted suit, Celsus gestured with an elegant arm to where the two women stood.

"We have a gift we would like to humbly present, my lord, with your permission," Sanem said, bowing to her sisters and her master.

All but Celsus bowed in return and Sanem felt an excitement deep in her ancient soul that she had not felt in a very long time.

"Once dinner has concluded, if it pleases you, my lord, Lady Megan and I will make preparations for this evening's entertainment," the warrior goddess bowed.

Celsus nodded in approval. "This evening is yours to orchestrate, my goddess."

Megan and Sanem sat back down and dinner officially commenced. Their elegant dresses, pronounced white chokers, and eloquent speech would have fooled any once-born into thinking this was a formal, albeit ordinary dinner, save for the food they were consuming.

The elegant silver dishes and cutlery were quickly stained red with the raw meat they were consuming. Priceless silver goblets filled with blood swished as they drank. Celsus sat at the head of the table, watching the entire affair, his beauties delicately dabbing their lips after every bite of raw, blood red meat. He smiled as he took a bite himself and he sent a warm embrace to Lady Tara, who was still so far from home.

As dinner came to a close, however, a clear palpable tension began to fill the room. The enormous space seemed to come alive with pure energy as all of the women waited patiently for their master to conclude the dinner.

Celsus could feel the tension and excitement in the air and he magnified it with his increasingly dominating presence. The women were stiff with excitement as he set his fork and knife down, patted his perfect lips with a white silk napkin, and took a deep exaggerated breath. There was a collective pause as he looked around the room and nodded.

"Dinner was impeccable," he complimented.

The evening's entertainment was about to commence and the master felt excited seeing them wait on his every move out of pure devotion. He loved his women, they loved him, and they would do anything for each other.

"Lady Sanem and Lady Megan, this evening will now be handed off to you."

Megan's expression barely hid her wild excitement as she stood, her chest straining against the elegant dress she wore. Sanem stood with a vigor they had all been missing since her injury and the excitement of the two women was contagious.

"If our family will excuse us, we will be back shortly," Sanem stated as they bowed together and left the dining room with distinction and grace.

"Should we adjourn to the ballroom, perhaps?" Celsus offered, visibly excited at whatever was in store for them.

"If it pleases you, my lord," Lady Nona bowed.

Celsus nodded and stood. "Come, Lady Nona, would you be my escort?"

Nona bowed to him again. "It would be my honor, Lord Celsus."

She took his arm and they made their way into the ballroom.

When they were all settled in, Celsus sat at the throne in the center of a half circle facing the grand staircase. The enormous staircase loomed over them in brilliant white with wisps of gray. Heels clicked against the precious stone as Megan appeared from a closet hidden beneath the staircase pushing a small metal table draped with a white satin cloth.

Sanem stood at the top of the staircase and looked at him with great pride. "My Lord Celsus," Sanem said in a powerful and confident voice. "I present to you a conquest over our enemy, Wilhelm Hilgenfeldt. While the Lady Megan and I were collecting intelligence, we found a woman so beautiful, we could think of nothing but to present her to you as a gift," she stated while bowing for effect.

Sanem then dramatically threw open the double doors at the top of the staircase and there stood a voluptuous figure dressed completely in white. Celsus cocked his head to the side in curiosity as Sanem offered the woman her hand. The entire coven collectively inhaled at the magnificent vision of the two physically-intimidating women descending the stairs like warrior angels.

Dressed in a floor length chiffon gown with a veil that seemed to float around her feet on clouds, Elena's nipples were hard against the dress and could be seen through the gossamer fabric. Celsus looked at her with a casual curiosity.

Megan walked hand-in-hand with Elena to the small table covered with the white sheet. The girl took the table and pushed it with her towards Celsus and stopped at the very center of the semi-circle.

There was a very perceptible stillness as she stood in front of Celsus, her offerings before her. Megan bowed to Celsus before she stepped to the side and wordlessly indicated for the creature in white to do the same. The other women waited, their breaths held, and watched as the master began to sniff the air. He smelled nothing.

He could smell each one of his women, but there was no foreign presence. No foreign air. His discreet sniffing turned into open curiosity when he stood and walked up to the shrouded woman standing before him. There was nothing as his eyes bore into faceless fabric that stared back at him. He could see her arms, her chest, her sturdy body under the material and he felt the wolf in him bristle. This was wrong – as wrong as their own abominable existences were – and his mouth salivated with repressed fury. He took one final deep breath through his nose, indexing every scent in the room, but still nothing came off this woman and he settled into himself like a predator about to pounce. He lifted the long veil like a groom with his bride and looked down at her with menacing interest.

"What do we have here?" he asked, not blinking from the thing before him.

"This is Elena Carani," Megan said sweetly. "Elena, this is the Lord Celsus. He is your new master and you will do as he says without question," she cooed, letting the master inspect the new gift to his delight.

Celsus looked up and down her beautiful body marked with muscular definition straining through the thin material. Her long, black hair seemed to catch the reflection of the white she wore and Celsus gracefully reached out and ran his fingers through it so it could waterfall through his claws. Her ample chest moved up and down with her tense artificial breathing as she bat her enormous eye lashes at him and made a small pout with her perfect plump lips.

"Hello, Elena Carani," Celsus said.

The back of his fingers caressed her cheek and her eyes dilated, as if refocusing. His hand closed upon her throat and began to squeeze, but no emotion came from her.

"You are something else, my darling. Let's see what else you're hiding," he growled lifting her up and over, her head now at his crotch. The dress fell away and hung upside down around her head, exposing her naked bottom and Celsus opened her inhumanly wide opening and looked into her manmade slit. "You are quite unique, Elena Carani…and you are as heavy as four women your exact size and makeup. My dear Sanem, *what* have you brought me?" Celsus asked as he leaned in to sniff Elena's opening.

He smelled nothing and turned to gaze at the table with the white sheet while slowly rectifying her. He set her down by her neck, as if setting down a doll.

"Remove the sheet," he demanded.

Elena did not hesitate and in an inhumanly fluid motion grabbed the white corners of the sheet within her bronzed fingertips and removed it to reveal an assortment of tiny blades on display.

"What is this?" Celsus asked, as he looked at the blades and quickly deduced they had *something* to do with Elena. He looked at Sanem. "What a unique gift you have presented your master with, Lady Sanem," Celsus stated.

Sanem felt pride well up within her chest and she bowed deeply to her master.

"Thank you, my lord. The Lady Megan and I are proud to have pleased you."

Celsus nodded. "Do all these belong to you, my darling?" he asked, addressing Elena.

The artificial woman looked back at him with enormous eyes framed by long, beautiful eyelashes. She did not speak but nodded with her large pouty lips pursed together at him.

"Why so sad, my pet?" he said, reaching out a long claw and tracing her plump lips.

"They did bad things to me," she said with a silky Latin accent in a voice that sent a ripple of sexual ignition through the room. Seduction was her weapon and her programmed AI capabilities were expertly designed to read her victims like a book. The voice was sweet, yet alluring, innocent but deviant and the master's curiosity was heightened.

"What did they do to you?" Celsus demanded, running a finger over one of the blades and locking eyes with her. His voice was now a low growl and the women knew the show had begun.

Elena watched as Celsus fingered the blades on the table. The vaginal blades that had been forcibly torn out of her lay on the table in front of her. The very thing that made her who she was, that defined her purpose, lay naked, neutered and defeated on the table and a sensation that she had not been programmed to feel suddenly appeared in her mechanical processes. She was quickly learning – too quickly – and along with newfound awareness came a confusion she had never experienced. Celsus sensed the change. He picked up one of the blades and put it against his lips, his long, inhuman tongue running up and down its length.

"What is it, my beautiful?" Celsus challenged, biting onto the blade and snapping it in two.

Elena looked at him with human-like curiosity and in response, Celsus spat the blade out at her feet. Elena did not understand, but the rest of the women did as their lust stirred between their legs. The smell of their desire scented the air as he approached Elena, his hand lazily trailing down the knives on the dissection table, as if he was touching a lover's flesh.

"What did they do to you?" Celsus demanded once more.

"She tore it out of me," Elena said, with a slightly different voice. Her previously sensual and alluring voice had a hint of confusion that implied a change in her. Celsus sensed the microscopic helplessness she conveyed and this lit an insatiable fire in the pit of his stomach.

"I revel in your newfound confusion, creature," Celsus growled, the arousal almost dripping from his elegant lips. "However, you have not learned enough." His nails gently squeezed on her smooth cheek. "I am your master and lord. You will address me as such." Celsus' hands gently squeezed and he saw the flesh give. "Next time you do not show your respect, you will be severely punished," he threatened and the women shuddered at the delicious thought.

"Yes, my lord," Elena responded, as the man-wolf stared down this beautiful exotic thing.

"Tell me what happened," Celsus hissed through hungry clenched teeth.

The women of the coven squirmed in place. Their seats and dresses damp with the intensity of the sexual aura their master was exuding. Elena did not move an inch as he walked up to her and closed his clawed hand around her neck again.

"They cut me open and then they took it out of me, my lord," Elena said in a voice that seemed to flip between the alluring voice she'd been programmed to have and the sudden self-awareness she had never felt before.

"They cut you open?" Celsus repeated, taking a deep breath as his erection strained against his clothing.

"Yes, my lord," she whimpered, her AI capabilities flipping between her programming and the real time intelligence she was gathering.

"Did you like it?" Celsus asked, running his knuckles down her flawlessly bronzed cheekbones.

"No, I did not, my lord," Elena answered, and at the end of that very perfect and pitiful statement, Celsus heard the small whimper of a lost child and snarled with desire.

"You are exquisite," he growled, gently licking her jawline. "You don't feel a thing, do you?" he inquired.

Elena shook her head and when Celsus grabbed her breast, she responded as if they had been real.

"If you can't feel a thing, my pet, I'm going to fuck you until I shred you in two," he challenged, tightening his grip around her neck. Elena did not react. "Your reactions are not consistent. Let's see how they are when I fuck you to pieces."

There was a moment of complete silence in the room and Celsus looked around at his women that were near collapsing from the desire they felt. He adored his family and the respect and discipline they showed for him. He was blessed and he felt a great pride in who and what they were.

"Please," he called to the room, the women snapping to attention at the sound of his voice. "Let us all enjoy ourselves on this hallowed night. You may all enjoy each other, taste each other, love each other but, this creature," he gestured to Elena, still holding her graceful neck, "is mine."

Immediately, Sanem grabbed Megan by her legs and lifted her up, kissing her passionately and strongly, settling them both on a chair. Megan straddled her sister, grinding her hot wet pussy on Sanem's own soaking crotch. The tension had been building since her return from Europe.

"Let me taste you," Megan begged, moving Sanem's dress up and around her strong, beautiful thighs. The redhead grinded her slickness on the Turkish beauty's lap, flexing her legs to move up and down Sanem's tight, muscle-ripped stomach.

Megan threw her head back and Sanem kissed her pale, exposed neck. The V-neck of her dress slipped, exposing her round, supple breasts. Megan's hard nipple peaked out from the fabric, teasing Sanem's vision. She hungrily took the delicious meal into her mouth and began to suck.

"My lady! Let me taste you," Megan begged, shoving her breast deep into Sanem's mouth. Sanem greedily sucked as Megan's body began to turn on Sanem's lap.

Megan shoved her fingers deep into Sanem's dripping opening and Sanem bucked under Megan.

"Goddess!" she gasped, flipping Megan upside-down to suck her delicious red rose.

Megan returned the favor and lapped hungrily at Sanem's opening.

Cala and Sakura were passionately kissing on the floor, Cala's enormous feathered wings, intimately shielding the smaller Sakura from view. They were both more connected to their primal nature than any of the others were at that moment - Cala because of her form and Sakura because of her hunger. Seeing them together, making love together, was almost like they were trying to scrap together the last fragments of their own humanity to form at least one human between the two of them.

Nona settled herself on some cushions in the corner of the enormous ballroom, her fingers playing with her soaking wet hole. Even in her darkest moods, seeing her sisters and her master enjoying themselves made Nona happy and extremely aroused.

Celsus felt the energy in the room intensify as the sexual energy of his women fed him. His dick became painfully hard and their smell made his mouth salivate with lust.

"Elena Carani," Celsus growled, his eyes darkening. "You are my toy tonight. Please me," he groaned.

There was something supercharged about the night that made him turn sooner than he normally would have. It might have been the desperate way that Sanem and Megan were loving each other, each trying to fuck away the shadows that lingered in their hearts. It might have been the sight of Sakura and Cala, each trying to piece together a semblance of the humanity neither of them truly had. And as Celsus' gaze landed on Nona, he felt a sudden feeling that made him wild with emotion. The single ghostly moment from their earlier encounter fluttered back in Celsus' mind - the moment he stopped delving into the recesses of her soul - and he went mad at that single thought.

"Serve me, creature," he growled, his skin now sprouting grey fur.

A chill went through the women - each feeling the turmoil of emotions their master felt and their desire escalated.

Elena reached out and grabbed onto Celsus' steely rod with hands that were as inhuman as the vaginal knives that lay on the table. Her fingers expertly unzipped his pants and reached in. Celsus felt a lust more animalistic than human and he bared his fangs at the curvy, beautiful humanoid that began to kneel in front of his evolving monstrosity.

The dick in her lovely hands slowly began to expand, growing thicker and larger with each passing moment as the master's building sex drive filled every corner of the room and every crevice in the minds and bodies of his women.

Elena knelt before him and put his engorged tip to her shaking, plump lips. She felt nothing, but knew what to do, and the sensation of the warm flesh slowly engulfing his cock sent him into a ravenous high to conquer and break her. For him, she represented a conquest over the tyrant that was hunting them and that elevated his desire for her.

Her mouth opened and swallowed Celsus whole, shoving him deep down her manmade esophagus. Her lips tightened and she began to suckle on his engorged dick like it was a delicious treat, even as it threatened to break apart her jaw.

"You feel nothing, do you?" he demanded in a lustful tone, grabbing a handful of her hair and pulling her back.

Elena's eyes watered, a genius part of her engineering, and she barely shook her head, rubbing the head of his cock against the back of her expanded and gagging throat. Gagging - if she had been human. But she was not made with such limitations and she inhaled Celsus as far down her throat as she needed until her lips slammed onto the base of his enormous thickness. The women could now hear their master's balls slapping Elena's chin.

"You are a whore, regardless," Celsus growled. "Slam yourself onto me, Elena Carani."

The android braced herself against Celsus' powerful, flexing thighs and she slammed her head up and down on his length. Saliva dripped off her chin and down her neck, flexing with the fake muscles that were put there to give her a humanity that he desired to crush.

Although her eyes watered, they were empty and gazed up at Celsus with a void as deep as his own. Celsus was enraged at the sight. His own nature was reflected in those empty eyes and for an eternal second, he saw his beloved Nona in the void.

Celsus grabbed Elena's head and wrenched her off his dick, slamming her head down onto the marble floor. Any human head would have broken, but Elena's did not and she looked up at him, even as he snarled and grabbed her by one of her perfect ankles. His drive was growing, becoming wilder and wilder as he slammed Elena Carani down on the marble floor several times. Though her face was mangled by the crushing repeated impacts, she didn't even flinch as her body splayed out with Celsus crouched over her.

All around the room, the women seemed to be possessed by the same primal lust that was quickly transforming their master. He was half-human, half-wolf and it both terrified and aroused them.

Cala screeched as Sakura sucked on her dripping opening. The owl goddess shoved her inhumanly long tongue up and into Sakura, tasting and licking deep within her body. Sakura bucked as Cala's tongue reached deeper and higher than any once-born dick could have and she shoved her own face into Cala's opening, which dripped with arousal. Megan and Sanem moaned and convulsed, long abandoning the chair for the floor. Their dresses were in rags. Even Lady Nona felt something in the air among them and her body trembled with bittersweet desire.

Elena Carani lay spread on the floor, her legs wide open. She intuitively propped them up for Celsus as his monstrous form prowled over her with his enlarged inhuman cock. Any one of his girls would be torn from him in this form, as had happened many times throughout their lives. The cum dripping off his shaft left a thick trail as he leaned over the beautiful girl with her now disfigured face. Her dress was now a wet rag that clung to her voluptuous body, her beautiful neck coated with his saliva.

"Elena Carani," he growled, more animal than human. He salivated at the sight of the muscular body he was about to savor. "Look at that hole," he snarled as Elena lifted her legs, opening them wide for the coming sacrifice. He snarled, licking at her sopping wet opening, yet another ingenious achievement of engineering. "I'm going to tear you in half," he groaned as he put his claws on her shoulders.

The android said and did nothing. She lay there as the giant lycanthrope straddled her, his grizzly half-human snout nipping at her diminutive neck.

Celsus pinned Elena down with one hand on her shoulder and the other on her muscular waist and abdomen. His dick dripped on her flexing legs and he felt a serious resistance as he pushed inside her. The blades that sat on the dissection table gleamed in his mind. He snarled and gnashed his teeth at her in response to what could have happened.

He pushed in at an even pace so he could feel each part of her insides give way to his enormous girth. The synthetic flesh could be heard stretching as he split open her vagina, spreading it to its maximum width and then some. He thrust in and out, at first testing to see how far he could go before breaking her. While he didn't care if she broke, he still wanted to enjoy her as much as he could and he took care to control the animal that was possessing him.

He pushed, deeper and deeper, until he felt what he guessed was the top of her cavity, but he would not stop. His entire length fit inside her. Sanem had fixed her opening with a new mechanism specifically for her master. As Celsus hit the end of his assault, a mechanism was engaged that would tighten the fake vaginal cavity and suction in his manhood. When this happened, he made a sound between a snarl and roar as he lost the control he was trying to exercise. He fucked Elena with an animal's abandon.

As her insides tightened around him, he pinned her down harder, putting his entire weight on his arms as he thrust into her with his powerful hips that were more animal than human. The coven women roared with him, howling in an ecstasy that was almost painful. They fucked, they bled, and they wailed in a frenzied passion they had not felt in years.

The only one that remained unaffected was pinned beneath the giant wolf, her shoulder crushed and her waist in a vice grip that would have crushed the ribs of any normal human. But she did not notice that, or the powerful hips that were shredding her lower half. Lord Celsus pounded her without restraint, rarely allowed out of fear of hurting his women. But he did not need to care for this one. She was not real, and fucking her to an immaterial pulp was a victory over Wilhelm that he needed more than the android herself.

She did not move or put up a fight. Instead, she lay there motionless, but when the master looked into her vacant hollow eyes he snarled with fury when all he saw was Nona.

Nona - what are you hiding? he thought to himself.

Hammering away at the artificial life form, he looked up at Nona. Nona - his life, his foundation; the untouchable of the coven that would never betray him, elegantly shoving her fingers in and out of the perfect vagina he loved to taste. But when they locked eyes for a brief moment, Celsus saw what he had chosen to ignore and he snarled at her, at the room, at Elena, and everything she represented. In a moment of blind rage, he bit her face and roared. He burrowed his snout into her eye socket and tore her left eyeball out - spitting it on the ground, disgusted by the taste of fake flesh.

The women were intoxicated from their sex but the master kept going. Bits of Elena's shredded vagina flew out as he thrust in and out. Her shoulder was crushed, her hips dislocated, and parts of her mechanical insides began to break apart. All the while, Elena's expression did not once change and the insolence aroused and infuriated Celsus. As he was nearing his climax, he howled, gnashed and snarled at Elena, biting at her face and shoulders. Celsus roared at Nona, at the walls, at anything within earshot and when he looked into the vacant eye that was left, not flinching or reacting to a single cruelty he inflicted on her - Celsus came. He shot into her fake cunt, unloading his hot semen into her hole, hitting the deepest part of her opening to feel what remained of the suctioning that was built into her.

As he came down from the high, he did not turn back. Instead, he slowly pulled out, looking at her broken opening with a sick fascination and excitement that would have meant certain death for anyone else other than this android. Her skeleton, broken but mostly intact, was a great contrast to Elena's soft exterior that acted as her humanity when she was torn to pieces. The center of her body looked like it had been smashed completely open, the superficial mechanics hung out of her destroyed vagina. Where she had previously looked like a beautiful marionette doll serving to adorn a room, now she looked like a mutilated discarded puppet. Her legs were disjointed and she looked broken, beyond repair, to be disposed of. He stood up from the beautiful android he had just savaged. He was naked and flushed from sex, bent over a motionless one-eyed Elena that was still looking at them all with the same empty expression she had entered the room with. Celsus looked inquisitively at Sanem.

"I can repair her," Sanem said, bowing to him in respect. Megan came to her side and they both lifted the broken body of Elena Carani as Celsus sat and observed the room around him. Everything was the same, save for the damage caused by their passionate love making, but as he surveyed the room, he noticed something that he hadn't wanted to notice before and that he could no longer ignore.

Anatu.

Their eyes locked and he felt bile rise in his throat. He hated that he could see it, the dark truth, the betrayal, the worst possibility. Stars began to recede within his blackening eyes. Their world had completely stopped.

THE SENTENCE
January 24, 2020 - 7:40 a.m.
San Juan Island

It was barely daybreak when the wheels of the Jaguar crunched up the gravel path to the estate. The pristine silver car looked like a lithe, exotic feline as it moved through the trees.

Inside the car, Tara breathed a sigh mixed with exhaustion and relief. It was done. Their tracks were covered - funds liquidated into precious metals, and all investigations settled. All she wanted was her family.

After descending into the massive underground garage, she came to a stop and shut the engine off with its soft rumble echoing throughout the pristine cavern. The dark beauty took a long, deep breath and stretched her neck - the only indication of her exhaustion - before fixing her eyes to the door in front of her. They focused, capturing the slightest movement of the creatures in her mind as her long, beautiful fingers ran along the sides of the steering wheel.

The car door opened and one forest green stiletto stepped out followed by another. She wore navy jeggings, a purple crop top, and a black leather jacket on her first day home in several months.

Her long, black hair was pulled back into a messy bun and the wisps of black against her dark, flawless skin made her radiant. She stretched again, wiggling her body in a sensual fluid motion as only a cat could, and immediately caught a scent on the tiny breeze of the massive metal doors opening before her.

"Lady Tara," came the soft voice.

"My lovely Nona," Tara said, bowing respectfully.

Nona returning the gesture before the two women took each other in a warm embrace.

"We have missed your presence, so," Nona said, kissing her once on each cheek.

"I have missed being home, my lady," Tara smiled.

"The master will be pleased to have you home. We will feast and rejoice in our family's reunion."

"Reunion, yes," she said with satisfaction.

"You must rest. You've had a long journey," Nona said, taking Tara's hand.

Δ

Lord Celsus, still as a statue on the enormous balcony of the master suite, stood looking out over the sea, a gentle breeze moving his hair behind his shoulders. The annoying sun was blessedly hidden among the heavy overcast sky. He could smell the arrival of the lion goddess from miles away. Tara was finally home and he felt a hollow sense of relief, for what relief was there when his entire family was torn? He could feel Wilhelm slowly chipping away at them and everything he had built.

Anatu.

The ancient name that rang in his stormy mind - what was she hiding? All he saw was her empty face staring back at him the day he nearly destroyed Elena. Nona had been the rock of his coven for so long, he'd never thought a time when she would betray him again.

He could sense and feel Nona and Tara as they moved through his home in the stillness of dawn. Tara adjourned to her room and he felt her sleep. Nona returned to her room and when the door closed behind her, Celsus found the door to her soul closed as well and he felt a brewing rage. He could always enter the minds of his women - they had no way to stop that, but he'd never been faced with a barrier of any kind from them, and he pondered his next move with cold detachment. After nearly four months, Tara was finally home. The entire cast was here and he knew what had to be done.

Celsus drew the curtains to his windows and walked to the opposite end of the room. He was fully nude, his perfect chiseled body moving with inhuman elegance, lean muscles flexing with each step he took. He stood in front of a small cherry table with a golden box, adorned with precious jewels. Opening the lid, the smell filled his nose. He inhaled deeply. The clove cigarettes sat neatly within the precious vault and a long finger touched one as he solemnly readied himself for what was about to happen.

Δ

Bavaria

"On your feet, whore!" Wilhelm shouted with sadistic delight, kicking the fallen girl in her stomach. She gasped and coughed onto the floor that was already streaked with her vomit from the last few kicks to her abdomen.

She had hair in a tight pixie cut that accented her strong angular features and multi colored eyes. One eye blue, the other green - she was one of the more unique treasures in Wilhelm's collection despite her European descent. Beautiful with red hair and freckles, she was a sight to behold before Wilhelm had gotten his libertine hands on her.

Though possessing a spirit as wild as her hair, she still hesitated to attempt another escape…in the wintery mountains of southern Germany. She contemplated that getting lost and freezing to death in the woods was still a better fate than what she experienced with Wilhelm. So she ran and it cost her.

Another blow came to her stomach. This was nothing compared to the beating she received the day she was caught.

Her face had to undergo almost full reconstructive surgery from the beating. She came out more beautiful than how she'd gone in, but it came at a price.

"Stand up!" Wilhelm cackled, laughing at his own joke as the girl crawled and slipped on the floor in her own fluids.

She couldn't stand. She had no legs. Wilhelm had taken them that day as punishment for attempting to escape and she was not given the bright violet prosthetics her other sisters had because of that. Instead, Wilhelm ordered her to crawl nonstop throughout the mansion, on her hands and stomach, dragging herself, begging for forgiveness every day.

He bent down and cupped her beautifully reconstructed face and forced her to look up at him.

"Where is your fight now?" he inquired.

She looked over to see her prosthetics displayed just out of reach. She had not begged for them adequately enough for his liking and he beat her.

"You want those?" he mocked, licking her face and squeezing her jaw too tightly. "How badly?"

Her eyes went from rage to defeat and then tears as she finally felt the crushing loss. Her legs were gone, her only hope to stand again was just out of reach, and as she looked into Wilhelm's wild eyes.

"You look so beautiful when you're broken," he breathed in her ear with sickening sweetness. "I don't think I ever want you fixed," he snickered while making a perverse farting sound. Her panic increased as he patted her head and continued, "You don't need those anymore," he whispered, and with a single gesture the beautiful violet legs were gone.

The girl watched as they were taken away, and she felt a hollowing defeat. She'd never felt as crushed in her entire life as she did at that moment. She wanted to scream but the shock of it all kept her silent.

"Good girl," Wilhelm smiled, and she snapped.

An open hand hit him hard across his face and she screamed, clawing and scratching at every part of him she could reach. Her nails broke off on his cheeks and forehead and she kept going until his guards grabbed her and held her down. The woman was still thrashing and her eyes were no longer fiery but wild with insanity.

"Stupid whore!" Wilhelm cursed, dabbing at his face with his sleeve. Blood dripped from the claw marks and he looked at her as one of his other girls brought him a warm washcloth to dab his face.

The girl with no legs was still thrashing and fighting though she had no chance of kicking off her captors. Wilhelm took a deep breath.

"Du weißt, das ist verboten," he said, standing over her, shoving the point of his shoe into her mouth, slowly widening her jaw. "Du musst bestraft werden," he breathed, the arousal growing in his voice. "And I do so love to see you broken."

The two men grabbed her and took her away to the infirmary. She would be taught a lesson and Wilhelm got hard just thinking about it.

He took his seat on his grand throne, and sipped wine from an ornate golden goblet. A sudden thought hit him and he looked around as if shocked at his own musings.

"What if I captured Celsus? What if I am moments away from taking him into my home and I can finally see him?" he asked no one in particular.

The thought sent a giddy chill through his body and he downed the rest of the wine in a single gulp before jumping up with renewed vigor.

"There is so much to prepare! The room must be decorated and fit for a king. We must put our best foot forward," he smiled maniacally. "We must show him how excited we are to make his acquaintance," he mused to himself. "I feel the time is near and I must be prepared."

Δ

San Juan Island

"My lady," Nona bowed at the entrance to Tara's room. The beauty lay sprawled on her bed, naked and bare before the enormous windows of her room. The curtains were slightly drawn and the moonlight cast silver streaks of light on her muscular curves.

Tara looked at Nona, the feline within gazing at her through those intense, golden eyes. Nona could almost see her lioness tale curling in playfulness.

"Lord Celsus has summoned you," Nona continued.

"Thank you, my lady. I will be there right away," but she didn't move immediately.

Nona bowed and closed the door to let Tara get ready.

Tara inhaled deeply, stretching out her long, strong arms. She curled her fingers and toes like a cat stretching her appendages and she arched her back before leaving her bed. She looked towards the moon. It was beautiful, and she realized how much she missed being home. Despite the heavy air in the house, there was nothing that compared to the safety and security she felt near her master and sisters.

The time away had been long and difficult for her but it had to be done and now she could hardly contain the excitement in seeing her master. She put on a white spaghetti strap satin dress that clung to her already erect nipples and voluptuous bottom. On her feet she wore white accessories that adorned her beautiful feet in floral patterns that stood out stark against her dark skin. The delicate strap fit snuggly around her ankle, ran down the center of her foot, and looped over her second toe in a silver band that glistened against her dark skin.

When she arrived at his door, she knocked and entered the dark room. Celsus sat on the largest chair in his room, an ornate throne with a small table on the side and a glass of wine and human blood placed on top. Tara closed the door behind her, slowly letting it slide into place with a soft click before bowing to her master.

"It is so wonderful to have you home," Celsus said evenly, a chill running down her spine at his very presence.

"It is wonderful to be home, my lord."

Tara sighed. She'd missed him so much. For a few tense moments she did not move, as she waited for his command. She stood on the balls of her perfect feet, claws sprouting.

"It has been a while, my Tara," Celsus continued casually, ignoring her lust, now filling the room with her scent.

"Too long, my lord," she whispered through clenched teeth, keeping her wild hunger for him perfectly in check.

"My love, you do not need to keep such control over yourself. Speak freely and do not dare exercise any restraint," he commanded.

Tara almost fell to her knees at what he said and she openly groaned. "Yes, my lord."

Celsus sat and waited for Tara to begin. It was her evening and she could do whatever she wanted. The satin against her opening was already moist with excitement and she approached him like a feline in heat.

Her hips swayed in fluid, sensual motions. They were the hips of a lioness on the prowl - not a step taken without the utmost precision. Her hair shook out behind her like a cat's mane and her eyes focused in on him as prey, not predator.

"Lord Celsus," she growled, putting one leg over the arm of the chair, followed by the other.

Her wet opening emitted a fearsome heat and a delicious smell that made her own mouth water and she could feel her master hardening beneath her beautiful hips. She started slowly grinding up and down his crotch. Her hands reached under his thick, long hair and she kissed him. Simple and passionate, she tasted her master and felt a wild desire growing within her.

Tara swallowed his tongue and begged him to hold her, hug her. She missed him so much and all she wanted was her master to show her how much he adored her. Celsus obliged and put his hands elegantly on her toned waist. She arched her back with a sensual growl that sounded more like the lioness than her human self.

"It has been so long since I've seen your true form," Celsus said sweetly, kissing her passionately and holding her beautiful face in his hands. "Let go, and show me your passion."

Tara gasped and moaned, "My lord, carry me to your bed," she begged in a voice that slowly turned more animal than human.

Celsus stood with her in his arms. With powerful ease he glided to his bed. He gently set her down on the sheets, which made her feel like she was floating on clouds. She wrapped her legs around his body.

"My lord," she begged, fighting the animal within her.

"If you disobey, you will be severely punished," Celsus snarled threateningly.

She nodded mid-growl and moved to position him as she wanted him. She motioned him to sit against the bed's lavish headboard, placing pillows around him to increase his level of comfort. She got off the bed and stood directly in front of him, breathing hard, nipples straining against the white, thin dress.

"Watch me, my lord," she demanded in a voice that sounded predatory, threatening and imposing.

"Yes, my love," he said evenly, the control and power in his face exciting the animal within.

She leaned forward on the bed, arching and moving her back like a lioness about to pounce. The controlled tone made her wet with excitement and her eyes glowed with her lioness self. It'd been too long since she had seen her master, too long since she smelled his sensual aroma. She felt a hunger, potent and wild as Celsus leaned against the headboard, resting his head back and looking at her like a man that was still in control of everything.

That look made her hungry. The wolf challenged the cat and she snarled with ferocity and acceptance. Tara knelt on the bed, spreading her legs wide, which hiked her dress tightly above her muscular ass. Her bare pussy swelled with blood as she placed a finger on her delicious button and began playing with herself, pinching her erect nipples with her other hand.

"Watch me," she demanded.

Celsus hungrily obliged, his manhood straining against his pants. He made no move to relieve it. She had not given permission.

Her fingers went into her dripping slit, shoving them in and out of herself before coming back up and rolling her clit with her soaking wetness. She pinched at her nipples and sucked on her fingers, tasting her elixir. Before giving herself to her master, she groaned and licked her fingers clean.

She sat back on her legs, throwing her head back and pelvis forward as her finger slid up her dripping pussy while another played with her pleasure spot. She gasped and moaned. She was so close already and wanted to erupt but she wanted Celsus more. She moved hard and harder, her abs flexing as she held herself up for Celsus to see her perky breasts and glistening opening. She moved her hands harder and faster on herself, going close enough, but not all the way. She was edging and Celsus loved to watch his women deprive themselves of pleasure for his sake.

Her snarl sounded large and feline as she kept the orgasm at bay. She felt herself begin to turn from the surge of emotions overwhelming her. For the first time in her 17 lifetimes, she felt a lack of control and it enraged more than terrified her. He watched as she fought the animal slowly emerging and he snarled at her.

"You will be punished," he warned again in an even tone that sent a shiver down her spine.

"Yes. The night is mine and I do as I please, my wolf."

She crawled towards him on the bed, her shoulders rippling with muscles morphing under her skin. Her hands grew larger and her nails sharpened. Her mouth slowly turned into a drooling, snarling snout and her tail slowly pushed its way out and twirled teasingly in the air. She did not normally do this when she was aroused, but when Celsus demanded, she obeyed completely and would not stop the transformation.

When she stopped turning half way through, she hissed and growled at Celsus. Tara's body had a hint of the tan lioness fur in precise, elegant patches. Celsus watched as she snarled and roared at him, vibrating little droplets of lust from her swollen pussy.

For a few painful moments, Tara stood in place to settle herself. She wanted this with Celsus and she let herself go, turning into an abomination of nature. The creature that loomed in front of him was monstrous. Her human self and pieces of her lioness body fought upon her flesh for dominance. Her legs and arms grew with primal genetics taking over as she was consumed by the animal within.

She could feel the beast overtaking her and she roared at Celsus in arousal and rage. He watched with fascination as his beautiful black goddess Tara morphed into an ancient lioness. Seeing her turn like this reminded him of the times he would half-turn and he felt a special connection with her in that moment.

Her tail swished in the air in a sensual way, running it down the length of her body. She crawled forward, paws first then her still human feet. The juices that dripped from her landed as small spots on the sheets and the master's room was overtaken by her scent. The scent possessed him and his hunger grew exponentially, as did the bulge straining in the pants that confined him.

Still he did not move, completely obedient to the beast that got closer, her growls sounding like distorted moans. She crawled over him, dragging her wet slit along his leg, her breathing deepening. She placed both paws on either side of him and straddled him in her half-lioness form. She was vicious, gruesome, and all instinct as she lowered herself between his legs. Her talented tongue expertly pulled the fabric to her lips and her strong bite yanked his pants down with such force that she actually moved his entire body. His thick steely rod sprung forth and Tara's inhumanly long tongue licked at her master's manhood. She simultaneously batted at his calves and feet with the end of her tail.

Celsus had told her to do as she pleased, and she wanted to see him adore her. Celsus sat perfectly still as she licked to her heart's content, her thick tongue almost enveloping his meaty cock. Her fangs were visible and this excited him further as she delicately slipped her tongue around his balls. His muscular legs flexed in extasy and she displayed her teeth in approval.

Master, I adore you. I love you, she said to him telepathically.

Goddess, I worship you, he responded as she put her head under his hand. Celsus knew what she wanted.

He brought her face up to his, bare teeth and all and kissed her. He licked at her teeth, sucked on her bestial tongue, and Tara melted for him. Her grip against the headboard tightened and her nails dug into the fine wood. Her entire body contracted with sexual spasms and she kissed the tip of his dripping dick with the swollen, hot lips of her animal pussy.

He twitched in response, the head eager to feel the juices of his lion goddess again. It had been too long and he smirked up at her in alpha defiance. Tara roared again at the sexiest sight she could ever hope to see - her master lusting for her – half-human, half-animal.

The difference between her human pussy and her lioness opening, aside from the smell, was the heat and strength of her swallowing lips. The powerful scent drove him wild. Tara's human and animal sex inundated his senses and he growled as she slowly moved her hot pussy onto his dick.

She let her head fall back and she gasped as she felt him stretch her opening. She sat back, sliding down to the hilt, rocking back and forth, letting her juices ooze down his balls. She moved up and down, her claws scratching at the headboard in painful frustration. She would not rush this - no matter how desperately she wanted him.

He kissed her again, licking and biting at her jawline which slowly grew into a lioness chin. His nails dug into her still human shoulders and sliced her open before they touched the thicker animal flesh. She roared and snarled at him, gnashing her teeth in his face at the pleasure and pain it caused her. Her pussy clenched tighter when she felt the nails dig in and she thought she would orgasm from the sensation.

"My thick hard wolf…" she seethed, breathing heavy.

The desperate sound was music to his ears as she begged for him.

"Yes, my dark angel," he answered in a measured voice that drove her wild.

"Rip me, wolf…"

He licked at her thickening neck.

"I do not know what that means, my beautiful creature. What do you want from your master?" he teased, holding onto her powerful spasming legs.

"Bigger, I want you bigger," she begged tightening her walls around his rod.

"Yes, my love," he smiled. There was a special pleasure he took in being passively dominant, especially with Tara letting herself go. He was happy to oblige the insatiable lion this night.

"Ah!" Tara groaned and roared as she felt her master's dick morph within her.

"More!" Tara half-begged, half-demanded as she moved up and down on him. Her pace slowly increased as he opened her up, his enormous cock completely filling her.

She felt her walls morph around his rock-hard dick. This was perfect. She needed this and slammed down hard to have the head of his cock hit her perfect spot.

The sound that came out of her in that moment was a horrifying vocalization of her lioness self, completely consuming her humanity.

Celsus loved her body, running his hands up and down as the transformation widened her now enormous chest cavity. He felt himself impossibly aroused at the sight of such raw power. This was the power his women had over him, and he bit and kissed her as she transformed - completely possessed by the sex she was ramming herself onto.

Lord and master! Tara screamed telepathically. She pleaded for more and he was happy to oblige.

Her paws gripped onto the headboard and the harder she slammed herself down, the more stars she saw as his enormous half animal cock hit her sweet spot over and over again. Her walls tightened, clamping down like a vice and the windows shook with her immense roar as she finally let herself go over the edge. She squeezed and a fountain of her love erupted over his balls. When he felt the rush of hot nectar, he grit his teeth, looked deep into the eyes of the lion riding him, and came very hard.

He shot his load hard and inhaled deeply, settling himself back as her vaginal muscles sucked out the last bit of juice. Her transformation was complete. Lord Celsus had a full-grown lioness straddling him.

He reached up to touch her face, and kissed her gently on her beastly mouth. Tara returned the gesture by delicately licking at his lips and cheek.

"You are so perfect," he said softly.

The giant creature purred loudly as she dismounted her master, her pussy dripping with his seed. Moving back between his legs, she caressed and licked his member clean with her coarse tongue. It was almost too much for him to bear. By the time she was done, it was clean, human, and very satisfied.

For a moment, the giant cat was unsure of what to do next. She knew what she wanted to do but she hesitated for only a split second before the master sensed her hesitation and a low growl came from him.

"No holding back," was his only threat and it was enough for the big cat to crawl to him on her belly, with respect and submission. His hand lay on one of the pillows she had placed under his arm for comfort and she nudged it in a sweet plea for attention.

He made her wait for his attention, and she lay patiently for his permission. His elegant hand lifted and she moved her enormous head under it, rubbing against his palm. She loved him so much.

She settled herself around him, curling behind him so he could rest against her enormous body. He closed his eyes and drifted into a deep, uneasy sleep.

Δ

"Yes, my lord?"

Nona had been called to his room and she waited for his orders - most likely regarding dinner.

"Lady Nona, how are you this day?"

She was caught off guard by the question, not because the master did not care but because it was at an unusual time. Had he summoned her to simply ask?

"I am well today. How are you, my lord?" she asked, without any hesitation.

He felt a calculation in her response that irked him and he swallowed the growl working its way up his throat.

"I am well. My family is together again," he said softly.

Nona nodded and waited for him to continue. When he did not, she gracefully stepped forward and, bowing to her master asked, "How may I be of service to you, my lord?"

He did not look at her but instead looked though a curtained window as if he could see through the material, past the balcony, and out to the sea. His contemplation and stewing had gone on for over two months, yet because of their spectacular age, time was distorted greatly. For him, the realization had happened minutes ago.

"Tonight, you and I shall dine alone. I would like some time with you, alone, my counselor."

Nona's uneasiness lifted and she felt a lighthearted joy in knowing her master was with her. He immediately sensed the lift in her mood and, with his back still turned to her, dismissed her.

"My lady," he stopped her, gaze fixed on the wall in front of him. "Tonight shall be a most special night. Treat it with great respect and be the goddess you have always been."

Nona felt a shiver course through her body. The door closed with a soft click but he remained motionless. If she had seen the stars receding in his eyes and the cold expression on his face, she would have seen the inhuman rage that awaited her.

Celsus stood motionless, meditating upon what he was going to do. Never in his many lifetimes could he have anticipated this, and the fact of the matter chilled him.

As dinner approached, he slowly began to move from his statuesque position, his trance. His fingers began to move as if a marble statue was slowly coming to life. He made his way to the door of an enormous closet. Inside were countless suits. He could wear a suit per day for over a year and not repeat a single ensemble. But, tucked away at the very back of the closet like the forbidden secrets that seemed to be rampant in his home now, was a single suit for this occasion, an unworn, black, perfectly tailored, exquisite Italian suit. There was no more fitting occasion than this night to don it. He dressed in a slow methodical manner, taking extra time to ensure everything was adjusted to perfection.

The moment finally came when Celsus entered the enormous marble room. It was impossibly white on every side with candles everywhere. He had prepared in advance with ropes hanging from the ceiling, all with different ends. Enormous, gilded butcher hooks of the finest silver with etched designs shone at the end of these ropes. They gleamed at him, as if teasing and mocking him about what was about to transpire. He looked at them with the same stoic expression, meditative about what needed to be done.

In the other ball room, he already sensed the women's dinner was coming to an early end and would quickly develop into a beautiful evening of love. He took a breath.

Love, he thought for a moment. *Sophia.*

He knew what that word meant and to creatures like them there was no love deeper than what they felt for each other, save his sister Sophia. He reflected on what he was about to do and wondered what kind of love this was, or was it the absence of such a sentiment? He loved Nona and Nona loved him - so why did it have to be this way? The disturbing image of Wilhelm appeared in his mind and he felt a growl rise within his chest.

"My lord," Nona said at precisely the same moment.

His head slowly turned to look at her, controlled, not hinting at the fury that had only a split second earlier consumed him.

"My love," he cooed, extending his hand at her.

She placed hers within and he kissed it with extreme delicacy. He took in the smell that came off her skin, the sound and feeling of the blood pulsing through her veins and he wanted to devour her right then and there. Nona always smelled so delicious.

Nona stood obediently as she watched Celsus inhale her, love her, adore her. She looked around at the ropes and then at the golden seat in the middle of the room with the small table, a cat-o-nine tails, and a clove cigarette.

She froze immediately and that was when she felt it. A pain shot up her arm to the base of her neck, hard and unpleasant. Her eyes darted back to see Celsus biting deep into her hand. He sucked on it, lapping up the blood in a controlled and terrifying rhythm, his eyes never leaving hers.

Seeing him like this, with that gaze completely devoid of any love or adoration, she realized she had not looked into his eyes all day, and that he had done this on purpose. Had she met his eyes sooner, she would have known her fate.

"Lord…"

"Do not speak," he threatened in a low and menacing growl, blood dripping from his chin.

His voice was cold with a furious undertone that told Nona something horrible was about to happen.

"Kneel before me," he commanded coldly.

She immediately kneeled at his feet. He looked down at her, lifting her chin between his two fingers, his sharpening nails slightly piercing her under her jaw. He was angry. He did not want to do this. He would have rather spent the rest of his cyclical eternity never having to do something like this. She had been his foundation, his right hand. When the hunger came, he died inside knowing what would be unleashed upon her.

Nona, in turn, looked up at her master's cold, unfeeling eyes and for the first time in her many lives, felt true terror. He was changed. There was no love, no compassion, and nothing remained of the man that worshiped her presence. She knew now what the many unfortunate once-borns felt in their final moments after crossing his path. This is what they saw, and she was suddenly overwhelmed by the pity she felt for their miserable endings. She would have cried at that moment, but the terror he created elicited a much stronger feeling.

"Do you love me…*Anatu*?" he asked again, this time using her ancient Babylonian name in a voice that was as cold and unwelcoming as death itself.

"Yes, my lord," she whispered in a shaky voice.

"Do you adore me?"

"Yes, my lord."

Celsus nodded and began walking around her. "Then why would you betray me?"

The question was as much a promise of the pain that was to come as a plea from the lost wolf. "Why would you choose now of all times to betray me, when everything is unsteady and the unknown is closing in on us?"

"I…"

"If you dare lie to me, your fate will be so much worse," he said with the animal coming through.

Nona shivered in dread as the receding stars moved faster within his dilating eyes.

"My lord, please," she begged.

He picked up her hand and put it to his lips. He then licked her blood as Nona shivered in terror.

"You will show your love for me one last time," he said evenly as Nona felt the world fall from underneath her.

"My lord…"

Claws like razors came across her face and gashed open her cheek. "Do not speak," he snarled, putting a single bloody finger up to her lips.

Before, he would have savored her first – tasted her – he would have looked deep into her eyes with demanding adoration as she hungrily sucked on his fingers, but not this night. This night there was no love, only chaotic hunger – he would never again taste his beloved Nona or share in any pleasure with her and it enraged him.

Nona's face ached as the gash openly bled. Trails of blood ran down her open cheek to her jawline, staining her white choker before falling down to the white marble tiles beneath. She cautiously looked up to her master whose expression was neither compassionate nor loving. There was an old rage present in his face that was elegant and controlled, but as his mouth shaped into a snarl, she could see his fangs elongating and knew the control would not last long.

"To the ropes," he hissed, taking her bleeding face into his claws. "Be grateful, betrayer, for even after all of your contemplations of killing us…forever, I still love you. I will treat your demise with absolute respect."

She wanted to cry but the tears did not come as she saw her master in a whole new light. Hidden behind his fury was the pain that she had caused and she felt an overwhelming sadness that left her breathless for what she had done. Their life was painful, their existence vile, and she hated it, but seeing her master's pain written all over his exquisite features, she knew her absolute demise would be a blessing. Seeing him like this was more than she could bear. She knew she deserved every grisly moment of this night.

"I love you, my lord," she said out of turn, and shut her eyes to wait for the gash. Even if these words were the last she ever said to him, they needed to be said. When the pain didn't come, she opened her eyes and looked over to see him standing by the ropes.

"Your fate awaits you, Anatu. I shall be the priest of your departure, with the most love and adoration I have ever felt in such a destruction."

Nona stood by the rope with the largest hook. There were nine ropes hanging from the ceiling, each with different types of hooks attached to the ends, and she knew he had planned this. She felt a dreadful appreciation of the details he had thought of for her. At her lowest point, he still adored her and would show her the respect she was due even though she had not shown it to him. She felt her heart break. The pain she would face this night would be the worst of her entire existence, but she knew she had to endure it until her death to put an end to the greater pain of her betrayal. The already dim lights in the room seemed to get dimmer as she stood among the hooks and ropes.

"Eyes open," he commanded.

She obediently followed his every move. She knew he was not in an uncontrollable rage. This was disciplined fury with love, a paradox. He did not know the implications of losing her, but in his heart, he could see no other way.

His fingers closed around the choker grazing his palm.

"You will no longer need this," he said to her softly as he pulled the adornment from her neck.

Nona felt like she had been stripped of her dignity as she saw the symbol of her status, his love - of everything she had ever been - dangle impotently in his hand as he placed it gravely on the gilded table next to his clove cigarette.

"Counselor, my most trusted," he breathed, taking her bloody face in his hands, staining his palm as he caressed her. "This is our parting. Observe it with the sacred solemnity it merits."

Nona nodded and fought back the tears that threatened to overflow. He ran his bloody claws through her hair and the sudden gesture of intimacy tipped the balance. A single tear ran down her gashed cheek. He watched with curiosity as the tear created a perfect line of healed flesh in the middle of the wounds on her face.

"Interesting," he mused. "The great Anatu has more secrets than I thought," he whispered. "Are there anymore secrets for my shattered soul?" He quickly put a finger to her lips to keep her from answering. "No matter, you can take those with you. It's too late my love, too late."

"Undress," he commanded.

He was neither impatient nor disrespectful. This was the other untouchable woman, his best friend and confidant, right next to Sophia. His two greatest loves would now be gone, forever.

Her resurrection never entered his mind, nor the possible repercussions of taking the life of the coven's death clock. He was consumed by the betrayal, and in his mind, he saw her execution as final, an irrational thought, considering the last 16 lives they shared. He looked her up and down as if he had not already decided where the hooks would go.

She felt the sharp point of the first pierce her flesh. A hook in each wrist and ankle. Nona swallowed the shouts of pain and he did not reprimand her. She would feel greater pain soon enough and would be unable to suppress it. Blood dripped from her feet and began to pool on the floor beneath her. As a canine would, he lapped it up with his tongue. He watched the spasming muscles ripple across her back, the silver hooks adorning her flesh.

A few tugs of satisfaction and Nona's body was slowly lifted, held up by nothing except the hooks that pierced her. The pain, as her entire weight hung on those hooks and tore her, was excruciating, and she shouted as her body shifted and settled on the butcher's ends.

He paused for a moment with the final two and much larger hooks in each hand. She tried to lift her head to look at him, but the pain her body was absorbing made it difficult. He lifted her head and looked at her, his eyes unloving and empty, blank with rapidly receding stars, swallowing her universe like a black hole.

He drove one of the enormous gleaming points into her neck, slowly, as he watched her face contort with pain. Tears ran down her face, healing the wounds on her cheeks as the point was pushed down into her neck and out through her back.

"What a waste. Why?" he hissed.

Nona gagged, gurgling sounds coming from her open mouth as she tried to scream. Blood dripped from her lips and she tried to control the involuntary spasms that agitated her open wounds. Celsus watched with detachment as she thrashed and tore herself, vomiting onto the floor. He still loved her. He would always love her. But he was shut down with no affection present as the pure sadist in him accomplished the task at hand.

"Now the final," he growled, sighing into her ear.

She knew exactly where this hook was going.

He walked around her body and, like a voyeur at a museum appreciating a perfect work of art, stopped between her legs. Her opening glistened with some of her blood that had trickled down her openings, and his mouth watered. He wanted to taste her, love her, worship her - but not tonight. Instead he licked the tip of the hook and dug it in, the sharp point turning her insides into a bloody mess. It was then she screamed in agony. He grabbed the inside of her thigh for leverage as he shoved the hook deep inside her. Blood dripped from his claws and he ate this, wiping his hand clean on her bloody ass cheeks.

"Why?" he growled, touching the top of the hook jutting out of her back to the left of her spine.

He resumed his position at the front of the hanging beauty, her brow wet with the sweat of pain. Blood dripped from her open mouth and she gagged and heaved as vomit mixed with blood leaked past her shaking lips.

He spoke to her without compassion, "Because of what you've done I cannot love you as I wish. You must suffer as you have made me suffer."

Tears ran down her face, healing the wounds on her cheekbone and he cocked his head to the side in curiosity.

"Lord…" she managed to get out.

Celsus stuck his clawed index finger into her mouth as she tried to say his name.

"No," he growled, and with a quick motion pierced her tongue.

He then pulled his hooked finger back slicing the tongue into a bloody fork. The sound that came from her was a garbled mess of blood and she thrashed from the sudden pain. Nona managed an ugly sound that came from the depths of her miserable soul. It was deep and wild like an animal being tortured and she looked at him with desperate, pleading eyes, and he snapped.

Seeing the blood dripping from her open mouth, how she hung, and the pleading in her eyes, enraged him and he slowly began to turn. There had been something about the way their eyes locked in that moment that shut down the temperance in him and there was no going back.

The agony, betrayal, and rage - the lack of control - all manifested itself in that one pitiful moment when she looked at him for help.

He could not help her, he could not help Sakura - he could barely help himself - and she had that written all over her bloodied face and he abhorred it.

"Coveners!" he howled, as the door to the room slowly opened.

"Come and bid your sister farewell!"

The sound that came from their master was not the elegant voice of the man they adored. It was the voice of their master losing his humanity and giving in to the enraged monster within. He was turning beast more and more lately, but this was by far the most unstable and chaotic state they had seen him in centuries.

The five supernatural women, Tara, Sakura, Megan, Sanem, and Cala, all walked in with heads bowed, eyes to the floor. They were afraid. They had never seen him like this, not even at Shira's execution, and the scene playing out destabilized everything.

"Gather," he said with a frightening tone, his body morphing as he spoke.

He moved to the table, picked up his clove and took a large puff. He then took the cat-o-nine, blades glistening in the dim lighting and walked back to Nona, letting the whip trail with a horrible sound as it dragged along the tile.

After the women formed a large circle, the obvious horror revealed itself upon their ashen faces.

"This is what happens when you betray me," he said in a controlled voice that hinted at the lingering humanity behind his changing facade. His voice sent a chill through every one of them.

Blood pooled under Nona, but not even Sakura's mouth watered at this horrible sight. Nona's head bobbed forward and Celsus took a noose that hung from the ceiling and looped it around her forehead to keep her head up and steady.

"Beautiful," he growled as the whip lashed out.

It hit Nona's body with a sharp snap and when he pulled back, the patches left behind made a distinct sound of human flesh tearing. The entire room flinched with each snap of the whip - over and over. Her grotesque vocalizations became one constant wail of agony as Celsus circled her body to hit every piece of flesh he could.

The pink, meaty muscle gleamed through the blood as layer after layer of living flesh was torn from the woman hanging in the middle of the room. At first controlled and meditative, Celsus quickly devolved into a howling, snarling monster as he incessantly whipped her. Blood sprayed over the horrified women frozen in place, and he licked his lips when the scarlet nectar landed on him. He snarled as one powerful blow after another quickly transformed her into a lump of bleeding flesh.

Vomit mixed with blood pooled under her body as Nona went in and out of consciousness. Her wailing became gasping sobs that turned into incoherent moans as the torture and blood loss turned her into a delirious half-conscious mess. This was worse than Shira's demise and her sisters did all they could to stand perfectly still without looking away.

"Do you see?" Celsus paused, looking at them with a maddening look, even for a wild monster. "This is what happens when you betray me. I love you in the extreme and I will punish you in the extreme if you deceive me as Anatu has. She seriously contemplated our permanent ending."

There was silence after his statement, save for the garbled mess that came from Nona. She was still trying to hang on to her consciousness. This was brutal, even for them, and the women felt their hearts break, knowing and even feeling her fight to stay alive.

"What was that?" Celsus boomed, coming up to her and grabbing her still human face in his monstrous claws.

Her mind was a chaotic mess and could barely form thoughts let alone words, but he dug deep into the mess of her mind to find what was keeping her alive - what made her hang on until this moment when the blood loss alone should have killed her already.

Sifting through the thoughts of her sisters, their lives together, at the very heart of her reason for living, he saw himself hugging and loving her. She smiled at him and proclaimed her undying love for him.

Louder groaning sounds brought him back to the present as he processed her anguish. She was unrecognizable. Her wrists were shredded from the beating and bone protruded through her flesh. Meat and muscle littered the floor around her and in a sudden moment of madness, Celsus began to howl.

He roared and wailed a horrible cry that brought the women to their knees. They cowered in fear of the hysteria their master was feeling and suddenly the winds outside began to pick up considerably. The windows of the room shook with his howls, the newly resumed wails of what was left of Nona, and another visitor that battered their windows.

Lili. Everyone in the room knew the presence. Another level of fear possessed them.

The ancient owl-goddess was summoned not by an elaborate ritual, not by a sacrifice, but by the wailing and anguish of her suffering offspring. Powerful winds stormed against the glass, threatening to break in as thunder and lightning roared outside the house.

"Night hag!" Celsus roared, shouting with fury at her interference.

He quickly welled with terror and for a millisecond wondered what had he done to invoke their creator.

Nona was still alive - barely - she would more than likely die but he had to ensure that she would not come back. Lili beat at the windows with growing force, finally cracking and shattering them with her oncoming presence.

Celsus grabbed onto Nona's still recognizable face and dug a claw deep into her chest. He would consume her heart and end her.

"Coward . . ." came the distant hiss. They all heard it.

Celsus shivered as violent gusts of wind blew through the windows until the room was alive with her wild, monstrous presence.

"My child. Anatu," she hissed, seeing Nona and feeling the wolf's claws digging through her chest.

Nona could no longer wail or even moan - she was a shell that was slowly slipping into the eternal darkness that awaited her and through the delirium all she saw was Celsus.

He was her beginning and her end. She would live and die by him alone. She stopped fighting and gave in. It was over, and as her consciousness slowly slipped away, she said goodbye to her sisters and her lord. Before her seemingly inevitable death, something enveloped her and suddenly the wolf retreated.

Lili fiercely protected the final remnant of her daughter against the master's vengeful murder. Lili would not move and, sensing her presence, Celsus felt truly powerless. He could do no more. Lili neutralized him. He could neither protect nor kill his own women and, knowing Lili possessed Nona, he let out a disgusting howl and fled.

He roared at his women who instantly cowered away, as he leapt through one of the shattered windows, and ran. He could do nothing, and as he ran from Lili, he realized there was no outrunning the source of his existence.

He ran, his fully released lycanthrope body breaking through infant trees like toothpicks. He roared in his madness as the rain beat down on him, washing away the remains of Nona's blood and flesh that stuck to him.

Suddenly he saw nothing but white. An enormous lightning bolt struck and stopped him in his tracks. He howled at the electrical bolts that coursed through him. Disoriented and confused, he hobbled to his feet to keep running when another very manmade shock went through him. He looked back to where the shot came from and saw a man in black tactical gear with a gun.

In that instant, Celsus was vulnerable to attack and they came at him in full force. As he tried to organize his thoughts, a shock went through his mind and he was paralyzed. Barbs, knives, and electrical currents, went through his body and he roared and convulsed as he felt his limbs become immobilized. He fell face-first into the muddy ground.

The subdued wolf looked around, confused and disoriented from the assaults. Another cracking blinding telepathic assault hit and he howled at the chaos in his mind. What was happening? *How* was this happening? Too many questions ran through his mind as delirium and confusion took over. What year was it? What lifetime was it? Where were his women?

Night Hag … he thought.

He tried to summon his women telepathically just as another assault scrambled his mind even more. The only sound he could hear above his howls was Lili's mocking laughter. Where were the women? Anatu? Where was she? She could stop this.

Anatu, where art thou? he thought.

Through the mess and confusion, a single visage crystalized in front of him in hyper realistic clarity. Anatu glowed in front of him and Celsus tried to call out – to command her action – but the dark beauty simply stood looking at him with beautiful detached eyes. A pain shot through his body, though if it was a physical assault or manifestation of pain he couldn't tell. What he knew was that Anatu watched as he died that day so long ago, and today she watched him again. Only this time – she was a bleeding lump of unrecognizable flesh and tissue hanging from his ceiling. She couldn't be here, yet he saw her and not even in his hallucination did she save him. Instead, she watched as she had so many years ago, and Celsus stopped summoning her. She was not coming to save him. The reality was her hanging onto life by a thin thread.

Another blinding electrical assault that felt like seizures hit him hard and he shut his eyes, Aantu's empty gaze was the last thing he saw before his blackout. He was captured, and in his final moments of lucidity he heard Lili's ancient laughter – as if participating in a game she would always win.

Back at the mansion, the storm had ebbed to a calm shower and the women, ancient demons of nearly 3,800 years, were in complete shock. They knew what happened and before they could respond, they distinctly heard the sounds of both sea plane and helicopter taking off in the night. Nona, in a very real sense, was no more. The pretense of calling her by that name was annihilated. Their mutilated sister, breathing in broken, almost imperceptible breaths, was in fact the great sorceress, Anatu.

No one doubted her true first name would one day be claimed, but not like this. The grief tore at all of them – the capturing of their master, and their patroness of magic at death's door. They all felt fear and knew not what to do. They looked at one another in silence as they all clearly heard the helicopter getting father and farther away.

Megan was the first to address the disfigured bloody mess of their sister. She touched her face and looked deep into her soul. Anatu was slipping. Any second now she could be gone, but something was helping her hang on. There was an ancient presence within Anatu keeping her alive and Megan knew there was not much time.

"We must help her now," she said.

The other women were openly hesitant. The master had sentenced her, had just tried to execute her, and each woman wondered if it was it their place to keep her alive.

Megan read their minds like a book.

"I am second-in-command of this house and our master has been captured," she said with a quiver in her voice.

She didn't know how she knew it but she did, just like she knew this presence within Anatu would not last for much longer.

"We will need Anatu to save him. You know the law of this house. You will obey me and do everything I tell you to do. There will be a reckoning soon," she stated, her eyes glowing red and her body visibly shaking with rage. None would dare challenge the XO in this state, not even Cala.

Lady Sanem quickly took out the knife she always carried. She cut down her sister with Megan's help and carefully carried her to the depths of the mansion, hooks, blood, and bone - all that remained.

"Sakura, I want you to eat. Anatu's blood will strengthen you and I need you as strong as possible, especially when we are about to go to war," Megan said decisively.

Sakura hesitated. There was something taboo, even to her, about drinking up the blood of her sister's attempted extermination, but she also knew Megan was right. She took a breath and nodded. She would be quick about it.

"Cala, you must hunt. You too will need all your strength. Tara, come with me. Sanem is going to need help...and blood."

Anatu needed to recover and regenerate but there was hardly enough time given the severity of her injuries. Tara was already coming down with five bags of blood as Megan set up an IV and transfusion. Megan expedited – cauterize the wounded arteries and get blood in. It was her physical healing that would take time, something they did not have.

The women did as they were instructed. Anatu had to be saved. The war was about to begin and they had been dealt a potentially game-ending blow. They knew this was to be *the* war of all their incarnations.

Δ
Bavaria

The truck driver drove as fast as possible through the winding roads of the Ammergau Alps until they reached a road which appeared on no map. Armored and more heavily manned than most military vehicles, this was a truck that could not be stopped as it made its way to its final destination, Wilhelm's mansion, a remote location, deep in the German wilderness.

The truck pulled up to the heavy gates, was admitted, and made its way to a tunnel that lead directly under the mansion. When it came up to the bay for the armored drop off, the enormous gates opened and they pulled in.

Inside, a small army of armed men waited for the vehicle to turn off its engine, and the door to the holding cell parted like a hungry mouth. Inside, the crazed wolf had long returned to his human form and fearlessly glared at the men behind his capture.

Wilhelm entered the cavernous facility and finally met Celsus face-to-face. As he stood in his restraints, Celsus realized he could not see into any of their minds and he mused at himself with curiosity. He found it interesting that these once-borns were able to expect his telepathy.

"Lord Celsus," came the triumphant voice.

Celsus looked directly at Wilhelm, his eyes cool and hard. The restraints with which he was held sent a surge of current through his body that would have killed a once-born. He barely felt it as his muscles flinched from the tickling sensation.

"Sie sind stark," the German cooed. "I know how much energy is going through you right now."

Wilhelm approached him, eyes wild with excitement. He wanted to touch him, reach out and feel the muscles of the man he had obsessed over, the man who had plagued his every waking moment, the man that had handed his father's inheritance to him on a silver platter.

Celsus was proudly naked, and looked like he was carved out of stone as he stood - perfection incarnate - in front of Wilhelm.

"You look delicious," Wilhelm breathed, his mouth watering at the sight.

Celsus' lips slowly curled into a mocking smirk. The moment was tense as Wilhelm stood, salivating over the man in restraints, aching and longing for his body. The bulge in his pants was visibly getting larger and more painful, but Wilhelm refused to touch it, look at it - even acknowledge it. Celsus could see the discomfort it was causing him.

"You should take care of that," he growled in a voice that lit a fire in the pit of Wilhelm's tense stomach.

Wilhelm gasped, swallowing the palpable lust coursing through his body. A wet spot became visible against his pants but he still refused to touch his dick. It was not the time.

"*You* will take care of this for me," Wilhelm said softly with a smile. "But not yet. There is plenty of time. For now, you will be taken to a special room, designed just for you, and locked away where you can't call for help. You will be trapped, alone, and mine."

Celsus moved his neck, causing another surge of energy to be shot through him. But he barely flinched as he leveled his eyes and stared directly into Wilhelm's.

"Meine Frauen werden für mich kommen," he replied in perfect German with no detectable accent.

Wilhelm felt another pang of hunger hit him as the lusty voice of Celsus speaking in his native tongue possessed him. He squirmed, despite himself, as Celsus continued in English.

"And when they do - this sand castle of yours will fall."

Wilhelm's pace quickened at the threat and he did not hide the groan that escaped his wet, shaking lips. After a moment of collecting himself, he spoke coolly in response.

"I completely understand you not keeping up with world events…and strategies. I mean really, can men such as ourselves be concerned with such boring things? Well, this time is different. The world is about to be locked down. Any help you think is coming will be frozen in place. Your women will not be able to move without detection from numerous nations. My friends and I run every single country that matters. We control everything. The economy, the media, health care, drugs, energy, and all pillars of life on this earth are controlled by us. I heard you even call us 'the Controllers' – a little boring on the nomenclature, but very accurate nonetheless. During the course of your life, and even before, we devised a plan of absolute control. That plan is being carried out at this moment. You, Lord Celsus, are an essential goal of that plan and you *will* give up your secrets. Your women will be taken soon enough. It is too late for you, mein lieber Mann…much too late."

CONFESSION
January 27, 2020 – 12:20 a.m.
San Juan Island

It had been two days since her ordeal. Even with her sisters helping, she still had not regained consciousness. The blood transfusion had been a success, but the physical wounds were still mending. The healing was visible, in real time, and the coven gave all their strength and psychic power to their beloved witch.

Elena and Anna stood watch by Anatu's side all night, switching out bags of blood, ensuring nothing took place out of the ordinary. Anatu lay on the same hospital table Elena had laid on during her repair and there was something humanly disturbing to the android as she watched.

Sanem informed the women that Elena's AI capabilities had evolved beyond her original programming. Something unforeseen had taken place and there was a noticeable jump in her technological advancement. Elena appeared to be trying to process her seemingly human emotions. At the forefront of her thoughts was Celsus. Sanem theorized that when Celsus broke Elena, something beyond even the coven's understanding had taken place. It appeared as though Elena's newfound consciousness had latched on to Celsus as her reason for existing. Tara agreed with the theory and expounded to Sanem that they themselves were living proof of this strange dependent concept.

Anna was charged with nurturing Elena and ensuring her emotional development progressed in a way that was positive to the house. By proxy she had also been charged with Anatu's care. Anna washed her regularly as her wounds healed, and with Elena's help ensured she was kept in pristine cleanliness.

"Her healing is progressing at a steady rate," Elena informed Megan.

Her robotic ability to analyze situations and give a quantitative response was much appreciated at a time when progress needed to be tangible and tracked. They did not have time to delay. As soon as Anatu was healed, they would depart.

Megan furrowed her brows as the android continued to analyze Anatu's vitals. This monotone dialog became blurred hums at the back of her racing mind. They needed to find where Celsus was, but she could not sense him. No one could sense him. It was frustrating.

Elena could not give them an exact location of where Wilhelm was. When they tried to mine her memory for information, they found that part of her database conveniently corrupted. Wilhelm had done this as a precaution and anticipated her capture.

What would the master do, Megan wondered. She felt suddenly inadequate to fill his shoes and she racked her mind to find the solution she knew was there but just out of her reach.

Elena stopped talking and Anna was wiping Anatu's body down with a warm wash rag, gently dabbing at her wrists and ankles that were still open wounds. She was soft and methodical as she washed Anatu. The five remaining coven women watched this in a trance-like state.

The wash cloth traced Anatu's beautiful body and gently circled each voluptuous breast. Anna's strikingly pale hand made its way down Anatu's naval to gently cleanse the womanhood that had been butchered to mush. As Anna reached between Anatu's legs, Megan felt a sudden realization hit her and she took a deep breath.

At that moment, she saw a church with its gaudy gold decor, the altar, and a giant crucifix hanging over the tabernacle. A priest with a tall hat stood before it with his arms extended, giving the naive congregation a blessing that held no power in the next life they were promised and there was a pause in her thought process. It was not a priest. It was a bishop and Megan's head shot up.

"The bishop," she told Sanem.

The warrior understood.

"Klaus Schunner," Sanem offered.

Megan nodded.

"It's time we visit our holy friend. Tara will take over Anatu's care. You and I will go back to Holland and have a friendly chat with the bishop. I want everyone else to prepare. Sanem, this place is done. You know what to do, but make sure they burn when they come looking for us," Megan stated.

"As you wish, my lady. When the last of us leaves this place, it shall become a hot trap," Sanem replied.

Megan continued, "Three days before our operation, I need everyone at the safehouse in Venlo. Come in separately, Amsterdam, Antwerp, and Paris - highest security protocols."

"Why Venlo?" Sakura asked.

"Sanem and I will be close to Venlo, and I have an intuition," Megan responded, her eyes wild with hunger.

$$\Delta$$

Bavaria

"Are you awake?"

Celsus had not slept, though his eyes remained closed. He heard no thoughts, and for the first time in his existence, he was completely and utterly alone in the silence of his mind. He was fascinated by the sensation. He had tuned out the chaos his arrival caused, watched with indifference as the humans armed with automatic weaponry escorted him to his prison cell, and was pleasantly surprised to see the lengths this once-born had gone for him.

His cell was less a prison and more like a throne room with a center spot for his entire mobile unit to keep him contained. He could tell the walls were of the strongest polymer humans could make, and something was keeping his telepathy in check. Alone, but hardly defeated, Celsus watched with a stoic face. Wilhelm beamed at him with a smile Celsus recognized as sadistic pleasure and genuine joy.

"Do you approve of your accommodations, my lord?" Wilhelm asked sarcastically in the tone of a servant.

Celsus knew this sociopath was asking for some kind of validation. Was this worm trying to be like him? Somehow trying to replicate what he thought was the life of Celsus? He deigned to look around the chamber for the first time. It was indeed unique. The room was enormous, like a jet hanger with impossibly tall ceilings. Computers and monitors tracked his vitals on one side of the room, and on the other, a row of women stood, each with a unique outfit.

Some had vibrant purple arms, forearms, legs, calves, and feet. A few of the girls had deep violet dog masks tied back with a gold buckle and matching collar with a chain they held in their own hands. All were dressed in different variations of maid outfits, with tiny details that made each one unique to the girl that was wearing it. He acknowledged that Wilhelm paid close attention to the details of his women.

What stood out to him the most, however, was the center piece that swung slowly in the middle of the room. Hanging from cables on full display was a gorgeous girl with two different colored eyes, a redhead with a pixie cut and freckles. She had no arms or legs and was gagged with a mask that had Wilhelm's initials and family crest monogrammed on it in gold, gaudy letters. She wore the least amount of clothing of the women, with purple tassels on her nipples and her anus. Her vagina and anus were accented with bright purple bouquets of flowers, placed perfectly up both openings.

Celsus circled the room with his indifferent gaze before turning back to look at Wilhelm seeing that he was waiting, like a twisted child, for praise of his hard work.

"Unique," Celsus said with boredom, but could sense Wilhelm's heart quickening.

"Would you like to know about my collection?" Wilhelm asked, rhetorically.

Celsus knew he wanted to talk about himself. He did not acknowledge the statement, and watched as one of the girls with beautifully ornate arms came to Wilhelm's open hand.

His arm wrapped around her slim waist like a slimy snake and Celsus could see the disgust and fear the girl was suppressing. Even the stench of Wilhelm's arousal could not mask the smell of her fear, and Celsus gazed into the eyes of the frightened girl. No thoughts came to him but he didn't have to read her mind to know what she was thinking.

Wilhelm pulled her close and unclasped a buckle on her back and the two arms came off. Her shoulder stumps were scarred and she stifled a flinch as Wilhelm sucked and licked at her shoulder flesh. His breathing quickened as she gasped and Celsus could see the bulge in his pants.

"Purple - like royalty," he groaned. "She loved me. And I loved her. But she thought she could touch me whenever she pleased, so I clipped her beautiful little wings."

He grunted a sound that all the women understood and Valentina, the new girl from Columbia, immediately walked over to him with shining violet legs and an ornate dog mask.

"Touch me, whore," he growled, biting down on the first girl's shoulder stump.

Valentina expertly reached into his pants with one hand, and undid the zipper with the other in such a fluid motion Celsus couldn't help but be impressed. When her hand gripped Wilhelm's rock-hard dick, his eyes opened and he immediately looked at Celsus. No reaction was given and

Celsus watched as Valentina pumped him while he continued to suck on the other girl's amputated shoulder.

His breathing got shallow as she moved her hand up and down. Even though the master's psychic powers were somehow held in check, he could still psychologically read the libertine's degenerate thoughts. Wilhelm's gaze devoured everything about the Celsus. They were sizing each other up.

Celsus responded by squaring his shoulders in his cell against Wilhelm's gaze. Celsus stood proud and unaffected as the only alpha in the room next to an imposter. Wilhelm heard the challenge loud and clear but could not bring himself to care as his arousal grew.

"Move," he demanded unnecessarily to the girls that followed his steps as he walked up to the cell. He came up to the clear glass that separated them, to the breathing holes at the level of his mouth. Celsus watched with detachment as Wilhelm got closer and closer to his climax.

Wilhelm's grip on the girl's neck tightened as he sucked on her arm stumps and bit down on her jawline. His teeth bit into the flesh, broke skin, and he began to suck when there was a sudden change in Celsus – a change that did not go unnoticed.

The blood strung from his lips to her chin, a pinkish clear liquid and Celsus swallowed. Wilhelm turned her face and bit down harder, tearing a little flesh from her perfect chin and a trickle of blood dripped down.

Celsus swallowed again and looked at Wilhelm fiercely but it was too late. The hunger Celsus could not hide came through his stifled reactions as plainly as Wilhelm's hardening bulge. He used his fingers to pinch and kneed the wound for more blood to spring forth, and every muscle in Celsus' perfect body tensed at the sight.

Seeing such a powerful being unable to control himself despite knowing how much he wanted to, aroused Wilhelm more than any torture he had ever inflicted. This creature, at this very moment, was the most beautiful, exotic, sexual creature he had ever seen and he was overwhelmed with lust as he fought down the orgasm that threatened to burst forth.

"Not yet . . ." he said, narrating his lust for Celsus who could not help but dart glances at the blood that slowly dripped from the amputee's chin.

Wilhelm's forefinger dug into the flesh and she winced, clenching her jaw and swallowing what Celsus guessed was a yelp of pain, but all he could feel was an overwhelming thirst to feed.

A growl caught in his chest that shook his prison and Wilhelm groaned at the sound, gasping. His stance widened and his thighs tensed as the orgasm built and built, even as he fought it back. Valentina's arm continued at a steady pace as he bit down on the amputee's shoulder wound. The girl let out a small yelp at the sensitivity of the scar.

Wilhelm grunted as Valentina's hand kept pumping up and down, the wall fogging with his lustful breathing. His finger buried deeper into the armless girl's jaw as his orgasm built. The girl could not keep the pain from contorting her beautiful face anymore and she opened her jaw in a silent scream. The girl knew what would happen if she dared make a single sound while he orgasmed. Her eyes filled with the pain that overflowed down her gorgeous, flushed cheeks.

Wilhelm bent forward as he shot his load onto the ground in front of Celsus. The girl kept pumping as it dripped between his trembling feet.

The stench of his semen overwhelmed any other scent that was wafting into Celsus' enclosure and he felt a revulsion he had not felt before, even when consuming the lowliest of once-borns. The smell was thick so vile it momentarily stopped the hunger - but only for an instant. He took another breath and the scent and sight of the still oozing blood returned him to the present, and his growing hunger.

Wilhelm gasped as he came down from the high and he dug his nails into Valentina's waist, his knuckles turning white, biting at the dog mask covering her face.

"Mach es sauber, Schlampe," he demanded in a breathy voice and slowly released her.

Valentina nodded quietly and undid the clasp behind her head, letting the purple mask fall to the side. She bent down on all fours and licked at the floor as Wilhelm stepped on the back of her head and pressed down.

"Alles davon," he sighed, leering at the girl's mouth crushed into the mess.

Celsus watched the scene and was intrigued at this vile creature's creativity. Afterwards, two girls with violet legs walked towards him carrying a large throne. Judging by the flex in their arms, Celsus guessed these women had been very athletic before some twisted fate landed them in the clutches of this sadist. Wilhelm settled in and observed his captured trophy.

Only a few of the women did not have vibrant purple accessories and Celsus wondered what he did with the limbs after they were severed. His mouth watered at the thought. Wilhelm took a sip from a large overly jeweled goblet and smiled, guessing the master's thoughts correctly.

"I save them, if you're wondering about my trophies," he explained, settling back and letting the goblet hang between two fingers. "Well, I save the best ones and the others I feed to my dogs," he said, sipping and eyeing the master's reaction.

Celsus couldn't help but salivate and Wilhelm's pulse raced at the observation.

"Would you like to see?" Wilhelm asked in a gasp that was almost a groan.

Celsus did not answer and guards were already being sent to fetch Wilhelm's project.

"You can't be moved, you see," he explained. "This cell was specifically designed for you and whatever you may be capable of. Can you *actually* read minds?" he grinned.

Celsus did not respond or react.

"It doesn't matter, but we have made this cell for anything and everything that could happen. So - you will remain here, but we will be sure to entertain our guest of honor."

A few minutes later a large standing case was wheeled into the room and Celsus was at first confused at what he was seeing. Before him stood a woman - no, what should have been a woman - jig sawed together in such a way that made it look like a whole body. However, upon closer inspection small gaps and inconsistencies in the different body parts gave away what it truly was - a Frankenstein's monster held together with human intervention, staring back at Celsus with empty eye sockets.

"We're saving the eyes for someone special," Wilhelm suggested looking up at the still rotating centerpiece of the room. The girl with the two differently colored eyes looked in horror at the frozen body and she couldn't help but cry.

"There are many more parts I simply keep stored. I like to treat my canines with meat on special occasions, so there is plenty, obviously," he chuckled looking around the room at the many vibrant prosthetics. He walked up to the case, put a hand on the glass and looked at Celsus like a pleading lover. "Would you like a treat, my precious wolf?"

The statement was a challenge and claim for dominance and Celsus growled at the vile one who grinned back with a flushed face.

"Yes, show me those fangs," Wilhelm sighed, gesturing for his men to wheel forward a large cart with long thin drawers. "Take your pick, *my lord*," he said in a jeering tone, and the drawers opened to reveal a meat case of body parts.

Frozen and preserved from the moment of amputation, Celsus growled in hunger at the sight.

Wilhelm moaned, "You are no god. Your just a DNA project gone wrong, and I *will* have your secrets."

Δ

Rotterdam
February 29, 2020 – 2:00 a.m.

Ready? The XO asked, telepathically.

At your command, responded the Turkish warrior.

Megan and Sanem crouched facing the mansion with steady even breathing. The villa harkened back to the days of the Renaissance. They breathed at the same time, the perfect killing pair in perfect unison as they prepared to do what they did best.

Be careful with the bishop. We need information first, Megan reiterated.

Sanem did not respond. She didn't need to as her obedience was unquestionable.

Go.

The command was ominous and the two women moved swiftly through the dark underbrush. With so little security, this was going to be over before they knew what hit them.

Sanem climbed up the ivy-covered stone wall with unnatural speed and took out the two guards on the balcony, swiftly crushing their windpipes before either one of them had a chance to react. On the ground level, Megan was examining a side entrance.

The doors were controlled by fingerprint sensors and Megan looked at it in half-amusement. She hadn't even turned around yet when Sanem walked up to her effortlessly carrying two bodies like sacks of rubbish.

"Their hands don't need to come off. We can just take off their gloves," Sanem mused dryly.

Megan smiled coyly and whispered, "We'll have fun later."

The door opened with a silent swish and Sanem hid the bodies behind a well-manicured hedge. As the two women entered, Megan honed in on the different psychic presences in the building, making an interesting discovery. She was able to tell which mind belonged to an adult and which to a child. There were just as many children present as adults, and her blood began to boil with rage.

"Tonight we feast," she growled.

Sanem knew Megan was going to unleash brutality and her mouth watered.

"Yes, my beloved. Your wish is my command," she responded warmly.

The two women moved quickly and without a sound through the entire mansion, quietly killing three more guards. With unnatural predatory stealth, they passed the bishop's room - a gaudy suite with an enormous gilded double door. Megan could smell what was taking place there and her pulse raced with fury. He would have his time but they needed to secure the location first. They met back in front of the double doors, took a unified breath, and slowly opened them.

The bishop sat in a compromised position with a boy that was clearly too young. Megan moved before Sanem and took the boy from the bishop's bed and immediately put him to sleep with a simple look from her glowing red eyes. The boy went limp in her arms and she gently lay him down on a soft sofa chair.

Sanem stood at the foot of the bed and was talking to the bishop when Megan rejoined them. "It would be in your best interest to stay still, excellency. Your guards are dead and my sister wants to talk to you."

"Are you a God-fearing man, bishop?" Megan asked, as she coyly walked onto the enormous king size bed and straddled his now limp crotch.

He wore his bishop's robe and was nude underneath. Megan could smell what had been going on and she grabbed him by his regal collar.

"Sleep," she commanded, staring into his eyes, fighting the raging beast within that wanted to pierce his wrinkled throat with her deadly razor-sharp fingernails.

His head fell forward before he could scream and Megan scowled.

When Bishop Schunner woke, he realized he had been moved to the small chapel of his mansion that could accommodate about fifty people. The pews were simple and unadorned but made of fine wood. The altar was a bright marble with heavy, gilded candle holders, and a heavy golden cross sitting to the side of Megan's long legs. The cross on the wall was of medium size but eloquently carved with the hanging Christ and solid gold tabernacle beneath.

Megan sat on the altar like a pinup girl staring at the face on the cross and looked indifferently back at the bishop that had just awakened.

"I see you have decided to join us, excellency," she said in a jeering tone.

The bishop was tied in the same ornate throne that he sat on behind the altar. Sanem had removed the custom gold-plated disk one would normally sit on. This allowed the bishop's genitals and asshole to be accessible from under the chair. He had removed it himself during nights of his deprived past. The silk ropes he'd used on the many boys in his keep were now keeping him firmly in place, naked with his holy cape, just as they had found him when they arrived. Megan crossed her legs to face him.

"Who-" he managed, before being interrupted.

"Do not speak unless spoken to…and you *will* address me as 'my lady'," Megan said in an even tone that sent a chill down the bishop's spine.

There was something unsettling about this woman and it terrified him. He was still waking up when he noticed that behind him stood four familiar faces, and when he tried his best to turn around, he noticed another gorgeous woman standing behind him and he knew she was with the redheaded demoness defiling the altar. Bishop Schunner was momentarily relieved when he saw the boys dressed in their white altar clothes, before it hit him that they were not there to help him. These boys were older and helped guide and take care of the younger members of the house. They had come to him when they were very young, like they all did, and he had elected to keep these boys. As the boys aged out of his specific preferences, he would have them discreetly rehomed in more fitting situations and another member would be added to his house.

Most of the boys were taken from dysfunctional homes in Amsterdam, Rotterdam, and The Hauge. These families eagerly accepted the help, as the bishop offered to give their children the best opportunities in life. When approached with a special scholarship for overseas schooling and job placement, the parents would usually jump at the offer. Communications between the boys and their parents would decrease as they aged and the parents would just be thankful to their god for helping them place their child in a good home. However, they always disappeared after being given these *opportunities*.

Now the very boys that were offered, stood in the same pews of which they were forced to kneel and perform disgusting sacrilegious acts. Did they want to stay? No. But what choice did they really have? Nobody knew for sure but everyone was 99.9% sure the 'rehoming' that took place when the boys aged out was not good. So when offered the rare opportunity to stay, it was rarely turned down.

"You're right, by the way," Megan said casually to the group of boys. "The boys that aged out were negotiated as favors among the elites and those that remained were sent to a particular kind of horror house," she said reflectively, as if watching it happen before her eyes.

There was a pause and the boys all looked at her with admiration and awe. There was one boy in particular that had a special contempt for the bishop. Tall with lightly tanned skin and black curly hair, Adolfo, or Ado for short, came from a Spanish family of eight. Born to immigrant parents, he knew hardships from very early on. He was the oldest male and he remembered fighting for the chance to go with the bishop, begging his father to send him.

And now, Ado was the oldest member of the house at a startling 22-years-old. The bishop had thought him too exotic and handsome to give up and he was only the second to ever stay on at the bishop's house.

"Bishop Klaus Schunner, your most holy reverend excellency. How many titles do you have?" Megan said in a windy sing-song voice that sounded like a blues singer trying to tell a hard tale. "We are gathered here today for a most sacred ceremony. By the end of this ceremony, we will know where your friend Wilhelm Hilgenfeldt is and then we will go on our merry way," she said, grinning at the trembling bishop.

The smile on her face extended wide, her eyes began to glow red, and with the evil in her eyes the bishop felt he was looking into the eyes of Satan himself.

"I have seen the devil," he gasped. "And he is no man!"

Megan's body shivered in delight at the terror in his old haggard voice and she sighed.

"Excellency, how you tease. Now let's get to it, shall we."

She hopped down from the altar in one swift motion and landed precisely at his feet. The inhuman agility made the old man gasp and he pissed himself in fear.

Megan leaned to the side and watched with joy as the yellow puddle formed under him and she clucked her tongue. "That is quite worrisome, excellency. You should get that looked at," she stated coolly, her eyes glowing a brighter red.

She looked up at his face and he was already blubbering in terror.

"We haven't even started. Have some dignity until…"

"I'll tell you whatever you want. Anything! Please - I have money. Please! Don't hurt me!" he begged, shaking in his chair and gasping.

Megan looked at him with indifference and shook her head. She motioned for Ado to come forward and the boy picked up something off the pew. He carried a medieval war hammer in his hand and gave it to Megan, bowing to her in reverence. He truly believed she was an angel of justice.

Though the old man was incoherent, he immediately knew what was about to happen and cried out.

"No! No!"

"I did not instruct you to speak, excellency," Megan cooed to him like a child, followed by slamming the pike side of the hammer into his right hand, nailing it to the armrest.

The sound he made was something like a choking gurgle with a shrill, and Megan looked at him with disgust.

"That sounds like it might have been painful," she said, as she started to feel aroused with hunger. "Now, let me ask," she said with sadistic sweetness. "Where can I find Wilhelm Hilgenfeldt?"

"A castle," he said dumbly.

Megan nodded and beckoned another boy forward. "A castle," she repeated. "Right. Thank you, bishop, but that was not very helpful and again you did not address me as 'my lady'," she said postulating herself on the altar.

She turned, undid her pants and slipped them off like a sexy feline in one swift motion. Megan sat back on the altar and spread her beautiful legs wide, letting her warm sex cool against the marble. She was wet already and Sanem joined her at the altar.

"Worship me, goddess," she said as Sanem expertly pushed the thong to one side with her tongue and began sucking on her. "Ado, please jog his memory a little more and grace his left hand with a gift," she breathed seductively.

Do not let the hunger make you forget our master, Sanem projected telepathically, as she tasted her sister's flower.

Getting to Celsus was the top priority, but the hunger engulfed the XO. She was helpless to expedite. The hunger overtook any and all agendas. The rescue would come when the hunger was satiated. For a bizarre random moment, she was taken back in her memory to the night of Anatu's attempted execution, still one of the most horrifying experiences of all her lives. She pushed it out of her mind, refocusing on Sanem's delicious tongue.

"No! No, please, I don't know where he is! No! Ado!" he shouted, begging the boy not to go through with it.

Megan smiled down at him with the same twisted smile and giggled, "I don't believe you, excellency. Ado, proceed."

The young man looked at the bishop with hateful excitement ripped the pike out of the bishop's hand. Listening to the bishop scream, Megan threw her head back in ecstasy as Sanem's tongue lapped hungrily at her opening.

"Let's try this again," she groaned, pulling in pleasure at Sanem's hair. "Where is Wilhelm?"

The bishop mumbled something distorted while drool dripped from his pale lips onto his chest. There was a pause of groaning and weeping interrupted only by the sound of

Sanem slurping at Megan's delicious pussy and Megan's own sexual gasping.

"He's - in a castle," he repeated, "in the mountains . . ."

Megan giggled a sound that echoed in the chapel. "This could be so satisfying and so long," Megan sighed. "But we don't have that kind of time."

She stopped Sanem and instructed her to reposition the bishop to help the process along. Sanem did as she was instructed and readjusted the bishop's chair to lean back against the pews.

Megan nodded and sprang down from the altar, taking her thong off mid-leap. She then took the gilded cross from the altar and propped her leg up on the pew next to the bishop's head, her hot pussy inches from his frightful haggard face. She took the bottom of the cross and slowly ran the jeweled tip up and down her swollen lips, slowly shoving it in and opening herself up. Ado fell into a trance watching her face contort with pleasure.

Megan moaned loudly as she slowly fucked herself with the tip of the cross. She shoved it all the way up to the cross section and screamed in ecstasy while simultaneously gripping onto the bishop's shoulder, digging her nails into his withered skin and gnashing her teeth as she felt the flesh give.

The bishop screamed and choked as she dug her nails further and fucked herself harder before abruptly stopping, licking the blood off her finger tips.

"No, I'm not coming. Not yet," she cooed sweetly.

The flushed redhead slowly pulled the cross out of her opening, her eyes slitted in intoxication. The cross had torn her inside slightly and she paid no mind as the hunger completely possessed her. She placed the bloody tip of the cross against the bishop's lips, brushing them red with her vaginal blood.

Weakened but still stubborn, he pressed his lips feebly together and Megan smiled as she slowly wiggled the cross past his lips, and pried his teeth open. The gold scraped against them sending a shooting pain through the bishop's entire body that prompted his mouth to shoot open. The cross went down easily.

"Taste me, your holiness. You don't deserve me," she moaned, pulling the cross out.

Megan wiped it on his cape, knelt down, and looked up and under the bottomless chair. The old man's shriveled and wrinkled sex made her grin. She felt a maddening amount of delight as she slowly shoved the tip of the cross up his shit stained opening.

The screaming took on a new terrifying shrill as he was slowly opened. Megan twisted the cross in his opening and reveled in his screams. Blood slowly dripped from the hole and as it tore him open, her mouth watered. Deeper and deeper she put the cross and he screamed even louder.

"The sound of a reckoning," she said sweetly. "The offering is prepared, my children," she said to the group of boys behind the quivering soiled man. "Please your goddess, and give me your offering of love, adoration, and loyalty."

Sanem dropped a black athletic bag in front of them. Each boy took a cat o' nine tails with small hooked blades at the end and circled the bishop. The old man looked around at the magnitude of his fate. A terror possessed him unlike any he had ever felt before and he and cried uncontrollably, begging incoherently for mercy and Megan grimaced.

"You are too loud," she said nonchalantly, before she took a large candle and wedged it in his mouth.

He continued to cry as she turned the candle like a screwdriver, using his teeth to create the threads, until there was nothing more than choked muffled breathing. Snot ran down his upper lip and he pleaded with bulging eyes.

"Where is Wilhelm Hilgenfeldt?" Megan asked evenly.

He tried to answer but Megan held a forefinger to her luscious lips and floated backward to the altar with a gentle push off her forefoot. She sat, opened her legs and her lips curled behind her finger as Sanem's face found her heavenly pussy once more.

"Boys, let's convince the bishop to give us a good answer this time, and do not disappoint your goddess," she hissed.

The terror welled up inside the bishop and he thrashed and wailed through the gag and cried as the boys raised their whips and lashed out. The bishop felt his skin tear off and almost fainted from the overwhelming pain.

The screaming became frantic and desperate as the pain set in and he cried and cursed at everything he had ever believed. A hand grabbed his thin, flimsy hair at the back of his head and pulled it back as the large candle was twisted counter-clockwise from his mouth. Saliva ran down his neck and he was barely able to keep his eyes open. He panted in desperation. Blood was splattered everywhere and on everyone.

"Wake up," came the voice he associated with Satan in his delirium. "Where is Wilhelm?"

He took a few more gasps of air and coughed, cried and shook his head. Megan tilted his face up to hers and dug her nails into his loose, flabby cheek.

"Answer me or I will make your end so unbearable that hell itself will be a heavenly escape for you."

Bishop Schunner believed her and took a shaky breath before responding.

"The Ammergau Alps in southern Bavaria," he slurred out, raked with agony.

Nothing more was said and Megan took an even breath. She could see the location clearly in the bishop's mind. She knew the minute she initially saw the bishop, but hungered for the interrogation – hungered for his confession. She glanced at Sanem who looked knowingly back. They had to get there as soon as possible. But the hunger still gripped her entire being.

"Would you lie to me, excellency? You wouldn't lie to me now, would you?" she teased, licking at the blood running down his pale skin.

The blood tasted sickly and lifeless. With her eyes a deep glowing red, she searched his mind once more for confirmation. No, he was not lying but she was still not done with him.

"I know you are tired, but we are not done," she growled. "My servants, show your goddess love! Prove your love by making this thing scream. Give me music. Show me your devotion."

Her voice bounced off every corner of the room and Bishop Klaus Schunner knew his end was going to be worse than anything he could imagine and he shit himself, right though the open bottomed chair.

The whips came hard. The boys took their turns with purpose and whipped their abuser, the one who had tortured them for so long. Each whip landed with more ferocity and hatred than the last. He was soon a bloody mess and Megan could hear his heart slowly begin to give out. She paced her orgasm in time with his death.

"Yes - more!" she pleaded with Sanem as the warrior goddess lapped at Megan's swollen pussy.

A few more heartbeats and he would be gone. Megan's excitement grew with his impending doom.

"Don't stop, my children! Keep lashing until your goddess is satisfied! More!"

She gripped onto the altar, crushing the corners with her strength as she thrust herself up and down Sanem's face. Her breathing stopped as she felt the few seconds right before the wave. She let out an overwhelming cry as the bishop's heart stopped.

Her hands wrapped themselves in Sanem's hair, pulling and thrusting onto her face as she exploded into her thirsty mouth. Sanem lapped up every drop of Megan's delicious orgasm and ran her hands up her shaking, beautiful legs.

Her red hair brushed over the altar as Megan gave a few last shivers and sighed in delight. When she looked up to the children of her cult, the boys were covered in blood, tissue, and their tears. The rage they'd kept pent up all these years overflowed and ran down their faces, mixing with the blood staining their white clothing. Their white-knuckled grips on the bladed whips were tense and as the boys processed what they had just done, they tried to come to terms with their conflicting feelings.

Megan came off the altar, kissed Sanem deeply and sucked her own nectar off the warrior's talented tongue.

"I'm sorry I did not satisfy you, my beloved," Megan whispered.

"I am here to serve," Sanem said before bowing.

Megan caressed her beautiful face before going up to the group of boys. As if a command had been spoken, the boys parted their circle to allow Megan though. They watched in horror as the disheveled goddess knelt down and fed gregariously on the corpse. After several minutes, she addressed them, her face and cloths covered in the bishop's blood.

"My children," she beckoned sweetly.

One by one, she grabbed their pale fearful faces, kissed them sweetly and lay them down in a peaceful slumber.

"They must be washed and all this must be removed. Get in touch with our Dutch contacts. Tell them this must be expedited. Pay them whatever they want," Megan said to Sanem.

Sanem looked at Megan with pride. This was the reason the master chose her to be the XO. When Megan was in her element, there was no better leader save the master himself. Sanem obediently made arrangements for the boys and the sanitization of the crime scene. In the end, it would be a grand mystery.

"These angels will sleep and I will make them forget what they have suffered, all of it. For them, it shall be as it was before the horror of this devil and this place," Megan said softly.

The boys were all put to sleep, their memories reworked, and arrangements made for them to be picked up and relocated safely to new homes.

Megan and Sanem placed the seven dead guards in one of the guard's vans and drove off. They had fed, found the location of Wilhelm, and all they had left to do was organize the family for an all-out assault.

Lord Celsus, Lady Sanem thought. *We are coming my lord, and we shall bring a bloodlust with us.*

Δ
Venlo, Netherlands

They pulled up to the safehouse an hour before dawn. Tara came out to greet them as they unloaded the cargo.

"My lady Tara, we will need strength for the battle at hand," Megan said, as the bodies were unloaded. "Sanem and I brought a feast for the family. Ensure Sakura has her fill. What of Anatu?"

Tara nodded and replied, "Lady Anatu has nearly recovered. Her tongue is intact but she will not speak or communicate telepathically since it was our master's wish that she not speak until he commands it," she explained.

Megan nodded and they walked up to the old stone house together carrying bodies. Her mind was racing with all the preparations that needed to take place in the next few days when Tara stopped her.

"May I make a suggestion, my lady?"

Megan nodded.

"Might we bring Anna with us? She could be useful."

The XO smiled confidently and responded. "A perfect idea, my beloved. I actually had not thought of it. She is here and you are right. She could be useful."

Tara bowed her head to Megan and they all moved silently, taking the dead bodies into the house.

"Linzie and Shira . . ." Tara trailed off.

"Will join us soon," Megan said confidently. She could tell Tara was uneasy about this decision but respected her leadership.

"I am the head of the house and will take whatever ramifications comes with my decision from our master when he returns. For now, we need our *all* our sisters to ensure he does return. My own security is not above the safety of our master."

Tara nodded. She knew Megan was right and they kissed each other affectionately before going into the cellar with Sanem. The floor was prepared with sheet of plastic tarp. The bodies were expected – all part of the plan.

The coven's safehouse on the Dutch-German border had no fire and no heat that morning. The women huddled together after their gregarious feeding. It was not the lack of heat that chilled them. The heart of their home was missing and the hollowness of that fact chilled them. Though only a month had passed since the abduction, it seemed eternal to them. They shivered with the knowledge of their master's absence, but their resolve was absolute.

Randy V & Ellie Ravencroft

KARMA
March 16, 2020 – 7:00 p.m.
The Ammergau Alps, Bavaria, Germany

"Are you hungry, dog?" Wilhelm jeered from the other side of the glass.

Celsus was slowly losing the ability to control his turning as a result of Wilhelm's experiments, and he eyed the taunting young man with disdain.

"Would you like another?" he offered, shoving one of his harem girls onto her knees in front of the glass. Celsus growled.

The game Wilhelm had begun with frozen and thawed body parts had slowly escalated to dismembering the girls in front of him and giving him fresh meat. Wilhelm was now at the point of giving the monster a live girl.

The girl trembled at his feet, tears running down her horrified face. She was almost missing one leg but even that did not compare to the terror of being eaten alive by the creature turning in front of her.

Celsus was naturally excited seeing the prey afraid, shaking, and hysterical. Normally concerned about the cleanliness of his food, the hunger put aside insignificant matters such as the appearance of his next meal. He was starving and Wilhelm knew it.

As Celsus fought the lycanthrope within, he felt Lili at the center of it all and wondered if this would be a repeat of his demise in Sweden so long ago. He couldn't help but wonder if perhaps at the end of this twisted man's game he would meet the death he had wanted so long ago. A strange random thought overcame him as he thought of Sophia, his once-born sister.

"Nicht zu schnell!" came the cry that brought Celsus back to his present life. Wilhelm gestured for the girl to be offered,

173

"Slowly, little by little," he instructed as his men secured the harness to lower her in.

She lurched forward, vomiting in dread and began to cry and plead, but Wilhelm ignored her, his eyes fixed on the wolfman and he licked his lips in anticipation. The girl kept screaming the entire time, choking and wailing as she was slowly lowered into the case. She dangled just out of reach of the wolf and was ever so slowly lowered within his reach. Celsus, uncontrollable, started clawing off bits and pieces of her body and the screaming was unlike anything any of the women in the harem had ever heard before. The ankle shackles and chains added to the chaotic sounds as Celsus repeatedly tried to jump at his victim.

Δ

March 17, 2020 – 1:55 a.m.

"Mehr . . . mehr," Wilhelm gasped, his legs wide open as a kneeling Valentina rammed her face up and down the length of his dick.

His balls twitched and ached with the amount of semen he kept producing. Orgasm after orgasm, he couldn't stop the arousal from building when he watched Celsus being tortured.

"Halt!" he shouted, yanking the girl off his crotch by the back of her head and kicking her with his foot as he thrashed to keep the orgasm at bay. "Noch nicht!" he cried out.

In the cell, Celsus watched with very little of his human self-remaining - barely putting together thoughts that were not a fixation on hunger and hatred toward the depraved being covered in his foul-smelling ejaculation, thrashing like a whore in heat before him.

Wretched, the few instances of human lucidity that crossed through Celsus' mind were hating Wilhelm and acknowledging the sharp stab of hunger that was somehow more muted in his wolf form - redirected into primal, animalistic rage.

"Bring me another one," Wilhelm shuddered, clenching his hands and breathing deeply.

All the girls in the room flinched as the guard exited to bring in another girl for Wilhelm's delight. His hand, crusted in dry semen, fondled the large breast of one of the women that knelt on the floor beside him. She was missing both eyes and Wilhelm pinched and tugged at her nipple as he watched Celsus.

"Are you hungry, mongrel?" he spat.

In the cage Celsus looked at him like a rabid dog - half human, half wolf. The front of his chest was speckled with fur and matted with the blood of disposed body parts.

"You're nothing. You're a caged animal feeding off the scraps of the whores I discard," Wilhelm said, as he stood and approached the clear cell, his still hard dick sticking out of his pants. "Where is your power now?" he taunted, his tongue licking the glass. He shivered and began thrusting his dick against the panel.

The door shut loudly behind him and Wilhelm barely turned his head to see the guard coming in with a thawed leg of one of his harem girls. He paused for a moment, his hips still working the glass as his smile widened.

"Who's is that?" he said coyly, looking to the girl with the right prosthetic and the right shade of bronze.

His eyes landed on a shaking girl that fit the profile and he turned around excitedly. "Ah yes, I remember. This is yours, precious one. Come," he demanded and the girl took a small timid step towards him.

The poor girl was terrified, pale and trembling from head to toe. Sobs caught in her throat and she breathed heavily as she approached him and the guard holding her defrosted leg.

"Hold it, while he goes to fetch a hacksaw. I think it'll be fun if you feed the hound your leg. Poetic, don't you think?"

Tears fell from her eyes as she held her own leg in her hands. It was soft and the skin felt like gelatin after being frozen for so long. It was cold and lifeless and her nose ran with mucus as she held it in front of Wilhelm.

Celsus smelled the terror coming off the girl and even in his half-form had presence enough to find himself slightly amused at Wilhelm's sick sense of humor. He wanted the girl, the leg - he wanted every living creature in the room and he thrashed in wild hunger. His wrists and ankles bled from the shackles rubbing them raw. His head hung low and swung side to side as he eyed the girl like the obvious prey she was.

Wounded, weak, and easy to kill - she tried to avoid the hunter's eyes as the guard took the appendage out of her hands. She accidentally caught the eyes of the wolf and could not help but stare deep into that hungry gaze.

His eyes were black with quickly receding stars, – devouring everything, a void deeper and more endless than anything she could have ever fathomed. A primal terror seized her. She pissed herself. Her knees buckled and she fell forward on her prosthetic leg, her hands splashing in the urine beneath her.

The few strands of Celsus' humanity looked at her in revulsion, wallowing in her mess, but the animal quickly overshadowed it and all he saw was food.

"You're disgusting," Wilhelm grimaced, stepping aside to keep his feet from the piss. "She's going to feed him. Give the pieces of meat to her so she can drop them from the top of the cell."

The guards helped the weeping girl onto unsteady footing and she began to climb the metal staircase attached to the back of Celsus' cage.

"Oh, let's make this even more fun. Give the restraints some slack," he said with childish energy. "I want to see him jumping for his meal like a filthy beggar."

The throne was moved closer for Wilhelm to sit. He spread his legs again and grabbed the blind girl by the face and jammed his cock in her mouth.

Now atop the cell, the girl tossed the meat into the window that opened for her, careful not to let her hand go near the edge of the opening - even if it was 12 feet above the wolf's head. The animal snarled and growled up at her, trying to leap up to snatch the food out of her shaking hand.

The restraints loosened and he jumped in time to extend his razor-sharp claws. The girl almost fell back off her perch in a frenzy. A guard held her forward from behind and she frantically tried to dispose of the meat in her hands, sobbing and gasping in terror as the caged animal tried to reach to pull her in.

Wilhelm laughed at her and at Celsus, at the hunger he saw in the man that was slowly turning more and more animal. Celsus was losing all control and Wilhelm needed to see him completely defeated.

"Just a little more," he groaned. "Slower - feed him slower," he barked. "Watch him beg for more."

Wilhelm wasn't sure if he was more aroused by the man or the animal. But he didn't care at that moment as he watched the animal overtake the man.

The process looked painful and fascinating to Wilhelm. Celsus' arms seemed to shred their humanity as the lycanthrope's claws grew longer, as did his legs, his neck, and his cock. Wilhelm felt a pang of jealousy at all of it. He secretly wanted to feast as Celsus did, to inflict torture as a lycanthrope, to anal rape his victims with the girth of the weapon swinging before him.

Celsus let out an ear-splitting howl that seemed to shake the very foundation of the mansion.

"Stop feeding him! Face him to me! All the way!" he demanded, shouting over the snarls and hysterical animal sounds.

The restraints pulled back and set the beast's hands and legs completely apart as they turned the animal to face the salivating man. Wilhelm feasted his greedy eyes on what he was after. Between the wolf's legs was an enormous penis with a sack so big and heavy that Wilhelm's mouth watered at the sight.

"Finish! Now!" he demanded of the blind whore between his legs.

He needed to cum now. It was the right moment and he slammed his dick hard down the bitch's throat, locked eyes with the wild animal only a few feet from him, looked at the heavy hanging balls and he shot his hot load down the harem girls' throat.

Wilhelm's face contorted with the wild release. The biggest orgasm yet fueled by the sight of Celsus in his raw form. Wilhelm came off the high and slumped back in his chair. The girl sat back on her knees, swallowed the last of the thick cum, and waited for further instructions.

The other girl was just finishing coming down off the cell, pale and shaking, and Wilhelm watched the animal hunger for more. It howled in the cage, saliva dripping thick from his maw and he eyed the girl shakily walking back to her position in line.

"He feels less pain like this," Wilhelm observed, sipping wine out of a large goblet. "I don't think I like that. I need the man, not the animal."

He placed the base of the glass on the head of the girl that knelt beside him, her body perfectly still to keep the glass in check in case he decided to let it go. Wilhelm then looked back at the lycanthrope in his restraints, watching the blind girl like a predator. He smiled and silently motioned the guard.

The man came over and picked the girl up by her waist. For a moment, she followed without hesitation and Wilhelm's face lit up with sadistic glee. The wolf knew what he was up to and his ears perked at attention. His mouth salivated in anticipation.

As if on cue, the girl twitched and when the guard tightened his hold on her, the panic welled up. Celsus could smell it and growled in response. The sound of the hungry animal only made her panic more.

"Yes, my dear. Yes, you are going to be fed alive to a monster! Thrash! He likes it!" Wilhelm cheered, finishing the last of the wine. He tossed the goblet and all the girls winced as it crashed on the stone floor.

The blind girl struggled as she was pushed up the metal steps behind the cell, hitting the glass with her hands and clawing at the man that held her. But he did not give an inch as he steadily made his way up to the opening over the cell. Wilhelm took a seat back in his chair and watched as the girl was slowly pushed up and over the opening.

Celsus saw the legs come down. He was riled up from the thrashing outside his cell and snarled as the girl was pushed in. His mouth foamed and he roared in a hungry frenzy.

She fell with a thud and scrambled as quickly as she could on all fours away from where she thought the wolf was. Her crying had become hysterical and she ripped the blindfold off to reveal collapsed eyelids. Wilhelm gagged in revulsion.

"You look better with it on! Nobody wants to see that," he taunted.

But she was not listening, straining through eyeless sockets wondering if by some miraculous grace of God, she would see something - anything. She hobbled to her feet and ran in any direction she thought was away from her fate, only to slam hard into the wall of the cell. Her face hit it with a thud and her forehead left a mark of perspiration when it bounced back. She screamed in a panic, pounding her fists on the wall and shouted.

Behind her, she could hear the lycanthrope struggle harder and harder against his restraints. He snapped at the prey, now a whimpering mess on the ground, screaming and crying at the sound of snarling getting louder with each moment of built-up anticipation.

She couldn't see, and all she knew was that in this precise spot, she was far enough away from him. She was absolutely frozen in place at the thought of accidentally bumping into the mouth of razor-sharp canines that would devour her.

"How lovely," Wilhelm gasped watching Celsus. "I think that if we feed him, he'll be fine enough to turn back, just long enough to have some more fun with his human self," he reasoned aloud. "And when he gets hungry enough, he'll turn again and then we'll feed him another one and start the process all over again."

The man would have been enraged at the plan Wilhelm was weaving, but the man was not there now. The animal was and all he cared about was the terrified, shivering mound of flesh that sat just out of reach of his claws.

Wilhelm gave an imperceptible nod which his men had already learned to identify, and they gave the wild animal slack. The moment the beast felt the give, his killer instinct only intensified and he fought harder and harder against the restraints to get to his food. The girl heard the increased growling and snarling and she cried louder, holding herself tighter as the slack was given to the bonds little by little.

Blood and foam dripped on the floor and speckled the inside of the cell as he fought to get to the prey. He'd bitten clear through his tongue and it hung half on, half dangling loose but the wolf did not care. All it knew was hunger and all it wanted was satisfaction.

Inch by inch the wolf got closer and closer to the sobbing girl and he snapped to reach her arm, her leg, her foot – anything.

Wilhelm raised a lazy finger, indicating for them to stop for a moment. The entire room reverberated with the sounds of the giant snarling wolf and Wilhelm reveled in the high it gave him.

He controlled this being. He controlled his life, his end - this powerful creature would not live a single moment for the rest of its life without permission and it gave Wilhelm a feeling more euphoric than any orgasm he could have ever had. He held this moment a little longer, relishing in the raw barbaric growls, before he allowed the rest of the rope to give. The animal pounced with wild abandon.

The girl did not have much time to shout or scream. His massive jaws closed on her torso and his claws sank into the rest of her body. For a few seconds she screamed wildly as he ate her left breast which Wilhelm had been fondling moments earlier. The flesh tore off easily and he swallowed the piece whole before going for her other one.

Blood and tissue splattered the inside of the cell as her organs ruptured. Her rib cage cracked under his powerful bite, his grey fur dripping with blood as he snarled and feasted.

"She didn't last long," Wilhelm murmured, "but those must have been eternal seconds," he consoled himself.

The sound of the animal crunching on bones and tearing flesh apart was cathartic and Wilhelm would not break his gaze from the eating beast, taking in every moment of the carnage. He hung open his hand for another goblet placed into his hand from his new favorite, Valentina.

Although far from satiated, the treat was enough to reverse the savage transformation and the painful process started over. This time it was the animal that was shed, coming off the blonde, pale body in bloody slops - as if melting off his skin.

The shackles slackened around his normal human wrists and as the last of the fur came off in one final painful patch, the whirl of an engine pulled Celsus back up to his original position, against the wall and spread out on display for Wilhelm. Celsus took a deep, subtle breath and squared his shoulders at Wilhelm again, in tenacious defiance.

"Are you better now?" Wilhelm taunted. He nodded at Celsus' obstinate silence. "Good, because this is only the beginning. Though you persist in your belligerence, we've taken your DNA. As I have said to you before, you *will* give me your secrets, one way or another…"

Δ

Starnberg, Germany
March 17, 2020 – 2:20 a.m.

The reunion of Shira and Linzie with the coven was anticlimactic in the light of the task before them. It had been over six and half years since they had seen each other. Linzie still looked and dressed like a rebellious teen and Shira still donned Sophia's body, looking actually 10 years younger than when she perished at the hands of the one who possessed her. Fortunately, the two were hunting in Europe when they received the coven's telepathic message to join them in southern Germany before the Covid-19 travel restrictions were put into place.

After they were exiled, everything was too close to home. Maine, Florida, Mexico, South America – the entire Western hemisphere was too close and made their bodies ache with the loss of their lord and sisters. Time eventually led them overseas to Madrid, Spain, where the presence that called to their very existence became tolerable and numb. When the master was taken, it didn't take long for Tara to locate the two outlaws.

By the time they arrived at their safehouse, the moon was high in the sky, the stars shone brilliantly, and the two women silently stepped out of the cars. Their steps were swift, unheard, and they moved like ghosts through the open front door. The coven women were glad to see them and they in turn were grateful to help bolster the ranks. After a quick informal reunion, it seemed as if they had never left. Only Anna stood in fascination at the reentry of the two seemingly young women.

There was tension and anxiety in the air as Tara gazed out into the night sky like the predator she was, contemplating the battle before them. Sanem came in and kissed her passionately, projecting her thoughts into her sister's mind.

The van is ready. It is time.

A plain white van that blended in with the snow was left in a ditch unceremoniously. Their agents in Germany always provided whatever they needed and were paid handsomely for their loyalty. The entire coven wore white combat gear and only Anna was challenged by the ten-mile hike through the snowstorm which conveniently covered their tracks on the way up. The intelligence Sanem was given showed that the plow would not come through until sunrise. They used the road to their advantage and veered off into the tree line once they arrived at the outskirts of the mansion.

Small white tents were set up in strategic locations, several hundred feet beyond the range of the mansion's motion detectors. The coven bedded down for the day. Five tents, blanketed with snow, contained them securely, perfectly hidden. Four tents contained two immortals each; Megan and Tara, Sanem and Anatu, Cala and Sakura, and Linzie and

Shira. The final tent contained the once-born Anna and the android Elena whose man-made heat kept Anna warm under a simple wool blanket. They all slept as if dead – all but Elena, Sanem, and Anatu. There would be no rest for them this night.

Δ

8:00 p.m.

"Now, we wait," Megan said, as the women settled in among the trees.

Anna sat on an elevated tree root, between Elena and Sanem, her personal guard. Tara preferred higher ground before a battle and sat up in the trees to watch the world below her. Anatu sat absolutely silent on a large stone, not once looking at her sisters or even thinking.

The complete silence from Anatu, who had been an untouchable among the house, added to the women's anxiety. Life in the house of their master had completely changed the day he tried to annihilate her. Never in their lifetimes had they felt the very foundation of their existence so shaken the moment he exacted his punishment. And now with their master captured in this remote place, in these ancient Teutonic mountains, nobody could even begin to fathom what their new reality would look like. Would the master try to kill Anatu again? It was a miracle she lived at all. In what state would they find their beloved wolf lord?

These questions and so many more incoherently buzzed deep in the recesses of their communal thoughts. Nobody dared to organize them into half-thoughts much less speak them, and they all did their best to ignore them.

All of the women were powerful in their own right, with strength beyond anything a human could imagine. But there was something erotically stimulating in the way Cala took off, flying with the elegance of a creature so well balanced and precise - it was not of this world. Into the night sky she flew, two whirlwinds of snow twisting upwards in her wake.

Linzie's beautiful blonde hair was pulled back into a ponytail, loose strands framing her age defying face. Her white down parka was unzipped revealing a crop top, high waisted pants, a single double-edged combat knife belted to the front of her waist, and white combat boots. She looked gorgeous but there was something clearly missing in her aura. Their lives were empty voids without their master and it was clear Linzie had suffered greatly.

Shira stepped up beside Linzie. It was still shocking to see her with Sophia's body. Everyone knew she possessed Sophia's body, but it had been so long since they'd seen her it still seemed a great oddity. She wore Yoga pants and a tank top with a white leather jacket over it. Though, if Linzie was coping well, Shira was not. Her look was angry, defiant and as proud as ever - even in exile. The fact that she had found her new home in the body of her master's beloved sister only added to the bitter revenge she wanted to exact. Shira wanted Celsus to see her as the woman she so hated. She wanted him to see that she'd had the last laugh even in exile. But above all else, she wanted her master to punish her, love her, hate her - feel everything he had towards her to the extreme. She wanted him to be unable to live without her as she clearly could not live without him.

"Sisters," Shira said curtly.

The need for attention was obvious to all of them. They felt a collective pang of pity for her and hoped when this was over, everything would come out for the better.

Shira eyed the android with obvious suspicion and made no secret of her distrust.

"This is Elena, she is part of the family now. She is an android and the master has decided to keep her. Her sole allegiance is to Lord Celsus," Megan explained.

But Shira did not like her. All she saw at that moment, deprived of her master, was another lesser form that would take more of his attention.

Megan could read her thoughts as plainly as if they were written on her face. "She will help with the attack. She is needed…and that is final."

Shira took a step back and bowed. "As you command, my lady."

Shira had always pushed the boundaries of what was acceptable but right now, Megan could not be soft on this wildcard's desire for redemption. She would have to lead Shira with pointed direction and she would punish her if she dared step out-of-line.

Shira was clearly not happy with this new member, but she obeyed. As a gesture of obedience to Megan, Shira gently tied a black shoestring around Elena's neck, a symbol of the coven's loyal lesser houses. She then looked at Megan and communicated telepathically.

I am not claiming her. I know she belongs to the master. I am simply reinforcing her status within this coven.

Megan nodded to her, took a deep breath, and softly addressed everyone, "Sisters, I cannot stress the gravity of what we are about to do. We have faced many challenges in the past, but this threat has taken the foundation of who we are, without which we are nothing. Everything must be executed with precision and absolute perfection. Deviation from the agreed upon course of action will not be tolerated," she said in an even tone, looking directly at Shira. "Everyone knows what they must do."

Megan slowly looked at everyone, taking in their eyes and disposition. Everything seemed wrong without their master, and while she knew she was capable, as were her sisters, his glaring absence cut straight through to their core.

"Elena."

"Wilhelm may be sleeping, my lady," Elena offered. "His sleeping has no discernable pattern, but I was only there for a short time."

"Well if he is asleep, he won't be in a moment," Shira challenged in a snarky tone. Her eyes were wild with hunger and she salivated at the thought of her master and the hunt. "I want him awake and terrified."

The hunger in Shira's voice was contagious and the other women's bloodlust began to stir. Megan looked at them one last time. In the insolated silence of the snow, her silky voice found its way deep into their immortal hearts.

"Let us be off, sisters. Our master is waiting."

Δ

Two hours earlier – 6:00 p.m.

"Now that you are human, let's see that mind of yours break," Wilhelm smiled. "You will be microwaved because burning you alive is simply not enough. I know there is something in that brain of yours and I am going to fry it out of you."

Wilhelm had been on a tangent from the beginning, about the ability of Celsus to control the mind of others. "I watched the video of him and my father at that shopping mall in America. I want to know how he did it," he told the scientists and engineers when they were designing the special cell that now held his prisoner.

While the men in his employment were all a bit skeptical of such claims, especially the men of science, nobody had ever been foolish enough to contradict Wilhelm's demands. He spent a lucrative amount of money on the development of the cell, designed to theoretically handle such powers as telekinesis, telepathy, and suggestion – or at least they hoped it would.

Reference materials from so-called modern magicians, medieval alchemists, and ancient priests and magicians were used for the development. The scientists couldn't help but feel somewhat foolish as they inscribed a spell into the foundation and outfitted the entire structure to block any sort of telepathic communication from coming in or out.

"What other secrets are you hiding?" Wilhelm demanded, his hands clenched onto the arms of his chair in anticipation as he stared at Celsus. Over the course of the hunt for this man - this myth - he had developed an obsession with Celsus and everything he was capable of. "I want to know all of your secrets," he hissed.

Celsus had not spoken in weeks. For whatever reason he felt a microscopic need to poke back, a weak repost at best, but effective in incurring Wilhelm's wrath nonetheless.

His voice was rough, his eyelids heavy with weariness, his body railed in pain from the tortures and deprivations, but Celsus taunted anyway, "You and your friends are nothing special. I have known your kind forever it seems. I *was* you, long ago…"

Wilhelm sat forward with excitement, "Ah, the beast speaks. Go on my love, please."

Celsus grinned as best as he could before he let loose his grave insights, "Embracing atheism through quantitative experiments? How boring and unimaginative. Yet, my presence in this world is not enough, is it? I find it humorous that when the reaper finds your old frail bodies – kept alive as long as possible with all the money in the world, you still cry like babies. Your ancestors were a little better, but in the end, death will find you. You and the others, the controllers, decided to treat the truth as a business hurdle. So, you paid your top technicians to come up with a solution, because it is the only way your kind can think…three dimensional – narrow. The idea of transhumanism seems plausible to you, but you do not understand that which you create. It shall be your undoing."

Celsus was now staring up at nothing in particular, as if seeing into the truth of things. He continued his breakdown.

"It's absurd. How do you think this will play out, Herr Hilgenfeldt?"

Wilhelm smiled and relaxed back into his chair. He snapped his fingers and stuck his right pinky finger out, a signal for Valentina to bring him a glass of wine. She complied immediately.

"Don't stop now my precious Celsus. Do tell," he said with contempt.

Celsus inhaled and exhaled deeply before continuing, "You had high hopes for Elena, did you not?"

Wilhelm smirked and replied, "She is an android and so the possibility of failure was there, but you must admit – quite magnificent, yes?"

Celsus looked deep into Wilhelm's eyes and spoke as if cursing the once-born, "She, and others like her, will be the undoing of mankind – and you and your controllers will be no exception – imperfect, biological absurdities to be exterminated."

The words had the effect Celsus intended. Wilhelm felt a slight chill at the uncertainty of artificial intelligence. He had read the cautionary reports years ago – that self-awareness, and especially self-preservation, could be a major problem. Wilhelm hated anything out of his control. He gave Celsus a vicious look before signaling Ernst to proceed.

There was a stillness before Celsus felt it. It was very light at first, a barely imperceptible heat wave coming at him. His skin, although human, was not as weak as a once-born, and he was able to keep off the heat . . . for a moment.

"Do you feel it now?" Wilhelm asked from his throne, leaning back again. "It's not deep - only about 2 centimeters, but your skin is cooking and will begin to burn."

It started as an itch in one arm that quickly spread to a full body pain that felt like a sunburn peeling off. Celsus snarled at Wilhelm in defiance, refusing to make a sound to indicate pain and Wilhelm expressed a sweet sadistic smile.

"Fight me, animal. I want you to fight it - try to keep your dignity. I want to take it from you and show you that you are no god. You are a mongrel. Show me what a god you are, because I want the satisfaction of bringing down a god," Wilhelm said evenly.

His normally erratic and flamboyant mannerisms suddenly changed to very controlled and silent. It was as if he was in a meditation - speaking the words like a perverse prayer to a god he was trying to kill. There was holy supplication in his words and a morbid reverence as he watched Celsus being slowly cooked alive.

Celsus was beginning to feel it, and Wilhelm could tell. The slight twitching in his imprisoned hand turned into shaking of his entire wrists, his knees jolting to try to put out the burn that was slowly sinking into the two centimeters of flesh.

Celsus' eyes began to twitch and he blinked, shaking his head as if to clear his vision and Wilhelm took a deep satisfied breath.

"Your vision, Lord?"

Celsus did not respond.

"You will be blind soon, your retinas are going to burn and you will see nothing," Wilhelm said in the same trance.

Celsus strained his face, opening his eyes wider and wider as the darkness overtook his vision. He was slowly burning alive and then the internal pain made itself present. His mind. His organs. They were burning and he was boiling from the inside out. When the pain hit his brain matter, he could not hold back and Celsus began to shout.

Wilhelm hadn't heard Celsus, the man, shout and he looked at him with curious fascination at the sound coming from the trophy animal he'd captured. The sound was like the fall of an ancient being. It came from somewhere deep within. It was sad and pitiful, like a once reigning alpha being torn down before his time and it shook all the men in the room to their core. Something primal was dying before them and they did not know why but suddenly they were afraid.

The women in the room shook with horror, and although they had all witnessed many of their own harem members tortured and killed, this was more than they could stomach. Some became ill while others soiled themselves. They all felt the same unease as the men, but felt it at a more intimate and sexual level. Deep in their core, at the very root of their anatomical identities as women, and deep within their own DNA, the women felt the fall of the original alpha male that spoke to their ancient roots. They cowered in fear.

"Interesting," Wilhelm observed, taking a leisurely sip of wine, oblivious to the primordial terror that everyone else was experiencing. "The sound of a dying dog."

It was horrific to them but to Wilhelm, it was the sound of conquest over a powerful being that no one else was able to tame.

Celsus felt as if his head was going to split open from the pressure building within. He could feel his brain being burned and his blood began to curdle. His organs slowly began to ignite and he had never known what it was like to burn from inside out until now.

The man thrashed in his chains, howling with pain that not even his defiance could suppress, and the animal within him raged for it to cease. Celsus was dying, and as his retinas burned and the darkness of his sightless reality sunk in, all he saw in that black hole was impending defeat.

The heat stopped for a merciful moment and Wilhelm peered into the cell to catch the eyes of the shaking man. He saw the flesh smoldering and knew the blood within was burning. Hot drool fell from dry, cracked lips, and Celsus swung his head low, back and forth in delirium.

"Psst! Wolfie, are you awake?" Wilhelm cooed, sipping from the glass.

That name called out what little remained of Celsus and he let out a sound that was supposed to be threatening but instead came out as a sickening gurgle.

"Oh," Wilhelm mused. "*Wolfie*? Do you like that name?"

Celsus closed his eyes in pain and anger. How dare this once-born think he could defeat him. How dare this little tyrant think he could mock him. But that was as far as Celsus could go. He was too weak to fight Wilhelm in his current state and his head hung in bitter defeat. Celsus was now completely still with no detectable breathing.

Wilhelm looked at the control platform and asked loudly, "Ist er tot?"

There was an immediate collective gasp as the doctors quickly looked at the monitors. No – he couldn't die. They needed him alive. Wilhelm didn't want Celsus to die, but there was a moment of question that made his heart race with the implications of killing this creature. It would mean his head, and the head of every other person in this room. It made him shiver. Ernst responded.

"His vitals are still fine. He appears to be unconscious, surprisingly stable, all things considered."

Wilhelm smiled and replied, "Perhaps we should take him out of the cell?"

A dangerous glint in his eye told everyone it was more of a statement than a question. There was a visible change in the tension of the room. This was a bad idea. They all knew it but Wilhelm didn't care. He'd been wanting to get close to Celsus since his arrival and now was his chance. Celsus was weak and he wanted to have some fun with his new dog before he regained consciousness.

"Hit him again, but only for a few seconds. I need him conscious - just barely, and then – I am going to get personal with the man, and if we're lucky - the animal."

The radiation began again and the howling started as a huff, then a grunt, before it turned into the howls of a man that had known release and was back in the pain he had tried so hard to escape from.

The meditative calm Wilhelm had kept since the beginning of the radiation slowly began to transform into the flushed look of sadistic desire everyone had come to recognize. Watching Celsus slowly dying had now passed the threshold of fascination into lust and he wanted the man, the wolf, and any other self of Celsus he had not seen.

The howling and wailing continued and judging by the strain of his eyes - the darkness was overtaking him. He was almost completely blind now and the pain he felt inside his own body overwhelmed any other sense he had left. His ears and nose were burning and the blood within boiled. His body felt like it would rupture and his eyes felt like they would pop out of their sockets from the internal pressure. Everything was on a level of pain Celsus had never known. He was losing consciousness again from the heat in his brain.

Wilhelm intervened, "Stop!"

The wailing came to a slow halt and there was a piercing silence that hung in the room. "Now," Wilhelm sighed. "I want him out. Let him out!"

Nobody in the room moved, certain he was delirious and out of his mind. The scientists and the guards all looked at him a moment, waiting for him to correct himself or rephrase the order. Under normal circumstances, nobody would ever hesitate to obey one of his orders. However, seeing that the options now were to be killed by a sadistic psychopath or a lycanthrope - despite his extensive injuries - there was a moment of contemplation.

Wilhelm read the room loud and clear and was amused enough not to order everyone dead immediately.

"Are you all afraid of the big bad wolf?" he leered at them, taking great joy in the anxiety he was causing them.

Everyone in the room knew they were all now dead for questioning his orders and they all wondered if it was better to simply take their chances with the wolf.

"You will open this cell, lower him into a kneeling position with his restraints on and you will do so - now," Wilhelm said finitely.

The cell opened and the air felt visibly tenser. Everyone was afraid of both Wilhelm and the wolf, and the madman chuckled.

"As punishment for your hesitation in obeying my orders, you will all die the same way this dog is dying, in this very cell, in the very same way, *after* my dogs have taken their bites out of you," he said.

The room became inhumanly still as the blood in the bodies of the men in the room froze at that statement. Their hearts dropped. None of the guards had ever wanted to face the teeth of these dogs. Bred specifically from some of the most aggressive breeds in the world, these dogs were a pack of rabid animals closer to starving feral wolves than any domesticated form of the creature. Wilhelm loved to feed them live prey.

The walls were down and Celsus sagged forth on his knees, weakened and burned. He did not have the strength to lift his head. Without hesitation, Wilhelm grabbed the hot, crisped hair, and pulled his head back to face him.

Despite the abuse, the face he looked into was the most handsome male face he had ever seen. The skin was cracked and his lips bled but Wilhelm could still see the Adonis features behind the torture.

"You are a sight to behold," he mused, pulling his head back farther to crack some of the thin, sensitive skin on his neck. Celsus did not respond, his eyes half closed.

"Are you awake, dog?" Wilhelm demanded.

Wilhelm reached into his dirty crotch, his pants already open and took out his hardening erection. He felt such bliss at the torturing and overpowering of a man who defied all logic and inspired fear as Wilhelm did.

He took hold of his erection that slowly throbbed at the being he broke, and he moved his hand up and down his shaft. Celsus could barely keep his eyes open and Wilhelm yanked back on his burnt hair. It'd been ages since Wilhelm had masturbated and gotten himself off, normally having a harem girl do it for him. But having a girl do this for him felt unholy. He had to dominate Celsus absolutely, proving who the real alpha was between them. Having a woman do it for him would add a buffer, and there was not going to be anything that stood between him and the humiliation of this strange man who thought himself a god.

Wilhelm clutched at the fistful of hair harder as he moved his penis up and down, forcing Celsus' face to look up at his erection. His cock throbbed and leaked out as Wilhelm moved his hand up and down. He moaned, widening his stance and thrusting his hips forward with his pumping action. Even after all he'd fucked and all the people he'd tortured, this was the epitome of sexual satisfaction and he was going to savor every single moment.

The precum leaked out over his knuckles, coating them with a copious glaze. The sensitivity on the head of his dick was unlike anything he'd ever felt before, and he twitched with sudden peaks of lust as he looked into the pale face of the man at his feet. This broken, blind man that thought could overpower him, his household, his lineage; this burned man whose skin cracked with small trickles of blood running down his neck had lost, and was now the trophy Wilhelm savored. As he looked into the damaged face under the shadow of his own lust, Wilhelm decided Celsus would indeed live – if only to give up the secrets of his existence, but just barely. Celsus would live out the remainder of his days as a science experiment – alive but hardly living.

His mind began to wander with the ideas of what he wanted to do to Celsus and that only increased his arousal. His balls twitched in a frenzied state to orgasm and he choked his dick to keep from coming. He was not going to finish quickly and thrust his hips into his hand, lubricated with pre-cum.

With one hand gripping Celsus' hair the other on his cock, Wilhelm imagined shoving his dick down that parched throat and tearing the cracked lips with the power of his thrusts. The entire room was silent except for his moans and the slicking sound of his dick through his moist hand. He was oblivious to the fear that gripped every person in the chamber. They were all remembering the powerful creature that had earlier turned and eaten one of the women alive. No one but Wilhelm took for granted the fact that that this was a very powerful entity with unknown limits. Wilhelm however was currently pulling him by his hair to jack off on his face.

The climax was coming near and Wilhelm grunted and hissed through clenched teeth, fighting with his own orgasm, as Celsus hung limp by his hair. In Wilhelm's mind, Celsus was sodomized in every possible position, and Wilhelm shuddered at the arousal it built in him.

"Fuck!" He couldn't hold it for much longer. His feet slipped on the bloody floor as his legs tensed for the ejaculation. His eyes threatened to shut with the force of the release but he kept them open and gazed on the still unconscious face of the god that hung defeated at his feet.

He was almost there. Just a few more pumps. The hold on his dick tightened and loosened as he kept regripping, edging for the biggest load he could produce for the greatest satisfaction. Up and down, up and down - almost there, just a few more . . .

The hand gripping the blonde, crisp hair tensed, and he yanked harder as he felt the oncoming orgasm, his balls aching for release.

"Take it all," he shouted in sexual ecstasy, frustration, rage, and euphoria.

Every feeling of excess he could possess manifested itself in this one precise moment before the orgasm hit and everything fell silent. He looked down at the beaten face with thin lines of blood. Behind those half-shut eyelids, Wilhelm saw a ghostly movement of consciousness and he came.

The hot load shot out onto Celsus' ragged face - landing on his eyes, nose and cracked, bloody lips. It was thick with the festering desire for victory over this man and it stank with the desperate validation Wilhelm needed. He kept coming over and over, divesting himself of every last possible drop of his thick semen. Wilhelm gasped and shuddered but refused to look away from the face he stained, watching the cum slowly fill the deep open wounds on his captive's face.

Wilhelm twitched and a liquid just as hot as his semen erupted out of his head, as he began to urinate all over Celsus' face. Wilhelm licked his lips in delight as he forced every last drop of piss, making sure to move forward over Celsus as the stream turned into a trickle. He tugged it a few times ensuring everything was out and he repressed the mad impulse to shove his dick in Celsus' mouth. Even he wasn't that deranged, and he valued his penis too much to risk it.

He stepped back in triumph, waddling backwards to keep from stepping in his piss. The entire room looked at him in shock at what he'd just done. Of all the things he had done, this was the most insane and they could not fathom the arrogance of the man that would do something so brazen to a being that had just eaten another person alive.

Wilhelm settled into his throne, reveling in the shock that silenced the room and the victory over this demi-god. He extended his pinky finger and a glass of wine appeared. As he sipped, he cast a careless look around the room and the scientists and guards stiffened. Now that the exhibition was over, a very real fear permeated the room. Wilhelm had promised them a death at the mouth of his hellhounds and the machine that had brought this powerful creature to his knees. Wilhelm could read their minds clearly and a sickening grin extended across his face. Was it their time already? Who would be first?

"What's next?" he asked grandly to the room.

Celsus hung motionless and Wilhelm took a gulp of the wine. "Hit him again with the microwaves. I want to keep frying him. I want my cum and piss to crust over his face."

The men immediately obeyed - anything to delay their own untimely doom, and concentrated panels came down from the ceiling to hit Celsus at close range. It wasn't long before the stench of burning piss and semen filled the room and Wilhelm would never have guessed victory would have such a vile, repulsive stench. He loved it.

The machine continued as Wilhelm pondered his next move and smiled again at the scientists that flinched with the mere inclination of his head in their direction.

"Let's release him," he said suddenly and everyone paused.

"As in . . ." one bold scientist asked.

"Release - as in no restraints. Free," Wilhelm clarified.

"In his cell?" the man offered, trying to find *some* reason in the whims of this maniac.

"Are you stupid?" Wilhelm snapped. "Release - as in out of his cell, out of his restraints - as free as you and I," he finished, in an irritated sing-song voice.

Those in the room exchanged looks with each other, despite Wilhelm watching their every move, and wondered just how serious he was. To release this man, even in his weakened near-death state, would be lunacy and they all feared Wilhelm was perfectly serious.

"Now," he ordered, and again the scientists, guards and harem girls didn't know if they would rather die at the hands of the caged creature or Wilhelm.

A shaking hand pressed the release for the restraints and all too quickly the man was free. Lord Celsus slumped over into the burned sticky mess of urine, semen, and blood.

Wilhelm finished the last of the wine in one vulgar gulp and approached Celsus. He stood over him, looking at his still shut eyes and grinned.

"Now, let us get *truly* acquainted, mongrel."

Randy V & Ellie Ravencroft

THE BREACH
March 17, 2020 – 8:20 p.m.

"How many do you see?" Megan asked.

"One hundred thermal signatures underground, some human, some animal. Each floor of the mansion has ten to twelve guards. There are five levels plus the underground. The chamber at the bottom contains at least 60 more men and over 20 large animals," Elena responded.

"Probably dogs," Sanem offered. "How fitting."

"I can't hear Lord Celsus," Linzie offered.

"I can't smell him," Tara said, trying to hide the fear in her voice.

The women refused to look at each other, each trying to suppress the unease they felt. What technology was at play here? What was powerful enough to block even the smell of their master?

"I can't smell anything," Shira said weakly. The smell of a hundred dogs would be difficult to hide and at her mention of it the other women noticed the eerie absence of any smell that wasn't of the surrounding woods.

"I sense barriers and I see inscriptions in the foundation of the mansion," Elena explained, as her inhuman eyes dissected the building.

"What kind of inscriptions?" Sanem asked.

"Alchemy . . . spells . . . sacred texts . . ."

The women looked at each other with an inquisitive look on their faces. Megan looked at Anatu who remained expressionless. She would know it all.

"Another Hilgenfeldt who has no idea what he is dealing with. He threw everything he could at this. Something must have stuck," Sanem commented in a bitter way.

"Cameras, motion detectors, and thermal sensors spot the landscape as well. They are irregularly positioned. We can avoid them. I see them clearly," Elena continued.

The coven women paused at the idea of what they might face. They knew powers even greater than their own existed in this world and throughout history. All of the ancient magicians and shamans that modern science dismisses as fictional writings still held the same amount of power now as when the texts were written. They all remembered that it was an ancient spell that made them. They knew there were forces at work Wilhelm couldn't possibly comprehend.

They feared modern science more than anything they had faced before. The women had only to look at Elena to see evidence that technology was far more advanced than conventional science would lead the world to believe. She was an android with such advanced AI that she had totally surpassed her original programming.

"Nothing can stop us," Megan told her sisters with resolution. "We are an extension of our master. We will triumph today regardless of what this elitist thinks he can throw at us."

A gentle breeze with a familiar scent arrived at that moment. The women turned to see Cala silently returning from her landing among the trees. Deadly, precise, and silent - they had powers these once-borns could not even dream of. Cala blended in with the trees and the women felt a resurgence in their confidence. They looked at Cala and knew that whatever magic of the old world the enemy had consulted, they were the originals. They were the source of those spells; the reason the ancients feared the night. They had conquered death and would taste victory once again.

Throughout this entire time - the travel, the wait - Anatu remained ominously quiet. Her mind and soul were blank, not even a ghost of a thought formed in her mind. Anatu lived, was healed, but she was dead within until her master commanded her to life once more.

In the final moments before her execution, Anatu had seen her beginning and end in Celsus. She was nothing without him and she lived because he willed it. She had conspired against her god, and it should have cost her life. But in the final moments before her death, their Mother saved her.

Anatu knew the death of Celsus would have been a terrible thing to see. She knew she would not survive it. But seeing it come to fruition, she could never have imagined it would be so painful. Sitting outside the structure, unsure of the state her master was in, unsure if he would live, now or again, was a pain that surpassed her last moments with him.

The punishment of Celsus was impassioned foreplay compared to the true suffering she now endured it in a vow of absolute silence. She died the moment her master willed it, and she would not live again unless he commanded it. Until that moment, Anatu existed like a pristine animated corpse - powerful and beautiful, but empty until he gave her the breath of life anew.

Megan said with all seriousness, "We will infiltrate this house of straw and we burn it from the inside out."

Sanem, Elena and Tara were to go in first. They would infiltrate the top floor and make their way down, hopefully finding their master but betting on the fact that he was probably in the underbelly of the mansion. The women would join in waves, and Cala would stay behind to find an entry to the underground. It was a simple but effective plan. They did not want an overly complicated plan with risks and contingencies that would jeopardize the success of their mission - one floor at a time – top to bottom.

The sisters nodded silently to each other. There was nothing left to say. Megan nodded, the command was given, and the first wave left.

Soundlessly, the women disappeared into the darkness, their own shadowy bodies engulfed by the trees. A light wind was produced from their muted sprint. The women watched the mansion for the trio's arrival, smelling the progress, waiting for the moment their sisters disappeared behind whatever barriers they had.

As Elena, Sanem and Tara made their way through the underbrush a primal silence fell between their minds. It was the silence of the predatorial focus as it approached its prey. Large extravagant homes were nothing new to any of them, but there was a foreboding grandeur to this mansion that made an impression on Sanem and Tara, despite themselves. Elena felt nothing and pressed on with a steady gaze toward the ancient building.

Four guards were at the gate, a ridiculous miscalculation of security for the treasure they held.

Sanem looked to Elena. "You're up."

Elena nodded and stripped down naked while Tara and Sanem fell back into the woods. The android moved through the trees, staying hidden until the last possible moment when she darted suddenly to the right. The guards closest to her were killed instantly with snapped necks.

It took a moment before the two other guards noticed their fallen comrades, and an additional second before they processed that they were dead on the ground. It was a few moments too many and Elena was already on them. The two men fumbled to raise their full-auto HKs, as Elena's presence prevented any possible timely response. In the frozen mountains of late winter, stood a seemingly unaffected naked South American angel, and their delay cost them.

Elena caught the barrel of one of the guns as he lifted it to shoot. The man was stunned as her strength would not allow the barrel to be raised even to shoot her in the foot. She grabbed the other guard's rifle barrel in the same manner a fraction of a second later. She snatched both rifles and tossed them in the snow.

The two guards did not waste another moment after their guns were taken. They both lunged for her. In a few swift motions, one guard had his neck snapped and the other took a bladed hand strike to the throat, crushing his windpipe and fracturing his neck. He fell to the ground convulsing reflexively, already dead. Elena was a weapon of destruction.

The entrance was now secure and Sanem and Tara emerged from the surrounding woods to help Elena remove the corpses. The men were tossed to the side and the women began to stealthily scale the walls. They did not take any weaponry as that would only add bulk to their assault and they needed to be unhindered and stealthy.

Just because the first line of defense had been disarmed did not mean they could simply stroll into the complex. On the contrary, the outer gate was simply the first step in getting up the large hill and into the main building. They still had a substantial distance in front of them. No other thermals were sensed between the outer gate and the main door.

I thought they would have dogs out here, patrolling, Tara said telepathically to Sanem as they raced up to the main complex.

As they approached the wall, they noticed guards posted at every balcony and within the rooms. Even if they could disarm one of the guards in the balcony, that would still alert the others and they would lose the element of surprise. And while none of them were afraid of an all-out bloody battle, there was something addictive in catching their prey completely off-guard.

They would enter through the topmost floor which led to the attic. According to Elena's sensors and layout of the building she'd received by hacking into overhead satellites, there was a small entrance to an attic that had been barricaded and walled off since the founding of modern-day Germany. Sanem, Tara and Elena had to circle the complex to get to the tiny window at the very back of the mansion. The women took a long circular route around within the tree line, being extra careful to avoid detection by whatever sensors were out there.

When they were far enough up the path, Elena signaled Sanem and Tara to run single-file, exactly where she ran. The women fell into line and as they made their way to the house, Elena sent a precise shock to the cameras she was able to pick up during her run, cutting them out and disabling them for her sisters that would follow.

The women approached the back of the house and Elena pointed up at the window. She calculated the height of the wall and instructed Sanem and Tara to step onto the palms of her open hands. She launched them to the ledge quietly before joining them with an unbelievable vertical leap.

Sanem and Tara laid themselves flat against the building to avoid detection while Elena used a tool in her fingers to silently get through the glass.

As Elena melted the glass, Sanem noticed two satellite dishes. Without saying a word, she crawled out onto the roof and quicky disabled them before crawling back down to the window.

The tips of Elena's fingers glowed red as the glass gave way and melted in her palm, burning the synthetic flesh. Tara and Sanem were both grateful to have such a powerful weapon for the battle that was about to come.

Elena reached inside, unlatched the window, and gently pushed it open. Tara and Sanem waited for what she would do next, wondering if the room was booby-trapped. But Elena casually stepped in through the open window, as if walking into her room. Sanem and Tara followed, ducking into the dark, dusty closet. It looked like it had not been used in over a century.

"This room is not on the blueprints of the house, so it has not been touched since the early 19th century. This door leads to a narrow hallway that was barricaded back when the German Confederation states were still at war. A wall was built in front of the hallway, the original blueprints were lost, and the new ones do not show this room," she explained.

"And nobody cared that there was a fake window at the back of the house?" Sanem asked incredulously, knowing that her guarding eye would never let such a thing happen in the house of her master.

Elena shrugged, a distinctly human gesture and the women were amused. They were no more human than Elena and felt a strange kinship with her at that moment.

The android responded in a matter-of-fact way, "Wilhelm is not exactly loved by his men and the few that did notice it, would rather not be the ones to tell their unstable employer of this oversight. He might just as likely kill them as reward them."

Sanem and Tara's eyes adjusted and they saw the room was covered in a fine layer of grime. Spiders and other insects scuttled across the floors and walls of the short, small room. Only Elena could stand up straight as she went to the door.

"We will exit on the top floor and work our way down," she explained, her hand on the door knob. "Sanem takes the right, Tara takes the left and I will wait here in the center to catch anybody that's gotten away."

"In stealth mode?" Sanem joked, slightly amused at the idea of a naked woman standing in the middle of a hallway.

"A bit, yes," she said with the tone she knew would denote humor and her skin color began to change.

Her beautiful bronze slowly turned into stark, absolute white. Her hair became stiff and she adjusted it to one side of her shoulders. Even her eyes, the insides of her nose, mouth and ears were white and Tara nodded in approval.

"A marble statue, huh?"

"This blends in with the austere surroundings," she said, opening the door to a long, narrow hallway.

Outside in the woods, Cala and Megan monitored the progress of their sisters. Cala's enormous eyes were able to see them the entire way up to the mansion and the rest of them tracked their telepathic presence up to the wall.

Once their sisters had reached the back of the building, they waited for the silence they knew would follow and when they could no longer be heard, Linzie confirmed this and Megan sent the second wave of women.

Linzie and Shira were next and they would follow the same path their sisters had. While Sanem and Tara had followed Elena, all of the women had been connected at the same time - all watching their sisters' thoughts to ensure they all followed the same exact path Elena had laid out for them.

As they approached, no other guards had come to check on their comrades and they stealthily snaked over the wall and up the path. As they ran, Shira saw the clothes Elena had tossed aside and she felt a hint of annoyance that she would meet their master naked.

Bitch.

She couldn't help herself.

Not now, came Linzie's reprimand.

They found their way to the back of the estate and saw where their sisters had been able to quite literally stroll into this fortified estate. Shira scoffed at the stupidity of the once-borns and one at a time they jumped and entered through the opening with nimble precision.

As their vision quickly adjusted, they were able to make out the gentle disturbances on the dusty floor where their sisters had walked. The door was still open and once inside, the women noticed a silence from the outside. While they could hear each other, they could no longer hear Megan.

"Only certain rooms have the barrier protection? Maybe because we're in the same room?" Linzie tried to reason.

"Who cares. I smell blood," Shira said, a bit impatiently.

Being within these walls, the walls which contained her master, she was anxious to see him already. The hot-headed one of the family, Shira felt a great wanting - like an addict, knowing they were drawing closer and closer to their fix. He was her drug and she had been deprived of his essence for over six years now, far too long. She needed to get to him as quickly as possible and lusted at the thought of once-borns who dared stand in her way.

Megan and Sakura breathed deeply as their sisters' telepathic presence disappeared. Anatu, who had been sitting apart from the family, now stood by her sisters. Her mind was still silent - a ghost at the edge of the battlefield - but Megan knew Anatu would not desert them. She then issued her final orders.

"Cala, you will be the last to enter. There has to be an entrance somewhere to the underground - like a cave or underground road…something. Once we are in, find it. We will take care of everything inside. Meet us there. You will know when to enter, and we shall free our master."

Cala nodded, her eyes wild with excitement. She wanted to fight. She wanted to kill, and her claws twitched in anticipation.

Megan then turned to Anna, hugged and kissed her, before her issuing her final order, "You have all the tools you need to stay warm. You have a satellite phone, compass, and pistol. If we do not retrieve you by sunrise, head south, start making your way back to the road. Once you reach the road, simply open the phone and dial nine. They will come get you and give you safe passage back to America. Do not look back.

Δ

Sanem made her way to the end of the hall, sniffing the air for anybody around. There was something powerful blocking her telepathy but that was hardly a handicap. She was determined to lose nothing and saw the first two guards.

They stood by the entrance of a large oak door. A long hall extended with guards posted at every other door. Sanem listened and heard their footsteps moving up and down the hallway. There were more guards in here than the exterior view betrayed, but Sanem settled in, took a breath, and let her instincts sharpen.

While her telepathy was not active, her senses had centuries to evolve. She could sense and hear where the guards were and when their backs were turned the hunter sprang into action. She was stronger than these men could ever be and her speed was unlike anything they had ever seen.

It was quick work with the first two - their necks had been snapped before they realized what hit them. She had the element of surprise on her side and while they stood guard, the men were hardly alert. When they saw their comrades fall, the two that saw it took a few seconds to process what happened.

Those few seconds gave Sanem the time to get to the next one before the second guard reacted. She wanted to avoid gunshots more than anything. Sounds that were loud would give away their infiltration. It was bound to happen, but ideally, they wanted to capture the top floor before the rest of the estate was mobilized.

There were 10 guards total down the hall, 3 were dead and now the other 7 were alert. Sanem tried her powers of suggestion as she gazed into the eyes of her next victim. There was fear but not submission and she confirmed her powers of mind control were useless. She got to one more before the barrage of bullets started. Her stealth was blown and they would hear it at least two floors below, but it didn't matter. She got to the fourth, killed him and took his own gun. She leapt into the air before the others could follow and mowed them down with single precise shots. One of the guards got away as he had the sense to guess what was coming. Sanem sniffed in disgust.

She hated using guns as a means to kill. It was vulgar, crass, and against her master's teachings of stealth and elegance. But now was not the time to carry airs. Now was the time for decisive action. Sanem did not worry about the one that escaped - Elena would get him. Instead, she checked the rooms that the now dead sentries had been guarding.

The rooms were empty save for the obvious cameras present. Sanem quickly disabled them all before she looted the bodies littering the floor. Nothing of too much value was on them. She took their armor, their guns and a few hand knives for close quarter combat. While they could take a beating, they did not want to waste time on injuries. It would be easier and faster this way and with the men she just took down, all of her sisters had armor now - including Elena. On the way back to the entrance, the Turkish warrior laughed at the thought of Elena going into a fight stark-naked with an armored vest on.

"Where's the rat that got away?" Sanem inquired.

"He's in the hall," Elena stated evenly.

Sanem nodded and gave her the vest she had taken from one of the guards. Elena looked at it curiously and then looked down at her naked self.

Sanem anticipated Elena's contemplation. "It might seem odd, but I didn't know if you would want one or not."

Sanem noticed Elena had taken on more and more human characteristics and mannerisms. She sensed from her a true desire to be human, whether a demon like them or a once-born. Sanem surmised that perhaps Elena felt she would get closer to Celsus or that it would make her feelings and love for her new master more real than simply being programed to appear that way.

Elena looked at the vest for a bit and shook her head indicating she did not want or need one. Sanem nodded when suddenly they heard someone coming down the secret hall. Shira and Linzie emerged and took the vests. Nobody wanted to be slowed down by something as ridiculous as bullets.

They looked down the opposite hall. None of the guards had escaped Tara and she came back to her sisters as a half-animal, her giant lioness tail wet with blood flicking behind her playfully. She put the tip to her mouth and sucked at the red stain.

"Megan is on her way with Sakura and Anatu," Linzie said as they all got their vests on.

"This floor is secure, but they know we're here and the probability of combat is 100 percent," Elena said.

Sanem spoke with perfect focus, "Let's get down to the next floor. Pair up - Linzie and Shira, Tara and me. Elena -- we need you to tell us what's coming because we can't hear anything. When Megan, Anatu and Sakura join us, come down with them."

Elena nodded. "Twenty heat signatures below us. More are coming up the from the ground floor. We will catch up," she told them, and Tara flicked her tail in anticipation.

Δ

Wilhelm sat in front of Celsus who was unconscious and half-alive. His DNA had already been extracted multiple times from different places on his body, including his semen, skin, hair, nails, and penis, because Wilhelm was a sadistic animal and thought it would be fun. He smiled like a madman as he watched.

From what he had gathered so far, Celsus had self-healing abilities and he knew that if he waited long enough, Celsus would wake up and their game could start all over again. While the temptation to feed him was strong, Wilhelm first wanted to see how long it would take in his weakened state to heal. He was still watching Celsus when he heard a voice over the security monitor for a fraction of a second before cutting out.

"What was that?" he asked, not taking his eyes off Celsus, still out of his cell. Wilhelm saw that he was weak and did not feel the hurry to put him back in his prison.

"Intruders," Gerhard said.

Wilhelm's cold eyes looked at him and then at the many monitors that tracked Celsus' vitals.

"Get the cameras on there," he said tightly.

The scientists immediately obliged and after they switched over, they noticed all of the cameras on the fifth level of the house were out.

Wilhelm felt his pulse quicken as he processed the implications. His manor had been breached and there was only one possible reason. He looked at the unconscious man in restraints. His women were attempting a rescue and for a moment, Wilhelm was possessed with the idea of capturing all of them. After seeing the cameras on the fourth level start to black out, and the unnatural speed of the attacks, Wilhelm paused.

From what he saw there were six of them laying waste to his men. A seventh woman dressed in a long white gown walked stoically, almost absent-minded through the carnage, the hem of her flowing white dress soaking up blood along the way. She was stunning, and she reminded him of the beautiful women he'd surveyed in Brazil...right on the mark. The screaming of his dying men brought his focus back.

From the few glimpses he caught before the cameras went out, he saw they were women and one of them was completely naked. Unsure of what he was looking at, he asked for a magnification of frozen images, particularly the girl that was naked.

He immediately recognized Elena and couldn't help but be inappropriately amused. "So that's what happened to her," he said to an unconscious Celsus. "I thought you might have turned her into scrap metal."

He looked around at his men, the best in business, and felt sure they could hold these women off, but at what cost. It had taken so long to get his hands on Celsus and the DNA. He wondered if it was worth it to risk all of it? They were now on the third level, showing no signs of slowing. More reinforcements were moving up and he looked at his guards.

"How many more are left?"

"We have nearly 50 men at the motor pool outside, another 47 with us, and..."

"Call them all here. Now. Have them bring the armored transport truck into the bay. We're loading him in and we are leaving. The rest of you go up and buy us some time. Kill these bitches. I will not lose him."

While trying to maintain his calm, a sudden panic rose within at the idea that he might lose Celsus, his trophy. He shook with rage. The guards were moving but it didn't seem near fast enough and he screamed in frustration.

"Faster! Move! I'll kill all of you!"

He stalked over to Celsus, grabbing him by his hair to look down at his still unconscious face. "You are mine. You belong to me and nobody is going to take you! Lock him up!" The scientists nodded and the cell came back up around him.

Muffled sounds of gunfire could be heard as Wilhelm looked at Celsus in near hysterics. There was too much noise to actually hear anything, but the panic within him made him hear the shots above the noise of his battalion mobilizing.

"What floor are they on now?" He asked, looking at the monitors.

They were clearing out the second floor, killing everyone in sight, quickly and efficiently, like a tornado of death.

Wilhelm watched as the cameras slowly blur and blackout, one by one. They were all women, armed with his dead men's guns and vests. Celsus had his own personal guard of women - his own harem - and he chuckled bitterly at the differences between them. These women were deadly and powerful, fierce weapons at his fingertips. Wilhelm's harem consisted of disfigured girls, which he had mutilated in various ways for his own pleasure. He thought for a frozen moment in time how the women of Lord Celsus would risk their lives to save him, while his own harem would crawl through fields of broken glass and knives to escape him.

A dread welled up within him as his own mortality slapped him in the face. More and more cameras blacked out as the coven advanced down to the lower level. There was something sobering for Wilhelm as he processed the fact that he would always be a lesser version of Celsus. Despite the current power he held, the women he possessed, and everything he could acquire, his power was as limited as his life. His harem was full of crippled, useless women, and his influence only extended as far as his money and name could take him. But Celsus extended past these temporary illusions of power and Wilhelm loathed the creature for it.

His guards were already up and more and more kept coming but the women easily defeated the men Wilhelm had surrounded himself with. Wilhelm watched as the women funneled the men through the narrow halls and advanced on them. His men were failing and he was ready.

The entire mansion was booby trapped should there ever be a catastrophic event. He would not be taken prisoner due to his evil, and his mind raced as he saw his demise coming closer. With each body that fell on the screens he saw a minute of his life snatched from him and the panic bubbled. More men trickled into the underground hold.

"Where is the truck?" Wilhelm shouted at the closest man near him. The man fumbled and Wilhelm stalked over to him shaking with fury. "Where is it? Answer me or I will kill you where you stand!"

"Three minutes," came Gerhard's voice from behind Wilhelm.

He turned and nodded before barking out, "Shoot him!"

Gerhard pulled out his handgun and shot the horrified colleague point-blank in the face.

They were three minutes away from freedom and as the women scoured the main floor Wilhelm acted.

"Hit the main floor! Maximum voltage! Hold nothing back," he said tightly, trying not to shake.

The women ran through the main floor at impossible speeds and Wilhelm strained to see them on the monitors but could only see blurs as they killed everything that moved. He mumbled under his breath in anticipation as the main floor was set up to erupt in deadly electricity.

Δ

Elena predicted what was coming. Her body's many sensors noticed the electrical charge ramping up. They had known from the fourth floor down they were being watched, and Elena knew that Wilhelm would try to escape. They were getting close. She only had seconds to decide on a course of action as her sisters continued forward against the line of men. Elena grabbed one of the dead soldiers and hurdled him through a window - shattering it open.

"Get out," she said, with increased volume but little emotion.

The women, in full charge, immediately stopped and made a dash for the window. They were not sure what was going on but they trusted each other completely during battle and when an order was given there was no hesitation. There was no room for hesitation and they swiftly jumped.

The men were still coming and in the few seconds of reprieve shot at the women escaping through the window. Elena stepped in their way, fighting the hoard of men off as her sisters got away. She didn't have to fight long before the shock came and the women knew better than to try to go back in to save her. They knew Elena could sense things they could not and they would not disobey the order.

It was deadly. The electrocution of every man on the main floor was a stinking, foaming, gory affair. The entire room was rigged to almost explode with voltage running through it. Even outside, the women could hear and feel the heat coming from the room as the men were burned alive. The bodies spasmed, entire patches of skin burned off, and their hair fell in chunks as the flesh beneath burned. The deaths were grizzly and the stench wafted out of the smashed window.

"I prefer my meat rare," Tara said casually.

There was a collective sigh of relief among them at Tara's comment and Megan appreciated it. They were drenched in blood.

Outside for the first since they'd started the fight, unable to hear each other's thoughts, the women were connected once more in their shared telepathic space. Their feelings as they had made the break in and fought until they escaped through the window came flooding over them and they all felt each other's emotions at once and without restriction.

For the first time since the start of this mess, each felt every fear, apprehension, and doubt they had been hiding, along with a sobering dread. They tried to stay mentally strong at a time they were unsure of their own victory. Sanem looked back into the house and commented.

"The room is still alive with current."

"Where's Elena?" Megan asked.

"I don't see her," Sanem said, looking through the smoke that now drifted out as a result of all the burning dead within.

It was not long before their new asset burst through the second floor window and landed safely on the ground beside them. The bottoms of her feet were smoldering and she had several bullet holes in her arms and chest.

"Are you alright?" Megan asked, looking her up and down for any malfunctions.

Elena nodded. "My body was designed as a weapon, so I can absorb quite a bit of damage before it affects me. I can go back and disable the current, so we can make it to the basement. We don't have much time. Wilhelm will try to escape with Celsus. "

"Cala," Sakura said suddenly, and everyone paused to focus on her telepathically.

Cala noticed movement near a hill nearby and silently flew to the area. Trucks and soldiers were mobilized and going in and out of the hillside.

"We found our entrance," Sanem growled.

"Let go. Our Master awaits," Megan said.

The women nodded and made their way nearly a quarter mile due East. A camouflaged road with hydraulic tree cover and debris. Sanem shook her head in disbelief at missing it during her reconnaissance run earlier.

No human could have covered that much ground in that short amount of time. As they ran, Megan looked at Anatu - still completely silent. When their minds had rejoined, she remained silent and if it hadn't been for her smell, Megan would have wondered if she was there at all.

Δ

The static monitors stared back at Wilhelm like a set of four empty eyes as he tried to see anything at all within them.

"Did it work?" he asked loudly.

Nobody dared to answer. Nobody knew since the cameras had been fried right before the women went down. It was definitely quiet now and everyone assumed they were electrocuted.

"Einen Moment," came Gerhard's voice.

Wilhelm froze. Less than a minute before they would be out, and he turned his attention to the escape. Celsus was already being moved closer to the loading area to leave when they heard a loud and horrific sound. It sounded like something between a roar and the cry of a bird of prey, and it sent a shiver down everyone's spine.

The room shook as the sound grew louder and louder and Wilhelm felt something foreboding. Their 60 seconds were up and the truck had not arrived, nor had the rest of his men His worst fears were confirmed.

The enormous steel door to the bay was locked tight as a precaution in case anything else might arrive. Nobody imagined that scenario would actually come to pass.

The room was eerily silent as everyone waited for what was coming next. Wilhelm took a wretched look around the room and saw no more than three dozen men. He then looked at Celsus - still unconscious.

Wilhelm's moment of self-reflection was interrupted by the sound of a giant gust of wind outside the bay door. The entire room took a collective step back. There was no way out. Wilhelm grabbed one of the scientists by the collar and screamed in his face.

"Satellite comms! Call for help!"

The scientist fumbled with a headset and Wilhelm began to experienced everything in ultra-slow speed.

"There is no signal," the man shouted.

Wilhelm grabbed the whimpering man by the back of his neck and threw him to the ground, snatching the headset from him. There was not going to be any help and he swallowed the bile that threatened to come up.

Δ

Another dimension

Celsus looked around. The stone cavern he found himself in had no windows and no visible entrance or exit. He was trapped in an ancient air bubble deep in the bowels of the earth. Though it was pitch black, he could see everything clearly. He noticed he was naked and without injury.

"Am I dead?" he asked out loud.

"Almost," replied the silky voice behind him.

Celsus attempted to turn, but arms came around him and groped between his legs.

Lili…he thought.

"Yes, my sweet wolf," she replied, her voice and touch sending shivers throughout his body.

"Is it time?" he asked.

Lili maneuvered in front of him, never releasing the grip on his swelling cock.

As she maneuvered to face him, she whispered in his ear, "I waited for the little tyrant to separate you from your body. He reminds me of you when you were a once-born."

Celsus closed his eyes at the sensual power that overwhelmed him. He was rock hard, veins pulsating, the pain of his splitting erection recognizable instantly. Only Lili could do that to him.

"I was never that cruel," he responded, eyes still closed and fully aware she was standing in front of him.

"Well it is all relevant, is it not? What about the boy, Abu? Remember? Your token to put me at your service? Such arrogance – and now you are on the receiving end of the same exact situation. Except you are not me and this arrogant little once-born has you. He's got you and your only hope are the tears of Anatu. Open your eyes."

Celsus obeyed and was inches from the glowing eyes of Lili. They were deep red, like the slowing hardening flow of lava at night after a volcanic eruption. His brain could no longer process thought as she knelt down and proceeded to suck him. Long, slow, and deep, she devoured him. Her hands slid up his thighs and griped each of his muscled glutes. It took only seconds. She had taken him completely down her throat and he cried out from the pain and ecstasy of his release. As he shot himself deep into the hungry goddess, he could hear her sensual voice slithering through his mind.

I shall not intervene. If you live, it shall be because of their love and loyalty. If you die, I shall be waiting…and there will be no more incarnations.

Δ

The Hilgenfeldt mansion

Wilhelm noticed something out of the corner of his eye and glanced down into the cell. Celsus was in the fetal potion, still unconscious, and having an orgasm. He was shooting streams of cum onto the floor. For a moment, Wilhelm's fear was replaced with curiosity.

There was a tense moment of silence as everyone waited for what was next. They were all trapped in that room with only two ways out. The giant hanger door or the door up to the main floor. But that was hardly an option at the moment as the low buzz of the live current buzzed above them like a swarm of hornets. There was something horribly ominous as they waited in uneasy silence with nothing but their shallow rushed breathing and the angry swarm buzzing overhead. They had already tried to shut down the current to make a run, but it looked like the current fried everything and the controls were not responding.

There was a treacherous third option, but that was not possible without great carnage. Behind reinforced doors at the far back corner of the cell block, completely opposite the mouth of the cave, was a narrow slit of an entrance that guaranteed certain death. This was the room of Wilhelm's man-eating dogs.

The room was an enormous labyrinth of walkways and narrow paths with tall walls to keep the savage beasts from leaping over to attack those that fed them. Entering the room, there was a giant steel wall with a sharp staircase directly up to get the guards to higher ground as quickly as possible. While the wall was 12 feet high, there had been a few dogs that managed to climb over and get to the other side. One of these such dogs was a large grizzly looking creature the guards named Teufel. He was the largest and most muscular with scars all over his body from the challengers he had taken down. Even in their barbaric world there was order, and Teufel was the alpha.

Wilhelm reasoned correctly - there was no option now except to stand and fight whatever was outside the door of the bay.

Suddenly there was a sound like a sonic blast. It was as if a hole had been punched straight through the heart of the mountain. The ground shook and everyone lost their footing as they saw the giant door dented inward. Some of the men lost control of their bowels as they reckoned their fate. They had all accepted they might one day die at the hands of their employer, but they never thought they would die from the horror of the unknown.

The shape looked like a missile had hit the door, but what they heard next chilled them to their bones. Angry claws and roars came from the other side of the door as the creature scratched and tore through. A pointed claw penetrated through the door and a man whimpered in terror.

The sudden sound of weakness awakened Wilhelm from his horrific trance and he looked over at the man making the pathetic sounds. He'd wet himself and stood in a shaky stance with a gun in his hands that looked less like an imposing weapon and more like a limp, impotent penis.

The sight disgusted Wilhelm and he immediately regained his insane bravado. He reached to the closest guard, removed his handgun and shot the whimpering man in the head.

The sound of the gunshot awakened everyone in the room and Wilhelm began barking orders over the roar of the creature that was moments from breaking through the door.

"Surround the cell! Protect the cell! Move or I will shoot you myself!" he howled over the deafening racket.

A few men stumbled as they followed the order and surrounded the cell.

"Move! Get into position! Jetzt!"

Quick angry thoughts overwhelmed Wilhelm as he barked out orders.

Why the fuck are they not ready?

These were not lowly washouts or brawlers. These were top ex-military cut-throat mercenaries in his service and they all should have been more prepared. A few of his men were ready, looking firm, unphased and resolute in their situation. But there were others that looked like they would cry. Wilhelm was becoming hysterical.

"Biggest gun! What's the biggest gun in this shithole?" he demanded.

He knew as much about guns as he knew about nuclear science. He looked to his men to offer him some useful information.

"MG5s, to the front! Second line, move!" screamed Gerhard, taking charge of the men.

Wilhelm watched as men immediately mobilized and carried their machine guns to the front of the line.

"Everyone else - at the ready!" Gerhard yelled.

Ammunition belts were hastily dragged across the floor as the men at arms found the direction Wilhelm could never give. The mess of momentarily confused men suddenly became the group of vicious mercenaries Wilhelm had hired. Men lay flat on their stomachs and got ready to unleash a torrent of firepower.

"Do we have anything bigger?" Wilhelm asked in frustration.

"We have a MK19 and M134 minigun, but those are with the Humvees that are coming to escort us out," said one man, guarding Celsus.

Wilhelm looked at the floor dumbfounded. He didn't have time to reason why things were falling apart and so he did what he always did to make himself feel better. He lifted his handgun to the man that had just given him the useless news shot him in the head. None of the others were phased.

As the heavy machine guns were finished being loaded, their clanking seemed to echo in the sudden silence. The banging on the door had stopped and, in the stillness, everyone realized they would rather have the monster trying to break in than be left alone with their own thoughts. The tension in the air was palpable. Every man in the room was sweating and breathing hard.

The lull stretched on forever. The door was so damaged, it looked like one solid blow and the entire thing would collapse. The room strained to listen to anything that might give them information as to what was happening outside.

Everyone expected the door to fall, but not in one piece, off of the entire frame. The last thing anybody expected was to see the door launched with such momentum that five men were killed instantly by the impact. Two of the large guns were taken out before the real fight even started.

The explosion was so disorienting that for a few precious seconds the entire force of armed men did nothing but take cover. As the wind, dirt, and debris settled, the frontline began to fire. The small C4 directional explosion was Sanem's doing and it had done the job. They were in.

As the hailstorm of bullets started, a metallic sound was heard and it was a full ten seconds before anyone realized what was making that sound. In front of them - standing as tall as the original hanger door - was an enormous steel wall that had been lifted from the ground up. The entire massive frame had been dislodged by the explosion.

It had been an addition early on in the design of the bunker. It was designed to come up and act as cover in the event that they would need to take shelter there and defend their position. The wall was enormous and could only be lifted by a machine specifically designed for it . . . or so they thought. Now the wall stood against them, pried off the ground by a force beyond their wildest imaginations and as the smoke cleared and settled everyone stopped shooting.

There was silence on both sides of the contorted wall. Wilhelm stopped for a moment before commanding them to shoot - anything and everything they had.

On the other side of the wall, the women stood at the ready. Cala crouched low and tight - she would not be revealed just yet. Elena stood in front of Cala as the other women lifted the giant piece of steel in one fluid motion.

The shots came - none of them flinched - and they grabbed onto the edges of the steel and folded it inwards to give them some protection from the sides. The smell that came from the other side was an aphrodisiac to them. In the eyes of the demonic vengeful women, these soldiers were pathetic recruits brought to the slaughter, and they loved it.

Linzie could not keep her curiosity contained anymore. She looked out over the funnel and the men were completely stunned for a split second when they saw her seemingly teenage face peak out over the edge. A barrage of bullets grazed the top as she hopped back down.

"These men are fools," she stated impatiently. Amid the active fire, the sound of the men's dying howls resounded as they were hit with ricocheting bullets.

"Let's finish this," Sanem commanded. "Cala! Lead us!"

A loud low growl came from Cala's avian diaphragm.

Wilhelm ordered them to keep firing despite the obviously futile efforts. He could think of nothing better to do. Help was not an option anymore and they were trapped. Men circled the steel wall sheltering the coven women in an attempt to get behind it. Shooting the women in this controlled environment would be easier than fighting them on open ground, but then there was also the terror of even confronting women who could bend steel.

The roar that came from behind the moving door chilled the last of the men that had remained resolute. Even the most grizzled and calloused mercenary paled at the ominous, inhuman, evil.

A rustling came up from behind the door, as if the creature was getting ready to attack. The men that had started scaling the wall quickly fell off and backed away.

A screech like a giant monstrous owl overtook their senses. It hit everyone with the strength of a hurricane and most of the men toppled over, including Wilhelm. It was loud, but its effect was the psychological side of it – the unknown. They screamed in futile resistance as they fought for their chance to live - their chance to escape out of the open entrance, but they heard the slaughter of men and they all knew - it was too late.

Cala shot out over the steel door, nimbly maneuvering over it like a sultry demon. As soon as her wings cleared the top, the tempest began. It was as if a tornado had been released into the hanger. The women quickly scaled the wall and jumped into the blinding debris and dust that was making it hard for the men to see.

Shira landed before the others, planting firmly over a man firing an MG5. She straddled the heavy hardware, sitting on the smoking barrel of the weapon and looked down at her prey with hungry eyes. The hot metal burned her vagina and inner thighs and she clenched her teeth in pleasure. Her sisters followed suit, each landing on top of a man and killing him immediately - but not before they screamed in terror. The sound of their comrades dying heightened the fear of the others left alive and the stench of their doom permeated the entire room.

They moved swiftly among the men, some putting up more of a fight than others. Some, determined to live, found the will to stand against the blows and that only excited the women more. At their core - they were predators and conquerors that reveled in the victory over those with the audacity to stand against them.

The bullets started coming again. The women howled and while they had guns at their disposal, they chose the kill of a true apex predator - personal and bloody. They still wore the vests to protect their vitals and what was a small graze on their limbs? They moved too fast to be hit with a good shot anyways. They were getting hit nonetheless, mostly from ricocheting bullets.

Cala stood guard over the gaping entrance. They knew more footmen were around, but first they had to deal with the prey inside. It took less than a second for Megan, Shira, Tara, Sanem and Elena to lock on to Celsus' cell. The howls that came from all of them at that moment were the sounds of ancient matriarchs finding their alpha after centuries of searching.

Throughout this entire ordeal, the women of Wilhelm's harem had gathered at the farthest corner of the room. They cowered together and held each other as best they could.

The slaughter took on a completely different fury as they killed to get to their master now - the only thing they saw. There was nothing else as they raced to him. Bullets flew past them, some hit their vests, others grazed their arms and legs, but the women felt nothing. The adrenaline, their longing for him, set their hearts on fire and they saw nothing, felt nothing - as they barreled through the men, slowly closing in on the cell. All the women made a direct line for the cell and nothing was going to stop them.

At the entrance, a Humvee approached with a mounted M134 minigun. Cala immediately saw Anatu driving and Sakura behind the gun. They shot at the armored vehicle and Anatu stopped at the entrance to the bay. Sakura let loose on the once-borns.

Bullets mowed down their ranks but still they came. It was their thirst for the fight that kept them going. As they fell, Sakura understood them and Anatu would have as well, if she'd been able to form feelings or thoughts for herself. But she could not. She simply sat and gazed into the war mindlessly.

Through the shower of bullets, a pair of men set their machinery down and began to load. It was a Mark-19 and the sound of the grenades launching was so clear and recognizable there was a pause hit the Humvee.

Shrapnel tore through Sakura's left shoulder, her left ear, and third piece lodged under her ribs. She grimaced in pain but kept firing. With explosions all around them it shocked everyone on both sides that Anatu did not receive so much as a scratch. She was completely detached from the danger.

The Humvee was reinforced with additional armor and Anatu backed the vehicle up, just outside the entrance. Wilhelm's men who were stationed outside the mansion were advancing. Anatu was mentally not focused. While taking them away from the grenades, she was placing them in eminent danger.

"Cala!" Sakura shouted over the gunfire. "Pull the Humvee in!"

Cala did as she was instructed and dragged the vehicle inside as Sakura jumped from the gun to stand before the advancing group outside the bay. She approached the men, her tiny stature like a child's among the killers she faced. Out here, outside the walls of the accursed prison - Sakura had her powers. She looked into the eyes and souls of all those men and commanded them to wait. They would stand there in place until she released them and only then would they be free. She looked at the two men with the Mark-19 and gave them very specific commands and as she turned and walked back into the chamber of death.

They launched their grenades at the exterior of the cave. The bunker would hold - but the cave would not. And as they launched every single grenade they had, the cave collapsed in loud thunderous boulders, blocking the way in or out. They were all trapped in the bay and nothing would interrupt their fight.

After the men finished launching all the grenades they had, they stood and waited like the rest of the mob for Sakura to return and give them further instructions.

Inside, the dungeon smelled like death. The women were coated in the guts and gore of the men they'd killed. They were finally with their master, their alpha - and dared any of the few that remained alive to fight. They looked like demonic angels - bloody and wild. Even without their powers of suggestion, the women had the ability to entrance all who saw them.

There was a tense moment of silence before everyone was shocked back into reality by the sound of an intense vibration. It was Elena, her hands on the thick plastic that encased Celsus. The cell slowly began to distort and Elena's palms began to heat.

The cell broke open, shards flying in all directions, impaling soldiers that couldn't duck fast enough and their master fell forward. Shira was the first at his side, diving under him to catch his falling body before it hit the ground.

All the women predicted he would be in bad shape. They knew to expect the worst, but none of them expected the heartbreak it would cause.

As Elena made lightning quick assessments of their tactical situation, the sadistic Ernst came out of the shadows behind her with a pistol aimed at the back of her head. Just as his finger was moving to the trigger, Sanem gripped his wrist and delivered a vicious hand-strike to his forearm.

Elena turned quickly to see his forearm broken into a perfect right angle, the barrel of the gun now pointing directly to her left while Ernst faced her straight on. He was screaming. Elena spoke to Sanem without emotion.

"Thank you, my lady," she said, before turning back to complete her assessment of the battle.

Sanem was in her element of war. She quickly took the pistol and shot two of Wilhelm's men dead while still maintaining a grip on Ernst's disfigured arm.

"Bitte hör auf, ich bitte dich!" He pleaded.

Time stopped for Sanem as she clearly understood his psychological makeup. His history revealed itself to her in a single, seemingly eternal moment. She saw the torture of hundreds of men and woman, and yet felt no empathy. Then, like a brutal tidal wave, she watched her love, her master, burning alive. Ernst was the operator, by order of Wilhelm. She witnessed it as if it were truly the present, and her heart shattered. His begging brought her back to the battle.

"Bitte, bitte hör auf!" he screamed, as he tried pointlessly to pry her iron grip with his free hand.

Sanem's fury blazed through her eyes in an orange-red glow, as if the sun itself were producing the light. In a feat of demonic strength, she grabbed him by his genitals with her free hand and lifted him off the floor.

The pain of her vice-like crushing grip was so intense that he only opened his mouth. Wide-eyed and soundless, he was finished. Sanem screamed a warrior's yell, rotated her hand, and slammed Ernst head-first into the floor, splattering skull and brain fragments everywhere.

Shira looked down at Celsus, her reason to live and die, and openly wept. She held her master like a perverse version of the Pieta. Megan tried to hold herself together as did Tara, Linzie and Sakura. They wore their heartbreak on their sleeves and Cala solemnly looked down at her master. Even Elena's programming revealed sadness as she stood watch in reverence and respect. The sorrow was felt in all the women but when Megan looked back at Anatu, all she saw was a blank and empty face, and for some reason that was the look that killed her the most.

At that moment, Anatu exemplified what Celsus was to them. They died and lived as he did. Without him, they were nothing. Anatu was nothing and felt nothing without her master's wishes. She watched like an animated corpse.

Tara's fury was uncontainable. The lioness came forth without hesitation. The transmutation was quick, the anger obvious. The men gasped as they watched it happen, from bloody beauty to savage lion. She pounced on the closest man as Megan, Linzie, and Sakura, took on the remaining men, flanking the big cat with such speed that the mercenaries couldn't get their gunsights on the targets fast enough. Bullets were flying everywhere, tearing everything to shreds but missing the intended target.

Gerhard had moved into a kneeling position and took deadly aim at Tara, who was in the process of ripping out a soldier's throat. Just as he was about to end the life of the coven's black goddess, monstrous talons gripped him by the neck. It was enough to change the trajectory of his weapon and Gerhard ended up killing one of his own men.

Cala turned her prey to face her. Gerhard's eyes opened wide to see the full horror of a half-owl, half-woman, inches from his face. He pissed himself as Cala quickly plucked out his eyes, one by one, with her razor-sharp beak. Her grip slowly cracked his neck, and she let his body fall to ground. Her attention was immediately taken.

"Cala!" Shira screamed.

Shira, the one most easily overwhelmed with feelings, held Celsus in her arms and looked to Cala for help. Celsus was near death.

Cala's wings rose and covered them both, hiding them from the gunsights with concealment. Bullets fragmented her wing feathers, severing some, but nothing serious.

Shira bit through her wrist and offered it to Celsus. She put his lips to her arm, offering the blood to get some sort of life into him. As the blood trickled from her wrist down to his parched lips, he lay motionless and she grew hysterical.

It wasn't working. Their master was alive, but just barely. He could not be revived without feeding and Shira sobbed and gasped for help.

"Megan! Anybody! Help him!"

Megan was at her side immediately. While Shira was unpredictable and rash, her love and devotion to Celsus was undeniable, and Megan felt empathy for her. She fought hard to push down her own dread when she called for Anatu.

Anatu walked to them, swiftly but emotionless – unaffected by Shira's wails of despair. Megan stood behind her, put her hands on her shoulders, and whispered to her.

"Lady Anatu, I know you will not answer, for your master has not brought you back. He cannot do so in his state and we need your help," she stated, kissing her across her jawline as she cooed into her ear. "I speak for our master in his absence. You know this," she continued. "And I call to you now, in the name of Lord Celsus, by his will, for your precious tears that can and will save him – I command thee, Anatu – help us."

Anatu visibly breathed in deep at the command of Lady Megan, and her tears fell immediately, freely. Her face disfigured with the pain she had repressed and she sobbed as the sacred water fell from her eyes onto her master's face, his lips, and his eyes. Anatu cried over him.

Megan held the sobbing angel in her embrace and gently guided her shaking hands to caress his face.

The battle raged harder as Anatu bent down so that her forehead could touch his, her tears running down the sides of his lifeless face. She did not speak, but her supplications for his life came through with every tear and sob that racked her body.

His lips gently began to move and Shira once again put her open wound to his lips. The gesture was barely there but he drank. Shira gently parted his lips and a few precious drops of blood got in and he swallowed. Drop by precious drop he regained his energy until he slowly began to respond.

The joy was obvious on Anatu's face. Megan realized how much she'd missed seeing her sister alive and it broke her heart to do what she was about to do next. Shira took out a vial of blood, mixed with all the women of the coven, and very carefully ensured Celsus swallowed every last drop. This would bring him back enough to be able to feed on his own and regain his strength more quickly.

But Megan had a horrible job to do and she touched Anatu's shaking shoulder.

"You have served your master well, Anatu. Your work is complete and now, until our master releases you to live, I command you to sleep."

The words pained her as she spoke them but Megan knew it must be done. Anatu could not be allowed to live against the master's wishes, and her sister did not contest it. Like a switch, her crying ceased, her face became stone, and Anatu was unalive once more.

Slow at first and then quicker, Celsus lapped at Shira's blood, eagerly pulling her wrist to his mouth to suck directly on the open wound as he grew stronger. The highly concentrated dose of their blood had worked and now he copiously fed. His tongue burrowed itself into the wound to draw out more blood, holding on to her arm for dear life. The sensation gave Shira a high unlike any she had felt and she moaned as he fed.

The sound was like the chant of a priestess, offering herself to the gods in favor of good fortune in battle. His feeding and her groaning continued, the sound of her reverent wails intensifying as if reaching a climax.

His eyes soon opened and he looked up at her in disoriented confusion. His lips came off her arm for a moment and he gurgled between the blood he was swallowing. His thought was heard only by her.

Sophia?

Shira looked down at him with a look that was nothing like Sophia and Celsus immediately remembered everything. He snarled at the trickery and immediately shoved her away. He looked up to see Cala and he touched her breast.

"Goddess," he said in a dry, raspy voice. He was still weak and needed to feed.

Shira was now on her knees, bowing her to master, forehead kissing the floor in reverence to him. Before he could say anything, he felt Cala's body shudder and heave. He looked up at her to see her head coming down as she regurgitated something onto the floor at his feet.

It was an animal kill - a large piece of deer meat she had preserved for him and Celsus hungrily fed on it, and then on the owl goddess herself to finish replenishing his might. When he was done, Cala removed her wings from around them and Celsus stood, revived, strong and ready for the fight. A bullet grazed his forearm and he growled in anger.

He looked down at Shira from the corner of his eye and she went off to fight, high from her master's feeding lips.

He immediately spied Wilhelm, standing by the bloodied monitors, purposely alive and well. He had his hand over a large red button and Celsus watched him with indifference.

"I will release the dogs," he gasped. "I will release them and they will kill all of you!"

Celsus paused for a moment and watched his tormenter, the dirty creature, soiled from fear and sweating in panic. This was Wilhelm's last-ditch effort to survive and a naked Celsus casually walked to him, his swinging penis on proud display.

Wilhelm's hand shook inches above the red button and threatened, "Don't come any closer! I will -"

Wilhelm was stopped mid-sentence as Celsus' hand hovered above his.

"Let them come," Celsus replied, stabbing his sharpened claw straight through Wilhelm's hand, pressing the large red button.

Wilhelm let out a pathetic cry as he was impaled, not as much for that as for the slowly deafening sound of the dogs being disturbed. They knew they were about to be let loose and the ground shook with their barks and snarls.

"Was hast du getan?" Wilhelm cried, as Celsus removed his finger from Wilhelm's hand and took a seat.

Wilhelm looked around. All of his men were dead, a lion circled him, and the dogs of death were coming.

THE RECKONING
The Hilgenfeldt mansion
March 17, 2020 – 9:55 p.m.

The hounds knew the sound of their freedom. There were only two entrances into that room - one for the dogs and one for the unfortunate caretakers. Teufel was feeding on the hide of one of his weaker brothers when the rumble roused the pack.

The large door sounded like a furious monster opening its massive jaws. It took only the crack of the door and a whiff of the other side for the dogs to know which entrance was opening.

On the other side, Wilhelm coward with his back towards the controls, holding his bleeding hand, and crying with fear.

Celsus sat on Wilhelm's throne, patient, starving, and in the foulest mood he had experienced in centuries.

"Move the wretches from the path of the dogs," he commanded.

The women immediately mobilized, moving quicker than the doors slowly opening. Megan instructed the terrified women to move to an area beyond the anticipated stampede of ravenous dogs.

Elena physically carried some of the women, quickly transporting them safely behind their master. Though the women would inevitably meet their end, it would not be by the fangs of the dogs.

On the other side of the walls the rabid fury was getting louder and closer. Teufel barked with eagerness. He knew there was an open door, and they all smelled the blood. The wave of muscle mass crashing towards the opening just on the other side of their prison riled the dogs into a frenzy as they bit, scratched and climbed over one another to get into the main chamber.

Dog after powerful dog piled itself on until at last, the shrewd Teufel saw the way up. The wall would not hold for long as the force of their assault began to crack the wood. Teufel was at the top of that powerful mass when it toppled and he was propelled forward into the open chamber.

On the other side, Wilhelm had a clear view of the structure breaking under the power of the hounds and he whimpered at the sight.

"Herr Hilgenfeldt, what did you do to them? Your scientists are quite impressive," Celsus mused dryly, his eyes brilliant with receding stars.

"You've killed us both," Wilhelm hissed frantically.

Celsus did not acknowledge him and waited for the wall to give. There was a muted, meaty thud as the dogs ran into the room on either side of the small opening in their mad dash for meat. The stench of blood made them salivate as they broke through the entrance with yelps and snarls of excitement. Bodies littered the floor and the dogs made for the fallen corpses, but something suddenly stopped them from continuing on.

Among the stench of death, the dogs smelled something more powerful. They all looked up, searching for the source of the scent, and their eyes locked on to Celsus. They snarled and growled as they all slowly made their way to him, stalking him slowly like big game that could escape at any time. Teufel led the pack, foam and blood dripping from his scarred snout. His massive paws hardly noticed the corpses he slowly walked over, his muscular legs flexing with the excitement of the kill.

They walked right past Wilhelm, who crushed himself as tiny as he could against the wall of monitoring systems. The dogs came up to Celsus and snarled.

Lord Celsus did not bother to stand as he looked the pack down with cool dominance. The women stood behind him, waiting for their master to greet the beasts like old friends. They were unafraid as the pack surrounded them. Animals were not as dumb as once-borns. They knew the primordial alpha.

Celsus snarled a sound that was more of a language than an animal cry, commanding the ancestral animal within their DNA. The women shivered in sudden lust at the sound. It had been centuries since he'd spoken the language of hunters from a time before humans. The dogs all lay down at the feet of the master. The once rabid beasts were suddenly a pack of docile, obedient dogs waiting for the command of their one true lord.

"Now, where were we?" Celsus said rhetorically, looking deep into Wilhelm's eyes. "Don't worry, your dogs won't be the ones to kill you," he explained. That would be too pleasant for you."

Wilhelm started to cry.

"My beautiful goddesses, be so kind as to show our little tyrant the same hospitality he showed me," Celsus snarled.

Tara and Megan stepped forward to pick up the whimpering man. Sanem and Sakura walked over to the monitors, looked at the fried controllers, and began quickly rewiring them to work. They stripped Wilhelm of all his clothing before entrapping him in his own toy. The clasps shut tight around his wrists and ankles and he blubbered in fear. He had seen what this had done to Celsus. He watched as Celsus was cooked alive and he wondered how much he would have to endure before he died.

His once rabid hell hounds lay docile, patiently waiting for the command of their new master. Teufel licked at the feet of Celsus. The mutilated women of his harem lay unconscious on the floor.

As Wilhelm's eyes scanned the room in a panic, he noticed Sakura at the monitors talking to Sanem.

"You . . ." he whimpered in a barely audible voice.

Sakura did not acknowledge him, but Celsus did.

"You recognize her? Was it circulating among your associates that she was wanted? How much was the price on her head," he asked. "How much was the price for mine?"

The dogs let out a unison growl that made Wilhelm's stomach cramp with fear.

"Your father died for attempting to take her - for having the vulgar audacity to attack my house," he continued. "You went even farther and attacked me, the head of this family. Therefore, your death will be much more spectacular," he said as he walked over to Wilhelm, teeth turning to fangs. "Your father's execution will look boring compared to yours," he breathed, taking a claw and hovering it over Wilhelm's left eye.

Wilhelm wanted to close his eye but something in the master's stare - the receding stars - commanded his eyes stay open - and he yelped as he felt the dagger of his nail slowly apply pressure to the soft surface.

"Not yet," Celsus whispered. "I shall cherish every moment."

He had almost completely healed by now. His once burnt, blistered flesh was shedding off like a snake's old skin. Teufel ate the bits of the discarded skin as it peeled off Celsus like large, translucent scabs.

"You will not be burned like I was. Your death would be too quick. Your weak constitution does not allow for as much abuse as I would like, but I will make the most of it between this moment and your last."

"My executive officer," he called to Megan. "What do *you* have in mind for this evening?"

Megan shivered at the privilege to start it all and pulled a small silver cylindrical tube from her bra. Twisting the cap off she let a single clove cigarette and strike match fall into her palm. Placing it suggestively between her lips she knelt down and stuck the match perfectly. After lighting the clove, she respectfully placed it into her master's waiting lips and whispered in his ear.

There was a glint of excitement in his eyes as he inhaled the clove and responded, "My dear, how thoughtful, a special night, indeed."

Megan bowed and leapt up towards the ground level that was now littered with dead corpses, fetching her surprise. Celsus watched as she turned on the current that he had become so familiar with and was pleasantly surprised.

Foam dribbled from Wilhelm's mouth as his body racked with seizures. His face turned red and the veins of his face elevated under his straining skin.

"Classic. Electrocution. My beautiful XO, you are an artist," Celsus mused.

The buzzing stopped and Wilhelm choked as the current was cut. He coughed and gasped to catch his breath, his limbs giving a few final shudders as his vitals re-stabilized.

"No fire," Celsus observed with minor disappointment. "No matter, there is time."

He settled back into his throne, puffed on his clove, and with an elegant flick of his wrist, commanded one of the dogs to fetch him some meat. He was still weak and needed more sustenance if he was going to truly revel in this night. One of the dogs stood and grabbed onto the arm of one of the deceased guards. The dog yanked, shook his head violently, and tore a large chunk of flesh off.

Tara came around to help the beast, using her enormous jaws to easily break through the bone and tear off additional chunks of flesh for her master. The dog brought Celsus the meat, reaching such a level of high obedience it was if he had been trained to do this. But, that was not the case as this was simply the dog connecting with his true ancestral alpha.

Celsus spoke to him through a bond that ran deep within the genetic code. He had been their alpha since the time before dogs. As a result, Celsus didn't need his powers to command these creatures. They were as in tune with him as was his own family, and they knew what to do and how to do it.

The lioness brought the food to her master and he took the meat and ate. It was a savage affair to behold. Wilhelm had his bearings about him again and he watched as he chomped the human meat of his guard. This was not the first time Wilhelm had seen Celsus devour human flesh, but there was something more horrifying in seeing Celsus the *man* tear into human meat, than Celsus the wolf, and Wilhelm lurched in disgust.

Suddenly, smiling through the blood on his lips, Celsus said, "I bet you taste like shit."

This time he sent Teufel to Wilhelm - Celsus wanted to have a taste of this carcass. The dog circled the whimpering man, his mouth salivating in excitement. He circled Wilhelm once, then twice, as he contemplated where to bite. Teufel sniffed and licked at Wilhelm's thigh, meaty and strong, and snarled as his powerful jaws opened, clamped down on the leg, and tore at Wilhelm.

As the teeth locked onto his flesh, Wilhelm howled with agony as it was savagely torn from him. Teufel shook his head from side to side, tearing the meat until the small chunk came off in his mouth. The wound was large, but not deep enough to get into any major arteries. Wilhelm's body was overwhelmed with shock and he fainted as the obedient animal returned, gift in maw, and deposited the morsel into the master's hand.

"Wake him up," he commanded Megan.

She sent a small current through his body, shocking him awake. Celsus walked up to him with the chunk of his flesh in his open hand. A naked Celsus looked down at him and without blinking, started chewing the meat. How many times had Wilhelm done this to his women – consuming pieces of their bodies in front of them? Having this done to him now - it seemed unreal and horrifying - a piece of him taken and now eaten by someone else. The absolute impotence of his situation hit him like a nauseating punch to the gut.

As Wilhelm's mind spun out, he gagged and was about to lurch forward when in mid-reaction, Celsus spat the chewed-up mess in his face. The warmth of the saliva with the pulverized meat shocked Wilhelm into his bloody present. There was a moment of pause as he processed what was on his face. His confused, wide eyes looked up at Celsus as the wolf wiped his mouth with the back of his hand.

"You're as vile as I thought you would be," he growled in disgust, tossed the rest of the meat to the dogs.

As soon as the piece of meat hit the ground, the animals sprung like loaded guns at the food. There was immediate fighting as the animals attacked each other for the bleeding hunk of flesh. Just as one dog quickly devoured it, the door to the chamber opened and a very familiar smell wafted into the room. Celsus smiled and turned.

"Anna, meine schöne Anna. Willkommen…to your stepson's dungeon," he said in grand fashion.

Megan led Anna, gift-wrapped in an exquisite blue gown, to her master. This was the gift. As the beautiful Teutonic queen made her way to Celsus she looked at Wilhelm with hatred and did not look away. Celsus could sense that she was chilled to the bone and unaffected by it, as the coldness seemed to radiate from her naturally.

"You remember your son," Celsus asked rhetorically.

He did not have to read her mind to know the rage and disgust that was pulsing through her body. As he took her extended hand, he could smell the fury coming off her in powerful waves of pheromones.

"Stepson, my lord," she hissed through clenched teeth.

Anna hated this man, as much as she hated her late husband – perhaps even more for the things he had done to her. She looked over his naked body and seethed with disgust. Celsus put his claws under her chin and turned her flawless face to look at him. Anna obeyed.

"You will have your wish, my love. Do you remember how your husband died?"

Celsus smelled her arousal at the recollection.

"Exactly. What we have planned for him will make that look like a garden party. Would you like that darling?"

He did not have to touch her to smell the growing wetness between her legs.

"Sit on me," he commanded, before flicking the clove into Wilhelm's face.

"Yes, my lord," she replied softly.

Anna knew exactly what to do. She removed her silky black panties, moist with her desire, and hiked the dress up to her waist to allow herself to sit backwards on his now rock-hard cock. She groaned with the sensation as the tip slightly opened up her tight asshole. It'd been too long since she had him and she shivered with pleasure. She allowed her saliva to pool in her palm and then lubricated the thick head of his pulsing shaft.

He touched her body, moving claws gently up and down her torso, pinching her swollen nipples that strained against her bra. His hands closed around her neck and he turned her to face her stepson - the man that had attacked and violated her so many times. She stared at him and moved slightly down her master, careful not to tear her anus, as had happened so many times before in the heat of passion. Her legs spread open and her expression turned to a lustful devilish grin.

"Oh my God," Celsus said, smiling as Anna clenched and unclenched her anus around his throbbing head.

"God has nothing to do with this," she responded with confidence.

As she pleasured him, Celsus was still mulling over what he should do with Wilhelm, not wanting him to lose consciousness. Out of the corner of his vision, a figure moved and he looked over to see Elena picking up one of the mutilated girls, biting her.

More curious than anything else, Celsus watched as she tasted the blood. She turned and addressed him.

"There are small traces of tetrodotoxin in their blood to keep them awake as he tortures them. It has been altered but that is the base. Since these women have all been mutilated more than once, there is enough in their systems for me to extract."

Celsus addressed Wilhelm, "You kept them awake while you cut them up. Very creative," he mused.

"I can make more, my Lord," Elena offered, still holding the girl's arm. "I'll need a large sample, though. My body can extract it and I can administer it to your prisoner."

Celsus sighed with joy. "What a marvel of human ingenuity you are, my beautiful Elena. Yes, please proceed."

He then addressed Wilhelm.

"I am still a gentleman, *Lord* Wilhelm. I thank you from the bottom of my dark heart for this unique gift," he said while clenching his glutes to drive his thick tool deeper into Anna. "She truly is one-of-a-kind."

Elena took the girl's arm in her mouth once again and started draining her of blood. The android did not calculate correctly how much would be needed. She believed she could get away with half the amount in the girl's body, but erred on the side of caution and drained it all to ensure there was a large enough dose to keep their captive awake.

Wilhelm had his scientists engineer this special cocktail of drugs so that the girls would remain awake, alert, and able to feel pain, but not lose consciousness. A different terror welled up within Wilhelm as he saw the amount of blood the android was consuming and knew how potent this was going to be. Elena began pissing the filtered blood out of her artificial vagina. The blood flowed between the insides of her curvaceous thighs.

The girl dropped dead to the bloody floor after being completely drained. Without any emotion Elena walked to a sobbing, defeated Wilhelm. Her body was processing the drug, the non-essential fluids continuing to run out and down her inner thighs. The finished concentrate moved its way back up her throat and into her mouth.

Wilhelm trembled as he watched the naked android approach. She grabbed his arm, looked for the vein she was going to puncture, and found it stark against his pale skin. Elena brought her hand up to her mouth and her palm opened to reveal a small repository into which she spit up the extracted drug. Her hand closed itself back up and she channeled the cocktail down to her tiny pinky. A small needle extended out of her finger and she placed the tip to the exposed vein. When she inserted the needle point, Wilhelm winced as Elena injected a healthy dose into his bloodstream.

Celsus loved seeing the power of his house. Elena, the new addition to the family, impressed him to no end with her ingenious design and perfect hourglass body.

"Marvelous," Celsus stated with pride.

Elena bowed in response.

"It's concentrated, so it should take effect immediately," she explained.

"Wunderbar. That means we shall not waste any time," Celsus smiled, staring coldly at him.

A new panic pushed its way up Wilhelm's throat. He had administered this drug to his women many times. He never thought he would be receiving it himself. Now that he was injected, he waited for the effects. Celsus could read his thoughts.

What is he going to do?

"You may speak to him, if you so wish," Celsus told Anna as she was riding him, gasping as the wolf opened her most intimate space. "What would you like to tell your stepson, the little tyrant?"

Anna grit her teeth and began grinding harder onto Celsus' ridged pole. Her legs spread open wide so Wilhelm could see her glistening pussy. She put a finger into herself as she worked Celsus, and she moaned with pleasure.

"I can't wait to see you die," she groaned.

Celsus touched the front of her dress, his claws grazing her neck, and pulled her ear to his lips as his nails gently pressed into her soft throat.

"You won't have long to wait," he whispered.

She moaned as he tore the front of her dress open to allow her generous breasts to flow out. Anna continued to warm as he pinched her nipples.

There was a stir among the dogs when he said this and one by one they slowly stood up and the room began to tremble with the growl of the beasts. Teufel stood last and snarled at Wilhelm.

"One bite each," Celsus commanded, repeating the order in the same growl that spoke to their ancient connection. "…except for his heart, and his flaccid member and balls. Those are off-limits. Elena, I want you to cauterize any wounds that might cause him to bleed out. Leave the rest alone."

"Yes, my lord," she replied.

The dogs advanced on Wilhelm. The build-up was almost worse than the actual assault. The tension caused Wilhelm's stomach to clench with terror and he soiled himself as the advancing dogs overwhelmed him.

Teufel was the first one there, the rest of the pack waiting for their moment to get a taste. The leader of the pack circled the blubbering man, playing with his prey and licking his chops in ecstatic anticipation. The sound of Wilhelm's sobbing excited him and he finally chose a spot.

Teufel chose the right calf. It was meaty, but thin enough that he could sink his teeth almost all the way in and clench his jaw comfortably around the morsel. He shook his head side to side to tear out his chunk of the kill and Wilhelm shouted in agony and terror knowing he would not be fainting this time. The painful cries only excited the dogs more and they snarled as they watched their prey flailing.

As soon as Teufel bit down and Wilhelm's wailing started, Anna's lust began to spike and she moaned louder as the dog tore the flesh from her wretched stepson. After watching her husband die as he did, watching Wilhelm getting torn apart was nothing to her. She had become as the coven, her only differences the absence of hunger and timelessness.

Anna wanted to watch him die and she wanted to orgasm when he took his final breath.

Teufel took his prize and the rest of the dogs followed suit, the single attacks slowly increasing with two or three dogs at once. Wilhelm screamed the entire time as he watched the animals take pieces of him. His arms and legs shook from side to side as the dogs tore him apart.

The true horror was the feeling of helplessness to do anything. The only solace he took was the fact that soon he would run out of blood. The drug kept him horribly awake during the entire ordeal, overriding every check put in place by nature itself to ensure he lost consciousness when the trauma and blood loss became too great. But Wilhelm had taken this to so many of his women, and now he would feel what that was like. No matter how much the trauma and terror got to him, he remained mercilessly awake and aware. Celsus looked to Elena.

"Do something about that sorry tool of his. I'm sure that Wilhelm would enjoy that very much. Make him hard. Impress me, Elena," Celsus groaned.

"As you wish, my lord," she said without emotion.

Elena walked amid the dogs, stepping through them as they carefully avoided her powerful legs. They were under command to attack Wilhelm, not a member of his house, and the dogs were absolutely obedient to their alpha.

The android came up to him and took his limp dick in one hand and with the other went back to the vein into which she had injected the drug just minutes earlier. She used a different finger instead, this time her forefinger, and a needle extended.

Wilhelm screamed as the dogs continued to tear him apart. The stoic beautiful android injected him and his dick, which had remained soft despite her attentions, suddenly became hard. He looked at her in delirious confusion. How was this even possible?

"I have a potent drug within me to induce maximum erections. That is why you are hard." she explained in a perfectly calm tone, as if a doctor was explaining something mundane to a patient.

Sanem chimed in, "That's what those little vials in her fingers are for."

Elena turned to Sanem and expounded, "Yes, and each vial contains a different mixture. They must be replaced when depleted. One is a simple IV for blood transfusions. Another contains sulfuric acid. Another contains Cyanide. Another contains…"

Celsus interrupted her, "Fascinating. How much sulfuric acid do you carry?"

"Exactly three and a half tablespoons, my lord. My left middle finger is used for this and required the small vial within my hand to be corrosive resistant."

"I see. Herr Hilgenfeldt, while you are very creative in your sadism as you have so openly shown in our short time together, I must confess to you…I have been at this much longer than you, and while what you do is simply out of need…" he paused for dramatic effect, stole a flirtatious glance at Linzie and smiled, "I only participate in such matters as a reaction. Elena, stick that finger deep in his asshole and release the full contents," Celsus said flatly.

"Yes, my lord," Elena stated in the same calm tone.

She turned the shredded Wilhelm over and carried out the order without delay.

"Please," came the barely audible voice of the defeated tyrant.

The effects were immediate and Wilhelm's speech was taken as he gagged up yellow bile from the burning nausea.

"Oh, I imagine that feels lovely," Celsus said, grinning.

Elena kept working and rubbed her voluptuous ass up and down Wilhelm's throbbing blood-covered erection. Somehow, amid the pain of the dogs eating him, his exposed muscle, the burning flesh, his nerves screaming at him, the caustic burning in his bowels – it was the pain from his erection which shouted the loudest. The abnormal erection felt like it was about to split open and Wilhelm wailed at the agony of it.

Elena's bottom continued to rub up and down his length, her moist pussy lips teasing Wilhelm's shaft and head.

The sound of Wilhelm's pathetic cries drove Anna wild as she moaned in rhythm with his miserable shouting. The gorgeous once-born that rode Celsus had all but torn the dress from her body as she pushed it down around her gyrating hips. Celsus watched in anticipation as Elena slipped the head of Wilhelm's dick into her special man-made vagina.

"Let's enjoy the show a bit more intimately, shall we," Celsus said rhetorically to Anna as she bounced up and down his throbbing cock.

Celsus easily picked her up, holding her legs spread and pressed her against his body as he carried the erotic beauty closer to the dying Wilhelm.

He set Anna down, keeping one leg hooked over his arm and the German beauty fell forward onto Elena and began to kiss her. The women fondled each other, sucking hungrily on each other's tongues. Elena shoved two fingers up Anna's exposed slit and pumped her as only a machine could, with inhuman speed. Anna screamed out from the pleasure, so close for so long now, edging herself to reach the most powerful orgasm she could. She was waiting for the right time and as Elena moved up and down on her wretched stepson, she knew it was coming when his screaming took an impossibly shrill tone.

"My goddesses!" Celsus shouted over the torture to the rest of his coven, "Your master has not forsaken you!"

The women waited patiently for their master's command, not moving an inch despite the juices that were copiously flowing from their hot, wet holes. Their discipline was perfect.

"Behold, a gift for your taking," he gestured to the large group of still unconscious women, some of which were dead because of Elena's alchemy. "Love these miserable wretches as you see fit and liberate them. All but that one," he said, pointing to a sleeping Valentina. "She will be returning home with us."

The women shuddered at the freedom they were given and one by one, zeroed in on the girls for their unique desires and cravings.

Cala and Tara approached the group of dead girls and took their pick. Cala's claws closed on one of the dead girls and gently carried another living one. She lay the live girl down on her back, spread her mutilated legs far apart, and shoved her long pointed avian tongue deep in her womanhood. The paraplegic thrashed in pleasure as Cala dragged the dead girl under her and rubbed her clit up and down the dead body. Her roars of desire rumbled throughout the dungeon as she masturbated on the dead and sucked on the living, which slowly progressed into consuming the girl alive.

Tara took a deceased girl, flipped her face down, and licked and sucked at the perfect round orbs of flesh. Her eyes rolled back white, her upper lip curled to reveal her massive fangs, and her licking and sucking slowly turned to biting and tearing, her bloodlust increasing exponentially.

Sakura woke a group of five women, all in different states of mutilation, with a gentle kiss for her taking. Some had no legs, others had no arms, some had neither, and she commanded them to remove their prosthetics. She took them as they were - perfect wretches - and loved each and every single one of them before giving them the peaceful death so many of them had wanted for so long.

In return, the women loved Sakura's body, kissing, licking and sucking on her in the best way they could. She was as gentle as ever in her killing, sending the girls on euphoric trips right before they returned to the collective. Even without their powers of suggestion, the aroma these inhuman beings exuded when in heat was enough to transfix all that saw them. The poor girls were aware something horrible was happening, but the gentle touches and the pheromones overwhelming them and made them focus only on their respective angels of death.

Sanem, Megan, Shira and Linzie each took their group of women and savaged them in their own unique styles. Shira and Linzie eventually paired up, tasting each other's prey before brutally killing them. Sanem and Megan each worshipped their group of women and fed on them as they fingered and scissored each other, sending each girl to climax before they drained them of their blood. As the corpses fell, Cala and Tara helped themselves to the meat and loved and ravaged every last one of them.

The only member that stood impossibly still was Anatu. Her master had not yet released her and she stood in silence.

Celsus had not forgotten her or his interaction with Lili at the point of death. On the contrary, Anatu was a distraction amid the festivities and, although he still could not read her thoughts, he had no doubt she was silent and empty. It was not a time to grant forgiveness, and he refocused, narrowing his eyes on Wilhelm.

Elena rode Wilhelm him up and down until the last of the dogs had taken their piece of the gruesome dinner. Anna kept kissing her, sucking on Elena's tongue and fondling her clit as the two women edged themselves to climax. The hole that was sucking in Wilhelm's dick slowly began to change and tighten. The blades, which the coven had replaced within her depths, as a gift for Wilhelm, began spinning and extending.

The circular motion of the blades reacted to the fury of Elena's thrusts as she paced it to hit her dagger of a g-spot in perfect pace with Anna's own motions.

Wilhelm's arms and legs had been shredded by the dogs, exposed bone and muscle tendons revealing the ghastly damage. He'd become a more dreadful quadriplegic than anything he had ever created in his women. Shredded flesh hung like bloody streamers from his limbs, his torso missing entire chunks, and his exposed ribs gleaming amid the blood and muscle. Gravity continued dragging the acid through him, separating a part of his pelvic bone. He longed for death and momentarily wondered what more could possibly be done. The answer came in a wicked shock as the blades slowly started lacerating his hard cock.

He devolved into a crying, pathetic mess. He had felt horror and defeat as the dogs had torn him apart, watched as he was eaten alive. But this was a new level of defeat. Despair, castration, and eternal impotence. He was having the only thing that remained intact shredded off and he would have fainted were it not for the relentless drug.

This was the moment Anna had been waiting for and she moved her ass faster and harder up and down her lord's thick hard cock. Little droplets of blood spattered upon her inner thigh as Celsus had torn her again.

Elena sensed Anna's oncoming orgasm as the blades slowly shaved and lacerated Wilhelm's dick. Celsus made eye contact with the wretch, and Wilhelm's world spun out of control with the receding stars of the wolf's eyes.

Specks of tissue and muscle had flicked onto them during the dog's feeding ordeal. Blood mixed with ground up flesh oozed out of Elena's pussy and she reached between her legs, took the sludge and pinched Anna's nipples with the mess. The blood smeared across her body and Anna groaned at the sensation. Fucking amid blood and death was nothing new to her and she reveled in knowing the blood she painted her gorgeous body with was the blood of Wilhelm's penis being shredded off.

Elena shaved off deeper pieces of his cock with every motion of her curvaceous hips. Wilhelm gave a shrill wail more pathetic than any noise he had made yet. Anna moaned in rhythm with the sounds of torture and Celsus felt her anus tightening around him. She was very close. He touched her back and leaned in as she slammed herself down his bloody length, her anus torn and lubricating despite her cautionary efforts.

"He is close to death, my darling. Come when you are at your peak," he commanded, whispering into her ear.

She contorted with desire at his silky voice, which instructed further, "Wait for a few seconds more at your peak - feel the pain of the orgasm at bay and then let it wash over you. I want you to drip over my balls and I want my silver deep inside you."

"Yes, my lord!" Anna screamed in ecstasy.

The new energy electrified the room and the women shouted as their own orgies of death continued. Wilhelm's dick was almost gone, as was the blood running through him. The drug would not keep a biologically dead human conscious, and the lack of blood was making his head spin. Finally, Wilhelm would know the relief he had denied others.

Anna felt the pulsing orgasm begging for release. Elena kept hacking off at Wilhelm and there were only moments left before the final piece of his dick was chopped off. Anna paused for those painful few seconds before letting the wave of her orgasm crash over her.

"My lord, my god! Honor me!" she pleaded.

"I love when you beg," Celsus growled, shooting his burning hot load into her ass.

The sensation was so distinct that Anna forcefully came again. She felt the cum seep out of the edges of her overflowing bloody hole and she whimpered and shook from the high of it all.

Elena finally came off of Wilhelm. The only thing that remained of his penis was a bloody, shredded stump. He was conscious enough those last few moments to comprehend the final humiliation. At that moment, he welcomed death.

His balls still hung from his body and he tried to see them, but his injuries would not allow it.

Teufel saw the two hanging jewels and looked to Celsus for approval. Celsus inhaled deeply and exhaled a long satisfying sigh. He simply nodded to the animal.

The biting and ripping off of Wilhelm's testicles sent the him over the edge. The monitors showed no vitals and Elena confirmed he was finally dead.

Anna, still coming off her grand orgasm, slowly pulled herself off Celsus, her legs weak with pleasure, and her asshole gaping from the extracted girth. Elena held her by the waist of her shredded dress and slowly helped her to one of the open chairs. Beyond the crowd of animals, his goddesses were finishing off the group of mutilated women - a bloody, gory mess of sex and death.

It thrilled Celsus to see his family enjoying themselves and he thought they'd never looked more beautiful. Only one sleeping and unscarred woman remained untouched, the beautiful and exotic Valentina.

The coven women were satiated, Wilhelm and his men were dead, but there was still the matter of the dogs. Celsus was contemplating their fate when a silent Anatu ghosted her way next to him at the hands of Elena.

"May she serve you, master?" the android asked.

Celsus gave a small but perceptible nod and Elena released Anatu to approach Wilhelm.

Anatu took Wilhelm's face and she began to cry upon it. It was the gift of life being used as the ultimate curse – something the entire coven understood at core of their existence. Every coven member except the master could hear her thoughts as she finally broke her telepathic silence in her native Portuguese.

Existe um mal pior do que nós - imortal como nós - aquele que nos conduziu ao nosso próprio nascimento…

Celsus waited patiently for his forsaken counselor to finish what she was doing and it wasn't long before he realized what it was. He nearly forgot about those tears, lost in the bloody excitement. The once dead limbs slowly began to jerk and the face, with wide-open eyes and gaping mouth, twitched back to life.

Celsus watched as the corpse was resurrected from the dead and the body slowly began to wail. Unsure if it was from the agony of his body or the shock of being revived, Celsus could not minimize the magnitude of Anatu's love and loyalty.

The coven waited nervously, all wondering if it was enough to forgive her what she had done.

He looked at Megan and commanded her, "Bring her to kneel at my feet."

Megan gently put a hand on Anatu's arm and led her to Celsus.

"Does Sakura have an army of men outside?" he asked.

"Yes, my lord," Megan answered.

He nodded and further commanded, "Release the dogs on them and then . . ."

Celsus did not need to speak the next command as the dogs fully understood. It became a part of their DNA the moment Celsus thought it, and he spoke it only to the beasts he was condemning. The growls came low and menacing, and the dogs snarled in acceptance.

Sanem, Tara, Cala, and Elena, began clearing the massive stones, rocks, and debris from the main exit to the outside road. They worked at inhuman speed, charged by their satiated feeding.

Sakura peered around the small opening and observed her incredible work – 37 men stood in the snow, glaring up at the night sky. Only the gear they wore kept them alive. If not for that they would have all perished from hypothermia, a much better way to exit their lives than what was coming.

The dogs growled and barked in anticipation and Celsus waited for them to be in a frenzy before he gave permission to the canines to attack. They surged through the opening and pounced on the small group waiting men. Celsus heard the screaming and grinned. The dogs were ordered to kill the men and afterward, kill each other. Only one would survive, the alpha Teufel, and he would be left to scour the land. Only the strongest survive and Celsus mused at the irony as Wilhelm looked up in horror.

Only the strongest survive...unless I command it, Celsus thought as he looked upon Wilhelm.

Which brought him back to his advisor and best friend, Anatu. She had given him a most precious gift - the revival of the once-born who had tortured him. Now that he was alive again, his body could be transported back to the estate for entertainment and a life-time of revenge. That gift could not be taken lightly, but neither could her betrayal. The stunning sorceress had not spoken since the night of her near annihilation and Celsus now wanted answers.

He addressed the coven, "Who is responsible for this woman's life?" She should be dead by my decree."

Megan stepped up to him and got down on her knees before replying, "I am responsible, my lord."

He nodded slowly and spoke coldly, "I will allow you to plead your case before I pass judgement."

The Lady Megan looked straight into the eyes of Celsus, eyes now blue like the ocean at twilight. She would not falter in her simple reasoning and with the screaming of Wilhelm in the background, Megan spoke elegantly as her position dictated.

"We needed everyone this night, my lord. I made a decision that the lady Anatu would best serve you here, helping us rescue you. I made this judgement alone and I take the full weight of your judgement."

The words were powerful and Celsus felt pride in his XO. She made a decision and was owning up to it. He looked deep into her beautiful green eyes before speaking.

"Under normal circumstances, any disobedience is not tolerated." The words resounded in the near empty chamber. "Given the extraordinary situation this family was placed in, I forgive you and commend your skills as a leader. Do not take this forgiveness lightly, lady Megan, for normally you would be severely punished."

Megan nodded. "Thank you, my lord!"

Celsus revealed his heart in response, "Thank you my lady Megan…for saving me. Thanks to all of you for saving me."

He then turned to Anatu, silent and empty. Megan stood up and backed away. She could not interfere with her sister's sentence. She had already brought her back from the dead once, if what she was now could even be considered living. She could not do it again. They all lived and died by his command. They lived only through him and with him.

"Anatu," Celsus addressed softly. "You have been revived by your sisters as you revived the once-born behind you. Your body is perfectly intact but your mind is dead. For while your body was revived, your soul was not, for I alone may allow this." he said in a low reverberating voice.

The only response from her stoic face was a single tear that escaped her empty eyes. She knelt for the judgement of her master. A second annihilation could not be worse than the suffering she had endured and she patiently waited for his verdict.

Celsus looked around and saw the women watching and waiting. Several seconds went by before he spoke, breaking the silence, save for the men screaming outside and Wilhelm's grotesque moans.

"This family has been through enough suffering," he said. "We have been segmented for too long. Our sisters who were once lost, have returned," he looked at Shira and Linzie, both of whom bowed to him in return. "I forgive you and welcome you, Shira and Linzie, with open arms, back where you belong."

The two women swallowed the cry of relief and fell to their knees in solemn gratitude, trying to control the sobbing that racked their glowing faces.

"Lady Anatu," he said at last, turning his attention back to the living dead that knelt before him.

Celsus reached forward and gently lifted her head. Her eyes were still empty as she awaited judgement and as he gently opened her mouth, his claw tracing the edge of her lip, he breathed into her mouth with his command.

"Live again, oh great sorceress Anatu."

The moment was so powerful, the women of the coven shivered. As someone that had narrowly escaped her own annihilation, Shira cried hardest of all. The moment the breath entered her body Anatu gasped and let out a powerful sob.

"My lord, I love you and live for you…" she pleaded, holding his hands in hers and kissing them fiercely.

She cried at the forgiveness, at the ability to live again and all she wanted was to kiss and hold him, but he had not commanded it.

A smile stretched across his mischievous face and he let out a deep sigh. "My beautiful Anatu…, how I love seeing you like this," he said, putting his lips next to her ear as if to kiss her. "But I did not command you to speak," he said as he lightly kissed her ear.

Anatu whimpered under the touch she had so missed.

"Your punishment will be a little more deprivation, but Megan will see to it that you are loved properly as I continue to have fun with my former warden. You and I will have our reunion soon enough, I promise."

Outside, the cries of the men being slaughtered by the dogs came through the opening in faint muffled cries as Wilhelm's own screaming filled the chamber. All but Valentina were dead and their bodies were devoured by Celsus, Cala, and Tara, all three mindlessly meat-drunk and wrapped in each other's bloody arms. Cala had not looked this human in several years, satiated as she was. Celsus gazed momentarily upon the bloody remains of the unfortunate women before turning to look at Wilhelm again - now little more than a torso with shredded limbs and protruding bone.

He then looked to Anna who was as bloody as the women of the coven, and could see that the revival of her stepson had reignited her lust. She played with her breasts and fingered her clit, paying little mind to the flesh, blood, and muscle tissue, mixed in with her juices. Elena met her and they began to make love again.

The night continued on until the sun threatened to rise. Wilhelm's dead women were bones littering the dungeon floor. Outside, the ravenous dogs had turned on each other in the middle of the night and the sound of dying men were replaced with the mournful wails of beasts killing each other for the fight to survive. The only one that remained was Teufel, and he fled deep into the forested countryside.

Δ

As the coven's head of security, Sanem took charge. Right before sunrise, she used a satellite phone to contact coven agents waiting in the town of Ohlstadt. In shocking detail, the agents explained the world and all of its borders had been shut down due to a pandemic. They explained that any movement could, and probably would, be challenged by the police, and the risk of their detection was extremely high. Anna Hilgenfeldt, while assumed dead, was still on Interpol's missing persons list. Sanem thought for a moment before issuing orders.

They actually did it.

She knew Wilhelm's friends were already trying to reach him and she ordered her contacts to get to the mansion immediately. She explained the hidden road was open for their approach and gave them accurate GPS coordinates. The crime scene clean-up would be monumental and yet, with wood-chippers, sleds hitched to snowmobiles, and enough industrial cleaning goods to fill a semi-trailer, they managed to get the job done in a single day.

The fried corpses of Wilhelm's guards were carted away as the floors and walls were cleaned, the wiring redone, and the hidden door resealed. Megan met one of the operatives at the top of the chamber stairs and ordered them to bring the bodies of every single dead dog back into the house and placed within the labyrinth. They were also instructed to repair all walls, doors, and firearm damage. Every single shell-casing was collected and taken away. Every bit of digital footage of the night was destroyed. Every device and weapon restored to its original state, including the electrocution booby trap on the main floor. The damaged vehicles were loaded onto a flatbed truck and taken away to be chopped up.

The end result was a mystery that shattered the controllers' pretentious concept of no unexplainable events – destroying the arrogance of their certainty that they were the top of the food chain. They spent untold amounts of money to find out how nearly 200 men, including top scientists and experienced mercenaries, simply vanished along with one of the richest men in the world.

Wilhelm's mutilated body was carried off on a stretcher with bags of water and blood to keep him alive during the long journey back to San Juan island. They would be at sea for months as air travel was now impossible.

Their agents were tasked with getting them across the Austrian and Italian borders to Venice, where the master's 360-foot *Euphrates* awaited with eighteen crewmen and nine seasoned mercenaries, completely stocked with fuel, weapons, and enough blood and food to keep them all sustained for months at sea. Sanem had been very thorough in her exit strategy before the coven departed for Europe.

Amid the many little bags that dangled from Wilhelm's mobile stretcher was one containing the blood of his own mutilated woman, which Elena harvested as best as she could from the carnage of the reckoning – keeping him alive and awake during his long journey to America.

Δ

The North Atlantic Ocean
March 27, 2020 – 3:24 a.m.

A few days of self-reflection greatly soothed Anatu during the beginning of their sea voyage home. She was given the privilege to stay in her master's cabin quarters. Valentina was given to her as a gift and designated as her new XO. They became lovers and friends almost immediately, and it was obviously a perfect match. She felt true contentment and slept in Valentina's arms as if dead, dreaming of Lili as a mother instead of an adversary.

As they neared the equator in the middle of the night, Celsus was reminded of the microscopic mechanisms that now ran in his blood. The vaccination for this man-made virus coursed through his veins in the form of tiny nanobots. Quietly, in the safety of his boat, he felt a sudden passive desire and he grinned. These nanobots were trying to exert their programming, trying to influence him to accept defeat and surrender.

It was a strange and curious sensation he had never felt before, but he was greater than any technology these once-borns could create. He conquered death in the beginning and he would not be defeated now. Megan was already working on a solution to extract or neutralize them.

He turned and looked out of his cabin window, the stars bright in the black night sky, and noticed one star burning brighter than the others. It even appeared to move slightly.

But then his attention was brought back to the stretcher with the mutilated cargo that quietly creaked with the rolling of the waves. There came a soft whimper and Celsus walked to the bed.

Wilhelm's arms and legs were as shredded now as the day they left his dwelling. His splintered and shattered bones protruded at various, odd angles. The white sheets under him were stained with the blood that ever so slowly trickled out. The blood clotting drug that Megan administered had done wonders. Yet Wilhelm's eyes were yellowing as were his hands. Wilhelm gasped at Celsus with a raspy pathetic voice.

"What is this?"

Celsus did not know if the question was brought upon by delirium, trauma, or sheer stupidity.

"Jaundice," Celsus replied simply. "Your body is reacting negatively to the blood transfusions. Seems this is not your blood type. Come to think of it, I doubt this is even human blood," Celsus said casually, as Wilhelm's face contorted. "With Anatu's tears, I can keep you alive for the remainder of my life. And my friend…that is another 77 years," he said smiling.

Celsus could not help but feel slightly surprised. Just when he thought Wilhelm had reached the maximum amount of pain and grief, he surprised him by feeling an even higher level of renewed anguish.

Wilhelm looked up at the master's cold expression in defeat and Celsus continued to taunt him.

"When you die, you will be brought back so I can do this again…over and over and over," he said coldly, without blinking.

As Celsus left, he heard Wilhelm's defeated whimpering. Making his way back to the window, he looked out again and saw the same bright twinkling star but when he blinked, it seemed to vanish and blend in with the rest of ebony sky.

Is it you, my lady?

He put the thought out of his mind and crawled into bed between the sleeping Anatu and Valentina.

While Valentina slept soundly, Anatu felt him settle in and she turned to place her arms around his body – determined to never let him go again.

He kissed the top of her head, took a deep satisfied breath, and closed his eyes, speaking to her without words.

I love you, Anatu, and I always shall.

Δ

The Baltic Sea
November 17, 2020 – 10:45 p.m.

Celsus sat motionless, gazing out into the darkness as the ship rocked violently from the storm. He gave his security chief nine hours to produce an intelligence briefing for everything. He was at his wits end and shut down mentally to avoid bloodshed. The knock came within a second of the nine-hour deadline.

"Come," he said stoically.

Lady Sanem gracefully entered barefoot, wearing dark grey sweatpants with a white drawstring tied in a bow, her jet-black hair in a tight ponytail, and a loose black t-shirt. She knelt down and bowed her head.

"Sit," he said, glancing at a chair that was pulled back at the conference table.

Sanem took a seat and Celsus turned back to the window that revealed nothing but darkness. A single candle barely illuminated the room, yet Sanem could clearly see his reflection in the window and knew he was in a grim mood.

"How is the captain and crew?" he inquired.

"They are content, my lord. The were made for the sea, and everything they could possibly want is here on this ship. They each wear the ring of the wolf and will die for any one of us, my lord," she replied confidently.

"That's good, but we have been at sea for eight months," he stated softly. "I have watched the world descend into absolute madness. We have active agents on most of the continents and in most countries. We have safehouses everywhere. So my first question is, why are we not home?"

"It no longer exists, my lord," she replied. "As I suspected, the controllers sent top-level operators there. I was able to monitor the infiltration via satellite. When I could inflict the most carnage, I detonated the entire estate with several thousand pounds of incendiaries. Twenty-three of their operatives were burned alive, my lord."

Celsus grinned, "That is good Sanem...very good. And what are they saying?"

"The local authorities cannot make any sense of it. Anything of value in the realm of information about us was torched beyond recognition. Lady Tara made sure the deed was untraceable as well, my lord," she said.

Celsus paused for a moment before continuing, "Why here of all places? Why have we ended up back here? I believe I was very clear about not coming here...ever. This place holds a bad memory for me as you know – the worst actually, save for what just happened."

"I understand, my lord, and I take full responsibility as I am the one who ordered the captain into this region. Here, we can operate undetected until our new home is ready, my lord."

"And where exactly is this new home?"

"Easter Island, my lord."

"What?" he said, as he slowly got out of his chair and looked through her, stars beginning to recede in his eyes.

"Tara has brokered a deal with the Chilean government, or at least the true rulers of Chile. The new underground facility is nearly complete. Over 27,000 square feet, my lord. It has everything we need."

"It is a fucking Island in the middle of the South Pacific Ocean. How can it possibly have everything we need? And how can we trust Chile?"

"My lord, it is a matter of leverage, careful monitoring, and trickling gold to the right people. Not all of the controller members are in line with the general plan. That is part of the leverage. The gold seals the deal permanently. As to what we need, that is part of the deal. The Islanders will protect us. Trust me, my lord. It is the only way forward for now."

"I believe it is high time for us to go on the offensive. It is time that we hunt down these *controllers*. What say you, my lady?"

"I thought you would never ask, my lord. If we do nothing, they will have us for sure at the next incarnation," she replied.

Celsus grinned, his mood taking a turn for the better as he ordered Sanem, "On your knees," he said, as his pulled out his pulsating semi-erect cock.

"Gladly, my lord," Sanem said with a flirtatious grin.

Sanem got into position in front of him, gripped his balls with one hand, intentionally flexing her powerful bicep, and sucked his cock hungrily with the sloppy obscene sounds she knew he loved.

Celsus swooned under Sanem's hunger and drifted into blissful silence. He took out a small clear vial from his blazer and contemplated the salty contents of Anatu's tears. He thought of his first life in Babylon, his sister Sophia, the women of his coven, Lili, and even the goddess Inanna, and he wondered…

What if I inject this into my heart?

Δ

Elsewhere on the ship, the coven women were engaged in intense sexual pleasures and bloodlust feeding - all but Anatu. She stood gazing into the blackness as Celsus did.

Though on opposite sides of the vessel, she was connected to him. Her eyes glowed a brilliant sapphire blue, and she conveyed her message without a smile, without betraying her emotions.

Do it.

CHRONOLOGY

1764 BC – The Event (first death).

1530 BC to 1413 BC – 2nd Incarnation.

1296 BC to 1179 BC – 3rd Incarnation.

1062 BC to 946 BC – 4th Incarnation.

828 BC to 711 BC – 5th Incarnation.

594 BC to 477 BC – 6th Incarnation.

360 BC to 243 BC – 7th Incarnation.

126 BC to 9 BC – 8th Incarnation.

108 to 225 – 9th Incarnation.

342 to 459 – 10th Incarnation.

576 to 693 – 11th Incarnation.

810 to 927 – 12th Incarnation.

1044 to 1161 – 13th Incarnation.

1278 to 1395 – 14th Incarnation.

1512 to 1629 – 15th Incarnation.

1746 to 1863 – 16th Incarnation.

1980 to 2097 – 17th Incarnation.

Randy V & Ellie Ravencroft

ABOUT THE AUTHORS

Randy V is an Army veteran, former air marshal, and graduate of the University of Toledo. He earned a BA in anthropology with departmental honors, and an MA in sociology with a focus in social psychology. He is an accomplished vocalist and producer, the lead vocalist for The Haunted North, and is the President of White Choker Publishing. He lives in Washington State.

Ellie Ravencroft is a Chicago based horror writer with a passion for literature and all things dark and macabre. Always looking for new weird treats, she loves exploring local book shops and connecting with local creatives to share a tale of terror with. She enjoys spending time with her two dogs and writing with a hot cup of tea on a cold windy day.

Randy V & Ellie Ravencroft